D0629398

THE MUSCOVY CHAIN

Recent Titles by John Pilkington

The Thomas the Falconer Series

THE RUFFLER'S CHILD
A RUINOUS WIND *
THE RAMAGE HAWK *
THE MAPMAKER'S DAUGHTER *
THE MAIDEN BELL *
THE JINGLER'S LUCK *
THE MUSCOVY CHAIN *

* *available from Severn House*

THE MUSCOVY CHAIN

John Pilkington

This first world edition published in Great Britain 2007 by
SEVERN HOUSE PUBLISHERS LTD of
9–15 High Street, Sutton, Surrey SM1 1DF.
This first world edition published in the USA 2007 by
SEVERN HOUSE PUBLISHERS INC of
595 Madison Avenue, New York, N.Y. 10022.

British Library Cataloguing in Publication Data

Pilkington, John, 1948 June 11-
  The Muscovy Chain. - (A Thomas the falconer mystery)
  1. Thomas the Falconer (Fictitious character) - Fiction
  2. Great Britain - History - Elizabeth, 1558-1603 - Fiction
  3. Detective and mystery stories
  I. Title
  823.9'2[F]

ISBN-13: 978-0-7278-6543-4   (cased)

All Severn House titles are printed on acid-free paper.

Typeset by Palimpsest Book Production Ltd.,
Grangemouth, Stirlingshire, Scotland.
Printed and bound in Great Britain by
MPG Books Ltd., Bodmin, Cornwall.

Prologue

The stranger had been seated in a shaded corner of the courtyard throughout the hot afternoon, waiting for the Seigneur de Maisse to return from hunting. The chateau servants who went to and fro glanced uneasily at the dark, thin-faced fellow in the travel-stained clothes. None ventured to approach him; his disfigurement alone made them shun him. When the Seigneur at last came cantering through the gateway with his huntsmen, a fine stag tied across his saddle, the stranger stood up to show himself; whereupon de Maisse's contented smile turned to a frown. He swung himself down from his horse, threw the reins to a stable boy and walked across the cobbles towards the stranger, who made his bow in perfunctory fashion.

'Well?'

The man gave a shrug, then spoke in the soft accent of northern Italy. '*Mi scusi, signor* . . . there are difficulties.'

The Seigneur's mouth flattened into a thin line.

'What manner of difficulties? No!' He held up a gloved hand abruptly. 'I refuse to hear of them! You were well paid – do you but come to tell me you have failed?'

The other's face bore no expression. 'It seems the goods have left France. Crossed La Manica – the Channel, to England.'

De Maisse took in the news with an impatient snort. 'Then what are you doing here?' he snapped. 'Why aren't you on a ship, crossing to Dover?'

The Italian retained his calm. 'I wish to know the *signor*'s pleasure,' he answered. 'I can pursue the prize as far as he wishes . . . I merely require the means.'

'Is that all?' The Seigneur's tone was contemptuous. 'Do

you not think my name is enough to procure anything, anywhere in Europe?' Irritably he fumbled at his belt, tugged a purse from its thong and held it out.

'Now be on your way – you've wasted time enough!'

The Italian took the purse, inclined his head and was about to take his leave, when de Maisse stayed him. 'Wait! That weasel of a jeweller – what did you do with him?'

The other man glanced about, then with first and second fingers extended together made a very quick gesture across his throat.

De Maisse gave a nod of satisfaction. His gaze shifted, beyond the chateau walls to the broad expanse of his lands. Woods, fields and vineyards stretched to the horizon, lit blood-red by a sinking sun.

'He won't be the last,' he muttered, almost to himself. He faced the Italian again. 'I told you at the start, Corvino, and I say it again now: I will brook no obstacle! Nothing matters, save that you find what I have hired you to find and return it – quickly!'

Corvino raised an eyebrow. '*Capisco, signor* . . . a little more time, is all I need—'

'You have until the month's end!' the Seigneur retorted. 'I expect you by the first day of August. But if you fail—' He broke off, allowing the other to read the stark warning in his eyes. Then without further word he strode away across the courtyard. Corvino watched him climb a flight of steps. Servants appeared at once, bowing and fussing like a flock of hens. Waving them away, the Seigneur swept through a doorway and disappeared inside the chateau.

Corvino walked calmly to the stables to collect his horse. While he waited for it to be readied, his mind wandered. England . . . he had never been there, though he had heard much about it. All Europe talked of the damp, misty little country across the Channel, where people drank ale instead of wine; whose famous queen, the mighty Elizabeth, had ruled for nearly forty years and was yet a maid. No matter – she had proved herself a warrior, who had defeated her enemies by land and sea. He nodded slowly to himself. If he had had time, he would have liked to stay in England a while. But he was a man for hire, who must go where he was bid . . . He weighed the Seigneur's purse in his hand, and a little smile played upon his lips. There was little doubt in his mind that he would succeed. How could he not, a man of his skills? Had he not served princes – even popes? All he had to do was to recover that which the Seigneur de Maisse had bespoke from a certain jeweller, who in his greed had sold it to another party without thinking of the consequences. For the Seigneur was not a man to forgive a slight, especially when it touched upon his family's honour. The jeweller had fetched up in the Seine, his body bleeding from a hundred gashes – but not before he had spilled all he knew to Corvino. In the hands of that inquisitor he had become a babbling fool – to Corvino's disgust, the wretch had even soiled his breeches. When it was over Corvino had rolled the body off the Quai d'Orsay with his foot, then walked away without another thought.

His horse was saddled; he took the rein and led it from the gloom of the stable, out into the evening sunlight. England it was, then. It should not be too hard to pick up the trail again. Once he had found the prize he would bring it back with all speed, collect the rest of his money, then put some distance between himself and the Seigneur de Maisse. He disliked his lordship intensely.

He mounted, and without looking back, rode out of the courtyard. By this time tomorrow he would be at the coast; perhaps already on a ship. Why, his task was half over.

After all, who was there in England who could stop a man like him?

One

One more day of rain such as this, and the Lambourn would burst its banks.

So Thomas the Falconer thought, as he stood upon the slope of Coldborough Hill in the downpour, and gazed at the river below him. Usually in high summer the little chalk stream was but a trickle – village boys from East Garston or Shefford splashed across it barefoot, or even leaped over it. But now . . . he sighed, watching the swirling water hurry by, and let his thoughts drift along with it. After all, floods were the least of England's troubles. A wet summer for the third year in succession meant yet another bad harvest. Already the price of grain had soared – he had even heard of riots in some towns. Where would it all end?

He shook the raindrops from his beard, pulled up his leather hood and turned to walk back to the manor. What sense was there in cursing the weather, when there was naught he could do about it? Though it troubled him that Sir Robert's falcons were sorely in need of exercise. The birds hated the rain, and despite his and Ned's best efforts they refused to fly. A few hours' respite was all he needed . . . He glanced up at the sky, looking westward where the Downs climbed towards Lambourn. But there was nothing to see save a sullen blanket of thick cloud.

After a while, having topped the hill he descended a long slope, and Petbury came into view. Smoke swirled from the chimneys, sluggish in the rain. Grooms were in the paddock, exercising horses. Sir Robert had been in London on some unknown business for the past week, but was expected back soon. Hence the more lackadaisical air that usually prevailed when Lady Margaret was in charge had given way to one of bustle and anticipation. Though there would be no hawking parties in this torrent, Thomas told himself. He skirted the fence, nodding to the grooms in their sodden clothes, then made his way past the stables towards the falcons' mews. As he drew near, two men emerged from the doorway. One was Ned Hawes, his young helper, while the other . . . Thomas stiffened, but managed not to check his stride. For the second man, a slim figure in a hat and fashionable cloak, was the last person in Petbury he wished to see. His name was John Doggett; and as far as Thomas was concerned, he was about as welcome as an epidemic of bird-pox.

He approached the two, exchanging a glance with Ned, who kept a straight face. He also cared little for Doggett, but his dislike of the man was mild compared to Thomas's. For Ned was yet unmarried and had no children, let alone a fair daughter of twenty-one whose looks attracted most males in the vicinity. And to Thomas's alarm, it had become common knowledge at Petbury that Eleanor had caught the attention of one of the manor's summer guests: the vain, smooth-faced Master Doggett, a Londoner in his mid-twenties, who served as personal secretary to a more important guest: Sir Robert's widowed sister Lady Jane Rooke. Moreover, Doggett's position was such that he was able to pursue Eleanor with ease about the house and grounds, and even further afield. For if Eleanor, as a woman-waiting, chanced to accompany her mistress Lady Margaret on one of her rides, Doggett somehow always managed to tag along. It brought bile to Thomas's throat to see how the simpering fellow fawned upon Eleanor and flattered her shamelessly, as he did his foolish mistress Lady Rooke . . . but that was a different matter, and one in which Thomas was powerless. With an effort, he pushed these thoughts aside and made his greeting.

'Master Doggett. It must be business of great importance, for you to visit us in such inclement weather.'

The young man retained his broad smile, though the sarcasm in Thomas's tone was obvious even to the guileless Ned, who looked away. Waving a hand airily, Doggett answered: 'It was you I came to see, falconer. But it seemed you were out for a walk . . . luckily young Ned here has been most hospitable.'

Before Thomas could reply he added: 'Firstly, I wished to enquire whether you are planning to go hawking upon Sir Robert's return. Secondly—'

'In this deluge?' Thomas raised his brows. 'I thought even a city fellow like you would know how the birds dislike water . . .'

Doggett was nodding. 'Of course – you interrupted me. My second purpose was to enquire after the whereabouts of your beautiful daughter. I have not seen her today.'

Thomas measured his words carefully. 'Nor I. Likely she's busy upon some task for her mistress. Being Lady Rooke's devoted servant, you know how demanding well-born ladies can be.'

Ned gave a snort, then tried to turn it into a cough. Muttering something about checking on the falcons he turned and disappeared inside the mews, leaving Thomas and John Doggett alone. But if the other was stung by Thomas's remark he hid it well. One of the many things that unsettled Thomas about this man was how skilled he was at smiling. His grin barely wavered.

'How true, falconer . . . though as you know I am Lady Rooke's private secretary,' he said. 'Kat is her body-servant.' He named Kat Jenkin, a timid little maid who had won the sympathy of all at Petbury for her devotion to a difficult mistress.

'As you please,' Thomas muttered, tiring of the exchange. 'Now if you'll allow, I've work to do.' He was about to follow Ned inside the mews, but to his irritation Doggett moved suddenly to block his path. His smile remained, but there was a look of defiance in his eyes.

'I am of course mindful of your deep love for Eleanor, falconer,' he said gently. 'Any man may admire such fatherly devotion, not to say the way in which you raised her alone, after her mother's death.'

Thomas froze. 'I'd choose your words with care if I were you, master,' he said at last. 'Else I might forget whom it is you serve, and treat you as I would any other young rake that tries to beat a path to my daughter.'

Doggett nodded briskly. 'Admirable . . . I barely expected

to find such sentiments here in the Downlands. Yet if I might speak as broadly . . . ?' The man's smile faded at last. 'Surely you would not have Eleanor – a grown woman of twenty-one years, who knows her own mind – mewed up like your falcons? To be carried on the leash, and only allowed to soar at your will?'

Thomas drew a breath, but remained silent. In an odd way, he felt relieved. This confrontation had been brewing for the past fortnight at least. Better to have done with it, and leave this smirking fellow in no doubt as to how things stood. He waited.

'You yourself have remarried,' Doggett went on, seemingly enjoying the sound of his own voice, and ignoring the rain that continued to drench the pair of them. 'A man needs a wife – and what a match you have made! The finest cook in all the county, I hear, and a handsome woman to boot. No doubt she's as skilled in her wifely duties as she is in the kitchens.'

Still, Thomas waited.

'So . . .' Doggett waved his hand again, allowing the rings upon it to glint despite the rain. 'Come, Master Finbow, let's dispense with this brabbling, may we not? We're both men who have lived a little . . . though you have twice my years, I'll wager we've the same appetites. Need I lay it out further? I'm devoted to Eleanor, and would walk through fires merely to kneel before her. And if I read her correctly, as I think I do, she does not dislike my company. Now is that plain enough, for a plain man like yourself?'

There was a moment, while the rain pattered relentlessly down. It ran in rivulets from the edge of Thomas's hood, as it did from the narrow brim of Doggett's high-crowned hat. Then it was that for the first time Thomas noticed that the hat bore a rather fine feather – or what had once been a feather. Now, the sodden object bore a closer resemblance to a dead mouse.

'Your hat, master . . .' Thomas found it hard to get the words out; for the urge to laugh, which had sprung up unbidden, threatened to make him break out in a roar.

'My hat?' Doggett looked puzzled. 'What of it?'

'It's . . .' Thomas struggled to restrain himself. 'It's very wet.'

'Indeed.' For the first time, Doggett looked impatient. 'Why would it not be?'

'The plume . . . I fear it's beyond repair,' Thomas continued. 'Perhaps we might find you a hawk's tail feather to replace it . . . though the stripes might give it away.'

Doggett frowned. 'Do you scoff at me, falconer?'

Thomas swallowed. 'As you've said, I'm a plain man, master,' he answered. 'Hence my humour's plain, too.' On impulse he added: 'And my daughter, you will find, despite the fine ways she has picked up from serving my Lady Margaret, is a plain Downland girl at heart, just like her mother was. She despises fluff and flummery, as do we all.'

Doggett opened his mouth, then closed it again. For once he seemed lost for words. Suddenly he shivered.

'I had a mind to try to get to know you a little, falconer,' he said in an acid tone. 'Perhaps I've merely been wasting my time.'

'Looks that way,' Thomas murmured.

'I have duties in the house,' Doggett continued, as if he had not heard. 'So I'll bid you good day.'

And to Thomas's relief, he started to go. But walking away, he paused to throw a parting shot over his shoulder.

'Tell your daughter when you see her that I was most eager to wait upon her, won't you?' he called. 'I have a new love song for the lute, which I've been at pains to rehearse. I shall change the words a little, to suit Eleanor . . .' And suddenly, the man's smile was back. 'We are now under the sign of Cancer, Master Finbow – surely even you will be aware of that? And Cancer, of course, governs the heart! Fare you well!'

And with that, the fellow hurried off down the grassy slope towards the great house, pulling his cloak about him.

When darkness fell, having seen the falcons fed and settled for the night, Thomas was in the cottage lighting a lantern when Nell at last came in from the kitchens. After kissing him, she slumped down tiredly beside the fireplace.

'No more suppers?' Thomas asked mildly. He dropped

the pane into place, allowing the flame to gain intensity, then hung the lantern on a peg.

'Lady Margaret is retired to her chamber,' Nell said, and gave a yawn. 'My Lady Rooke plays at cards with that popinjay of a secretary of hers . . . young Kat will take her up a posset. Let's pray that's enough.'

Thomas nodded and sat down beside her. Their duties were such that they saw little of each other as it was. When there were guests at Petbury, he seldom saw Nell from dawn to dusk.

'I had a few words with Master Doggett myself this morning,' he murmured. 'Tried to let him know I don't care for his chasing after Eleanor, though he had no mind to listen.'

Nell raised her brows. 'You'd best make it plainer, then. For I hear he's a rutting fellow, back in London. He's fathered at least one child – by a washerwoman, so young Kat says. Made her sell it in secret, like a whore's burden.'

Thomas frowned. After a moment Nell sat up, took off her linen cap and began to pull the pins from her luxurious red hair.

'Still – if he thinks to treat Eleanor in such fashion, he'll regret it,' she went on, favouring Thomas with one of her half-smiles. 'She's seen off better men than him.'

Thomas returned her smile. 'True enough.'

'Even if he does have a fine singing voice,' Nell added. 'To my mind, that's how he charmed his way into Lady Rooke's service . . . though the woman's half distracted in any case. She seldom knows what day it is. How Kat puts up with her ways, I know not.'

Thomas gazed at the rush-strewn floor. It was true that Sir Robert's sister, a childless, empty-headed woman in her mid-fifties, was a sorry figure at the best of times. When her husband, the sickly Sir Hugh Rooke, had died last winter, Lady Jane had all but lost her reason. Small wonder that, lonely and unhappy as she was, she had allowed the sly John Doggett to come into her home. That was only a few months back, yet the man had so won her trust that he had become a permanent member of her household. Though none seemed to know much about him, he behaved like a steward, ordering Lady Rooke's affairs much as he liked. The distressing part was that the woman had come to rely on him so much, she would go nowhere without him. Hence Sir Robert, who loathed the fellow almost as much as Thomas did, had been obliged to house him under his roof for the summer, along with his sister.

'Mayhap the cove will get his comeuppance,' Nell said sleepily. 'If the weather turns and Sir Robert gets up a hawking party, you could arrange a little accident for Master Doggett. Give him a frisky horse, or some such . . .'

Thomas threw her a wry look, whereupon she stood up, still undoing her hair. 'I'm for bed,' she said. 'Are you joining me, or not?'

He smiled, and nodded.

But an hour or two later, when all of Petbury should have been asleep, the two of them woke together in the pitch darkness. Above their heads the rain drummed on the thatch – but there was another, louder sound that startled them anew, and it came from below. Someone was beating upon the door.

'Who in heaven's name . . . ?' Nell sat up, her voice loud in the small sleeping space beneath the rafters. But Thomas threw the covers aside and rose swiftly from the bed. She heard his feet on the ladder. With a muttered oath, she fell back upon the pillow.

The knocking came again, heavy and insistent. Thomas stumbled across the darkened room towards the door. Now there came a voice, which he recognized at once – though it aroused alarm in him rather than reassurance: Sir Robert. But if it was indeed he, why had he returned home so late? And besides, for him to come to the falconer's cottage was unheard of, let alone at such an hour . . .

'Thomas! For pity's sake, are you not within?!'

The words turned to a mutter of relief, as Thomas gained the door and wrenched it open. There stood his master in his cloak, alone and soaked to the skin. His hair was plastered to his skull.

'Thank the Christ . . .' Barely waiting for Thomas to stand aside, Sir Robert ducked to avoid the lintel and hurried into the cottage. Quickly Thomas closed the door, looking anxiously at him.

'Sir, let me have your cloak, before you take a chill. I'll make up a fire—'

'There's no need – I will not stay.' Sir Robert wiped the rainwater from his brow with his sleeve. He was short of breath, as if he had run uphill from the house. Only now did Thomas's glance fall upon the object in the knight's hand. It was a small case perhaps a foot square, bound in black, tooled leather, with a brass clasp. As Thomas looked up enquiringly at his master, the other gave a short nod.

'This will answer your question, as to why I come here at this time,' Sir Robert said, tapping the case. 'For I wished no one to see where I brought it.' When Thomas said nothing, the other went on: 'In here is something of great value – I may almost say beyond price. But more, a great deal hangs upon its safe delivery, to—' Sir Robert broke off. Now Thomas saw how tired he was. He looked like a man who had been riding half the night.

'Never mind who it's destined for. What matters is that it lies safe, somewhere known only to the man I trust most.' He paused, glancing round Thomas's home as if seeing it for the first time. In fact, Thomas realized, though Sir Robert had ridden past the cottage door a thousand times, he had never before been inside. And suddenly the strangeness of the situation struck both men. Their eyes met, and Sir Robert gave a short bark of laughter.

'Your pardon, Thomas . . .' He shook his head, sending droplets of water flying. 'If I seem to have lost my wits, you'd not wonder at it were I to tell you what's happened in the past week. It's but a day and a night since I left the Queen at Richmond Palace. She's gone away now, on her summer progress. But not before she charged me with a task the like of which I never thought to undertake . . .' He sighed. 'I believe the matter will become clear to you tomorrow, when my guests arrive. For you too will have to share in the entertaining of them. And it seems we must deny them nothing!'

'More guests, Sir Robert?' Thomas showed his surprise. 'The house will be full . . .'

'Indeed it will,' Sir Robert agreed. 'And my poor sister will likely have to vacate her chamber for one of more modest size. For these are no ordinary guests.' The knight's brow had furrowed. 'Not even in my father's time,' he muttered, 'was Petbury called upon to host an ambassador and his train.'

Thomas kept silent. He knew Sir Robert well, and saw now that his master was eager to take his leave. But first he held out the small case, nodding to Thomas to take it.

'Hide it – anywhere you like, as long as it's somewhere dry, and as long as none but you can find it,' Sir Robert ordered. 'I will say more to you later . . . in the meantime, you must take my word that this is an object of grave import. Besides, who knows the Downs – the barrows, the pathways and the crannies – better than you? I know you will choose a good place.'

Thomas took the case from his hand. It was solid, and surprisingly heavy.

'You may go to your bed in the knowledge that it is safe, sir,' he said. 'None will know where it lies but me.'

Sir Robert gave a sigh, as if a weight had indeed been lifted from him. 'I know it,' he said. Then clapping a hand briefly to Thomas's shoulder, he turned and made for the door. His boots left a pool of water where he had stood.

Thomas let him out, pausing only to watch him hurry away into the darkness. Then his glance strayed towards the bulk of the great house below. A single light showed from the upper storey. Lady Jane Rooke always had a candle burning in her chamber, for she feared the dark.

He closed the door, and made his way thoughtfully back to the ladder. In his hand the leather case, still wet with rain, felt cold to his touch.

The next morning the rain eased off, though few expected the break to last. But Thomas and Ned seized the moment and were out early, taking their master's falcons on the gauntlet and flying them upon Greenhill Down. Ned was in good humour, having spent the previous night at the Black Bear in Chaddleworth in the company of a new sweetheart, but finding Thomas preoccupied, he knew better than to press him to conversation. As midday drew near the two falconers walked back to Petbury, having exercised the last of their charges. Thomas bore a tercel on his arm, while Ned carried a little saker. The tiny falcon, a lady's hawk, had been obtained at Sir Robert's bidding for his sister. It turned out that Lady Rooke had no inclination for hawking, yet Thomas had decided to keep the bird for the summer, in the hope that her ladyship might change her mind.

'Will you see them settled and watered?' he asked Ned. 'I've something to attend to at home.'

Ned gave a nod. It seemed to him now that Thomas's glance had been straying towards his cottage throughout the morning.

'Naught amiss, is there?' he asked.

'No.' Thomas stared straight ahead. They were descending the long hill, with the mews in sight below them. He felt the tercel shift upon his wrist, and spoke a soothing word to it before picking up his pace. The truth was that not for a moment had he been able to forget the mysterious case which Sir Robert had given to him, and which was now in a chest in his sleeping chamber underneath Nell's best gown. He had had no time yet to find a proper hiding place for it, which made him uneasy. He meant to take the object out of sight of the manor, perhaps as far as the Ridgeway, and conceal it beneath a slab of stone. He would mark the spot with a few well-placed rocks that only he could recognize. But now the rain had chosen this morning to lay off, obliging him to fly the falcons. Sometimes, luck could be a fickle jade.

They reached the mews, and Ned took his charge inside and placed it on its perch. As Thomas followed him into the semi-darkness the other birds stirred, then calmed. Ned took the tercel from Thomas's gauntlet, and asked: 'Have you heard aught about this party that's expected today?'

Thomas shrugged. 'An ambassador is all I've been told, along with his servants. Though what country they hail from, I know not.' Absently he watched Ned settle the tercel, then turned to go. 'Take a bit of dinner when you're done,' he said. 'Nell says there's an ox-tongue pie left from last night's supper.'

Ned grinned, seeming to savour the dish already.

Thomas went immediately to his cottage.

Once inside he wedged the door shut with a stool, then climbed up to the sleeping loft. He opened the chest and fumbled under the clothing, feeling reassured when his fingers closed upon the hard edge of the case. Then he straightened up, allowed the heavy lid to fall shut, and almost laughed at his own foolishness. None but he knew the case was here – not even Nell. She was still asleep when he had crept from the bed in the early dawn, taken it from under his clothes and stowed it away. Nell had not even opened the chest, but gone to the kitchens in her workaday gown as usual. He gave a sigh, and resolved to deal with the matter just as soon as darkness fell.

As he descended the ladder, it struck him how little time he had had since last night to wonder what was in the black case. What on earth could have caused Sir Robert to run through the rain in the middle of the night to give it to him?

He sighed; he was not about to let his natural curiosity, which had led him into trouble on more than one occasion, get the better of him this time. His master had been entrusted with the case, and he had entrusted it to Thomas; it was enough.

With a sense of relief, he left the cottage and walked down the grassy slope towards the kitchen garden, aware now of his own appetite. But as he passed through the archway he was startled to see an excited little group hurrying out of the kitchen doorway, spilling on to the path. Drawing nearer, he saw Ned among the grooms, servingmen and kitchen wenches who were making their way round the side of the house towards the front courtyard, talking in animated fashion.

Ned was gesturing to him to hurry. As he came up, the lad grinned. 'Thomas, stir yourself! The ambassador's come – and you'll not trust your ears when I tell you where he's from!'

The lad was so elated, Thomas could only smile.

'Well,' he answered, 'aren't you going to tell me?'

'Gladly!' Ned cried. 'For he's only sent from the Emperor of Muscovy! They say he's eight feet tall – and he's brought a white hawk with him that's big as an eagle!'

Two

The story about the Russian ambassador being eight feet tall proved to be a myth. The man was huge, with a great black square-cut beard like a coal shovel, but he stood little more than six feet, though his fox-fur cap made him appear taller. His followers, four or five of them in long coats of sheepskin, were similar: big men, one enormously fat, and all bearded save one who was slighter than the rest and had the air of a scholar. The Petbury folk would soon come to know him as the ambassador's secretary.

The part about the great white falcon, however, was true. Thomas stopped in his tracks when he saw the bird, sitting on the arm of one of the ambassador's men. He had never seen a hawk like it. It was, as Ned had said, the size of an eagle, with snow-white plumage, a speckled chest and a mighty tail. It was not even hooded, but stared about defiantly as if daring anyone to come near. In fact the Muscovy men wore similar expressions, gazing suspiciously at the manor folk who had gathered to look at them with unfeigned curiosity.

Fortunately the initial awkwardness would not last long. The Russians had dismounted from their horses, and seemed willing to hand the reins to grooms. But the small cart they had brought, loaded with intriguing-looking packages wrapped in hides, they would permit none to touch. They spoke among themselves in their tongue, but made their sentiments plain to the Petbury men with frowns and dismissive swipes of their hands. Only when Sir Robert and Lady Margaret, accompanied by their old steward Martin, emerged from the main door of the house to greet their guests did the atmosphere soften a little. Then the speeches began; whereupon curiosity turned to astonishment. For all of Berkshire, let alone the Downlands, had never heard the like.

First the ambassador spoke: a rambling tirade in his language, full of grand gestures and deep, rolling sounds that made the kitchen boy giggle. It seemed to be a greeting, which Sir Robert and Lady Margaret, standing stiffly together, heard in respectful silence. His master, Thomas saw, had seemingly recovered from last night's dousing, and struck a dignified pose in a new black doublet and wide breeches with silver stripes. Lady Margaret, elegant as ever, wore a summer gown of saffron and white, her hair dressed with a caul of pearls. And for the first time in days Thomas now saw Eleanor, standing in silence behind her mistress. His heart gave a jolt, for his daughter looked quite beautiful in a lilac gown, made over from one of Lady Margaret's. In the doorway behind, other house servants crowded – and Thomas's mouth tightened as he saw a familiar smiling face among them: that of John Doggett.

At last the ambassador finished and turned to the smooth-faced attendant who stood nearby. The company realized that this one would act as interpreter, and their relief was evident when it transpired that he spoke good English.

'His Excellency Grigori Stanic, Duke of Novgorod, Lord of Karelia, Warden of the East Forests and Ambassador to his beatific highness Feodor, Tsar of all the Russias, greets you!' the man cried. He smiled, and made a passable bow. 'He is pleased to salute Sir Robert Vicary, knight of Her Majesty Queen Elizabeth . . .' The secretary gestured to the cart. 'His Excellency has brought gifts from our far country, with great trouble over land and sea!'

There was a moment while the Russians waited. A silence fell, which Sir Robert quickly realized he was expected to fill.

'We are honoured, sir,' he replied, and made his bow to the ambassador. 'Lady Vicary and I extend our warmest affections to you and to your noble train. Welcome to Petbury, which we beg you to treat as your own home for . . .' He faltered only slightly. 'For as long as you please!'

The attendant translated swiftly for the benefit of the

ambassador, who merely nodded as if he expected nothing less. Thomas, standing beside Ned, saw Nell arrive at the rear of the little crowd. They exchanged meaningful looks. He knew better than most how much extra work this group would make for the kitchens.

'You are kind, sir.' The interpreter inclined his head towards Sir Robert. 'Permit me to present myself: I am Keril Yusupov, secretary to His Excellency. This man . . .' He indicated the fat, unsmiling fellow who stood at his side, sweating in his heavy coat. 'He is Mikhailov, a *sotnik* of the *streltsi*. He must go where the ambassador goes – and he will also taste his food.'

There was a murmur from the servants, which ceased when Martin, at his most officious, threw a stern glance at them. Clearing his throat, the old man hastened to assert his authority. 'I am Sir Robert's steward,' he announced, 'and there is no need for such practice here, sir. Your master shall eat from the same dish as mine, if he wishes – at Petbury we safeguard the lives of all guests as if they were our own!' He paused, then added in a less confident tone: 'And permit me to ask what a *sotnik* is . . . or was it a *strelli*—?' He broke off, frowning. But Yusupov smiled indulgently.

'Your pardon, master steward. Mikhailov is His Excellency's bodyguard, who will defend him unto death. The *streltsi* are the Tsar's personal militia, and a *sotnik* means that he is a captain.' He turned to Mikhailov, who made a stiff little bow. Then to the consternation of Sir Robert and everyone else, the man launched into an incomprehensible speech of his own. Mercifully this one was short and to the point, punctuated by frowns and sideways slashes of the bodyguard's hand – not to mention sporadic grasping of his sword hilt. The weapon was short with a curved blade, encased in a stout scabbard. Hence the meaning of the fellow's outburst was plain enough: he would cut to shreds anyone who dared to lay a finger upon his master.

Now Sir Robert bristled, but again Yusupov hastened to oil the wheels of diplomacy. 'Sotnik Mikhailov merely wishes to make it clear, sir, that he is at your service as well as our master's,' he said, keeping a very straight face. 'If danger should threaten, no matter how great, he would lay down his life for you, as if you were the great Tsar himself!'

Then to move matters on, the secretary looked to the man bearing the white falcon, and beckoned him forward.

'This is Kovalenko, His Excellency's chief falconer. He brings you a fine hawk from our country! Her strength and speed are such she will take wild swans, even cranes! In the domain of these creatures, she is truly a tsarina!'

And along with everyone else, Sir Robert could only gaze admiringly at the bird. Finally he glanced towards the servants and caught Thomas's eye. His master's words of the previous night came back to him: Thomas would indeed have to share in entertaining the ambassador, if hawking was one of his pleasures. Beside him, Ned muttered in his ear. 'Jesu, how do we manage a bird like that?'

But there was no time to dwell on it, for the ambassador was speaking again. This time, without waiting for interpretation, Sir Robert spoke up quickly.

'My thanks are inadequate,' he said, 'to do justice to the ambassador's gracious gift. I will have my own falconer take care of the bird . . .' He beckoned. And watched by everyone, Thomas emerged from the group and walked towards Kovalenko the falconer.

The fellow looked round. He and Thomas were both tall men, and as their eyes met, a look of understanding passed between them. Even if Kovalenko had not seen the gauntlet that Thomas took from his belt and pulled over his left hand, he recognized a fellow hawksman by his manner. The man relaxed somewhat and raised his arm slowly, permitting Thomas to place his own arm close. Then to Thomas's surprise, he spoke suddenly in English.

'Speak low, and she come to you.' He bent his head and muttered a few words to the great bird. Watched by the whole company, both Russian and English, Thomas nodded and began to speak softly to the white falcon. And sure enough, after a moment the bird raised a huge talon and stepped gently on to his gauntlet. It lifted its wings briefly, then folded them and sat staring into the distance.

A sigh went up. But Thomas merely took the leash which Kovalenko had unwound from his gauntlet, and gave it a couple of turns about his own. He nodded approvingly at the man. 'She's a wondrous creature, master,' he said. 'Do you have a name for her?'

The other shrugged. 'I call her *dushenka* . . . it's what you say to a woman, when you want her to do your bidding.'

The bird, despite her size, was light upon Thomas's wrist. 'Come to the falcons' mews when you may,' he said, turning to go, 'and tell me more of her.'

But the man looked aside, distracted by the ambassador. Stanic was now embracing Sir Robert like a long-lost friend, causing some raised eyebrows. Yusupov the secretary, who was clearly a very astute fellow, spoke up once again.

'His Excellency greets you as a brother!' he said to Sir Robert. 'And as for gifts – even the great hawk will seem of little import, when you see what else he brings! Seal oil from the Arctic, sable furs from our forests, caviar from our great river-fish!' He nodded towards the cart. 'Will your slaves now carry them inside?'

'Slaves?' Sir Robert threw a blank look at Lady Margaret, who had yet to speak. Now she summoned one of her most winning smiles and came forward. Ignoring the lecherous grin which stole over the ambassador's face – for at forty-eight years, the mistress of Petbury was still a strikingly attractive woman – she addressed him directly.

'Sir, you and your men have had a long journey from London. Now you must eat and drink with us – pray come into the hall, where a feast awaits!'

The effect was striking. If the ice had been somewhat slow to melt thus far, it now disappeared in a moment. As Yusupov translated for Stanic and the others, smiles appeared on all their faces, even that of the menacing Mikhailov. They were indeed hungry men, and they needed no further urging. Forgetting their cartload of gifts, the party promptly followed Sir Robert and Lady Margaret into the house. The servants quickly dispersed to their duties. Martin took charge of the cart, ordering grooms to wheel it to a side entrance where it would be unloaded.

And that, Thomas thought, was all he, Ned and the rest of the outdoor folk would see of their Russian visitors for a while. Now he had his hands full – literally, as he bore the great white hawk away from the house, and up the slope towards the mews. Ned ran ahead to ready a place for the new bird. As Thomas brought her in, the boy stared at it in wonder.

'What did you and the Russian say to each other?' he asked.

Thomas stooped and placed his gauntlet beside the low stump that would serve as a perch. From there the bird could drink without putting its tail feathers upon the damp ground. After a moment, the white hawk stepped on to the wood with such an air of lofty disdain, both Thomas and Ned laughed aloud.

'What a grand lady she is!' Ned cried. 'She don't care for us country folk much, does she?'

Thomas shook his head. He took an earthenware dish, filled it with water from a pitcher and placed it before the falcon. For a moment she regarded it, then to his satisfaction bent her head and began to drink.

'What did he say, then – the falconer?' Ned repeated.

'He said her name's Dushenka,' Thomas replied, keeping his eyes on the white hawk. 'And if you ask me there isn't a hawksman in England could tame her!'

Late that night, while Sir Robert and Lady Margaret entertained their guests in the great hall, Thomas at last got the black case away from his cottage, hidden under his jerkin. Confident that he had been seen by no one, he hurried uphill towards the Ridgeway, until Petbury was lost in the gloom behind him. When the narrow sliver of gravel appeared, a faint streak in the moonlight, he walked along it for a while until he came to a familiar hump, a rock that had lain beside the path ever since he could remember. Here he knelt, and with the trowel he had brought, dug a hole under the stone. Then looking about him, he brought out the case, wrapped in a piece of soft leather. He nodded to himself: though the damp would get to the case in time, he did not intend to leave it here long. If Sir Robert did not ask for it, he would move it in a few days to a better spot.

Carefully he placed the case in the hole, shovelled earth over it and patted it firm. Then he dug up a few tussocks of grass and replanted them in the fresh soil. Finally he stood, and looked down at his handiwork with satisfaction. Dusting his hands on his breeches, he walked back along the path, then turned and began to trudge downhill to the manor.

Relieved to have disposed of the business, he allowed his thoughts to turn to other matters. Uppermost in his mind were the Russians: Sir Robert had sent word that if the rain held off, he would go hawking on the morrow with the ambassador. The falconer, Kovalenko, would accompany his master along with the fearsome Mikhailov. Thomas should have birds ready for all of them.

Kovalenko interested him. He was surprised that the man spoke English, and looked forward to talking to him. He realized how little he knew about far-off Muscovy, though he had heard of the Muscovy Company, who with the Tsar's approval had traded English wool for such things as oil and furs for the best part of forty years. Otherwise the place was little more than a name to him. It was a poor country, he seemed to remember; dark and cold, with huge forests filled with wolves. He grinned to himself, recalling what Ned had said when they parted earlier that evening: that he had heard the Muscovites ate the bodies of their dead. Somehow he could not imagine the elegant Yusupov sitting down to a dinner of human flesh.

The great house was in sight, lights yet showing from some of the windows. Nell was still busy in the kitchens. He passed by the mews, hearing no sound and knowing the falcons were content. Then as he turned towards the cottage, he heard it – very faint, from perhaps fifty yards away: the twang of a bowstring, followed by the thud of an arrow. And immediately, he knew who had loosed it: Will Greve, once a companion of his boyhood – now Chaddleworth's most notorious poacher.

The park, beyond the paddock . . . there were a few fallow deer in it, for of late Sir Robert had taken to hunting again, to vary with his hawking trips. Who but Greve, Thomas thought ruefully, would have been bold enough to try his luck with the lights of Petbury burning a hundred yards away? And when, as everyone knew, the penalty for poaching a deer was death?

His keen ears straining to catch every sound, Thomas fell into stalking manner. Bent low, he moved soundlessly through the grass, still wet from the rain, until he had skirted the wall of the stable yard and reached the paddock fence. Now he heard the nervous snicker of horses: several had been left to graze for the night. There was too much cloud and little moonlight, but peering ahead he could make out the silhouette of three or four mares, bunching in the far corner. As he watched, they veered away to the left. At once his eyes swung to the right, beyond the paddock to the park with its few small trees, their trunks fenced about to protect them from the deer. He waited motionless beside a post, but there was no movement. Then, as he was about to creep forward, the outline of a human form rose slowly from the grass, barely ten yards from him.

The man had been crouching, as Thomas was, but he did not know he was being watched. He started to move; and now Thomas saw the shape of the bow in his hand. He waited a few seconds, then stood up and ran forward swiftly.

Instantly the poacher snapped his head round, then turned and bolted. But Thomas was quicker. In a short time he had closed upon his quarry, who was a head shorter than him: a stubby man with thick, brawny arms. As Thomas gained on him he heard the fellow curse, before accepting the inevitable. Whereupon he stopped and swung round to face Thomas. As he did so he put his hand to the quiver on his back, whipped out an arrow and fitted it to the bowstring.

'Easy, Will . . .' Thomas halted, catching his breath, and levelled his gaze at the poacher. 'You wouldn't want to spend a shaft on me, would you?'

'The blazes with you, Finbow!' Greve glared at him. 'Let me go – I've taken nothing!'

'I heard you shoot,' Thomas countered. 'I didn't think you'd risk all for one of Sir Robert's does . . . What's wrong with a hare, or a couple of rabbits?'

'Let it lie, won't you?' Greve snapped, with a nervous glance towards the house. His face was running with sweat, his lank hair loose to his shoulders. 'Are you grown so pious these days, like that whoreson steward, that you'd turn in one you've known all your life?' He sniffed, and drew a sleeve across his snub nose. 'You and me were close . . .'

Thomas returned his gaze. 'Aye . . . but our paths have diverted somewhat,' he answered drily. 'I'd condemn no man who's hard pressed to feed his family – but I stop short of wounding. Now lower your bow, you dunderhead—'

'You be silent!' Greve cried. There was a wild look in his eye. 'I'm no saint, Finbow – but nor am I a murderer, if that's the way your mind moves! I was tried once and took my branding, is't not enough?'

Somewhat shakily, he stuck his fist out. Thomas could not see it in the dark; yet he knew well enough, as did all of Chaddleworth, that Greve bore the letter T burned on the base of his thumb. A thief's punishment . . . and less than he deserved, many folk said. Once a traveller had been found on the Wantage road, killed by a bowshot to the neck, his purse taken. Though there was no evidence, many suspected Will Greve. When he was caught for the theft of a silver jug, some tried to raise the matter of the murdered traveller again, without success. For his part, Thomas had tried to convince himself of Greve's innocence. Yet he had seen the man's savagery, in a drunken fight over a woman . . . something he liked not to think upon now.

There was a moment while each waited for the other to speak, for Greve was no blusterer; and he knew Thomas too well to try bluffing. Finally he lowered his bow, loosed the string and stood to his full height. 'Come – follow me, see where the arrow fell,' he said in a softer tone. 'I'll wager I've killed naught. Will that not sway you?'

Thomas gave a sigh. 'By the heavens, Will . . . is it always to be so, year by year?' he asked. 'This cat-and-mouse game of ours can but end two ways: with me losing my place, or you on the end of a hangman's rope – or both!'

Greve shrugged. 'I'll retrieve my shaft,' he muttered. And berating himself for a soft-hearted fool, Thomas followed him across the park. The deer had already fled, for there was none in sight. Finally, guided by his instinct, Greve stopped and bent down, peering at the ground. As Thomas came up, he pointed.

'My eyes must be failing,' he said sourly. 'I mistook a log for something that lived.'

Thomas peered through the gloom, and saw that he spoke the truth. His arrow, fletched with the feathers of a wild hawk, protruded from the stump of a felled tree.

'If your eyes are failing, it seems your luck is not,' Thomas told him. 'What if it was one of Sir Robert's foals – or for that matter a farm girl and her swain, bucking in the grass?'

'Then the cove would've got shot in the arse!' Greve retorted, and bent to pull his arrow from the stump. When he had wrenched it free, he turned deliberately to Thomas.

'Well, falconer? What's your decision?'

'You know it already,' Thomas said, and looked away. 'You'd best lose yourself before I change my mind.'

Greve relaxed, and gave a dour grin. 'Then I'll stand you a mug in the Black Bear.'

'Nay, keep your money,' Thomas threw back. 'I'm particular who I sup with these days . . .'

But Will Greve had turned his back, and was trotting off in the direction of the Hungerford road. In a moment the darkness had swallowed him.

The following morning dawned misty, but yet the rain held off. So as soon as they had taken a bit of breakfast Thomas and Ned were at the mews. And they had not long to wait before several riders appeared from the direction of the stable. Foremost was Sir Robert, and with him as expected were the Russians: Stanic in fur-trimmed riding clothes, and three others: Kovalenko the falconer, the bulky

Mikhailov riding a very stout horse and another behind them, a younger man. Then as they drew near Thomas saw Lady Margaret riding behind – and was surprised to see Eleanor with her, on a chestnut mare from the Petbury stable. His daughter, it was true, had learned to ride in recent years to accompany her mistress, but it was rare to see her at hawking, though being a falconer's daughter, she had handled the birds from her childhood. Thomas, however, had to busy himself with the honoured guests. He saw with some relief that Ned had a hooded bird on his wrist already. As the party came up and drew rein, the lad made a stiff bow and offered the fine passage-hawk to the Ambassador. Stanic took it expertly upon his glove and favoured Ned with a curt nod. Then he turned to Sir Robert and spoke rapidly in Russian. There was a moment's unease, since Yusupov the secretary was conspicuous by his absence. But it seemed Kovalenko, with his limited English, would act as interpreter. Drawing his horse close to Sir Robert's, the falconer said: 'Sir – His Excellency ask if you take the great white hawk out, and fly her yourself.'

Sir Robert looked embarrassed, and turned to Thomas for help. He had no intention of flying any other hawk than his own favourite three-year-old. Thomas cleared his throat, and when Kovalenko looked round, caught his eye. 'I've exercised the bird already, master,' he said. 'She's resting now . . . will you tell His Excellency?'

Kovalenko hesitated, then bent his head and spoke quietly. 'Is wise not to displease our *batsushka*,' he murmured. 'He want to see Sir Robert fly the bird . . . you get her?'

Thomas caught Sir Robert's eye; and his master understood. 'Bring the white hawk out, then,' he said in a dry voice. 'It seems I must show my gratitude to our guest.'

Ned had busied himself getting Lady Margaret's merlin and taking it to her. So Thomas went into the mews and unleashed Dushenka from her perch. To his relief the falcon came readily on to his gauntlet. He brought her out, and watched by the ambassador, took her to Sir Robert, who leaned from the saddle. Mercifully, at a few soft words from Thomas the bird stepped on to Sir Robert's gauntlet.

The knight eyed her for a moment, then his expression softened.

'She's a duchess,' he said at last, and threw a smile at Lady Margaret. 'She knows she's among those of her own class.'

And so the matter was settled. The ambassador seemed content, and if his glance strayed admiringly towards Lady Margaret at times, Sir Robert pointedly took no notice. Quickly Thomas found a passage-hawk for Kovalenko, then took a tercel for himself. Mikhailov the bodyguard, it seemed, wished for no bird, but was here on duty. His stern expression did not waver as he observed the goings-on. Finally Eleanor urged her mount forward, smiling down at her father. 'Have you a bird for me?' she asked.

'Lady Rooke's little saker should suit you,' he answered, and glanced round. Sir Robert and the others were starting to move off towards the Downs. Only the young Russian, who had hung back, remained. When Thomas looked towards the man, he quickly touched heels to his horse and rode up beside Eleanor. Now that Thomas was beginning to see past the Russians' black beards to the men behind them, he saw that this was a handsome, sharp-eyed fellow, barely a year older than Eleanor. And then, as his glance flitted to his daughter and back to the young man, he understood.

'You have an admirer,' he said.

Eleanor met his eye. 'I know it. He wouldn't leave me alone, all through supper . . . he even sang me a song, in his language. Sang it on one knee. I thought it was a lament – but Master Yusupov swore it was to extol my beauty.'

Thomas raised an eyebrow. Nowadays he was not always certain when Eleanor spoke in jest and when she was in earnest. Frowning, he went inside, got the little hawk and carried it out again. 'Does he have a name?' he asked, tilting his head towards the young Russian.

'Piotr,' Eleanor told him, and held her wrist out to take the saker. 'It means Peter.'

She tugged at the rein and urged her mount after the others. Piotr followed at once. But first he smiled politely at Thomas, and by gestures gave him to understand that he wished no falcon for himself. His reason for being here was plain enough.

Thomas sighed, as he and Ned began to follow the party on foot. But then a thought struck him that brought a smile to his lips.

'What's tickled you?' Ned asked, and jerked his head towards the riders. 'Yon fat cove? I pity his poor horse . . .'

Thomas shook his head. It had occurred to him that Master John Doggett would likely have been there last night, in the great hall. No doubt he had brought his lute along . . . what then would his reaction have been when he saw young Piotr drop to one knee and sing his heart out to Eleanor?

His grin broadened, prompting Ned to smile in turn. And with a spring in their steps, both falconers strode forth towards the Downs.

Three

When the hawking party returned to Petbury some hours later, an unexpected trio of visitors awaited them at the mews. Thomas, walking behind the riders with Ned, saw Sir Robert frown and stiffen in the saddle. He fancied his master muttered an oath, and looking ahead, stifled one of his own. For there, resplendent in an old-fashioned velvet gown and a hat fluttering with black mourning ribbons, was Sir Robert's eccentric sister, Lady Jane Rooke. With her stood a tight-lipped John Doggett, and Kat Jenkin, Lady Rooke's maid. As the riders drew rein the girl made her curtsey while Doggett bowed. But Lady Jane, ignoring the Russians who gazed at her with frank curiosity, strode through the long grass towards Sir Robert. Her skirts were already soaked, but she seemed not to notice.

'Since you were at such pains to avoid me last night, brother, I asked word to be brought me the moment you returned!' she cried. 'As you see, my household insist on shepherding me . . . have I not the right to go where I will? This house was once my home, too – or have you forgotten?'

But the woman flinched as horses milled about her, snorting and stamping. At a glance from Thomas, Ned hurried forward to help him take the birds from the riders. Sir Robert handed the white falcon down, dismounted quickly, and leading his horse by the rein, took his sister aside. The knight's embarrassment was plain for all to see.

'Jane, my dear . . .' He threw a look towards Lady Margaret for assistance. 'You should have waited in the house.'

'Should I indeed!' Lady Jane's voice grew shrill. 'You mean in that cupboard you have forced Kat and me to inhabit, the pair of us crushed together like a pair of stock-fish?' The woman's large eyes, usually her best feature, shone like sovereigns. But the effect was spoiled by her garish white face-paint, seemingly applied in a hurry, and the grey hair which stuck out from beneath her hat like frayed rope.

'For pity's sake!' Sir Robert hissed, glancing at his guests, who sat their horses together, talking low. 'You know I had small choice in the matter. 'Twas the Queen and her council bade me play host to these Muscovy men – I was bullied into it!'

'As you have bullied me, into staying in a chamber fit for a wet-nurse!' Lady Jane retorted. 'My lady!' She swung her gaze at once towards Lady Margaret, who was walking her horse towards them. 'I know one of your sensibilities will understand . . .' Suddenly the woman's lip trembled, and those nearby saw that at any moment she would burst into tears. 'I cannot sleep on the north side of the house! That's where evil comes from . . . I fear even the wind when it rattles my casement! I beg you, prevail on my pig-headed brother to hear me!'

There was a moment while the little group stood in silence about Lady Jane, who now appeared a pitiful sight. The desperation in her eyes was genuine. Thomas had gone to take the saker down from Eleanor, when his glance fell on young Piotr, who was watching them from some yards off.

'Did you enjoy your ride?' Thomas asked quietly.

'I did,' Eleanor answered. She seemed distracted – and he knew why. As he took the little falcon on his gauntlet, he glanced towards John Doggett and hid a grin. For the secretary's winning smile had been banished today. He stood behind his mistress with a glassy expression, clearly praying that the present dispute would speedily be resolved.

And so it was. For Lady Margaret, unruffled as always, brought an end to the business. Helped by her husband she dismounted from the side saddle and walked to Lady Jane.

'Dear sister . . .' She laid a gloved hand on her arm, prompting the woman to shudder with a suppressed sob. 'You must not distress yourself. I will find another chamber for you, even if I have to give up my own – which as you know faces south.' She smiled kindly at her. 'Shall we go indoors now, and order the matter?'

To general relief, Lady Jane melted. After throwing a hurt look at the ambassador and his men, who seemed puzzled by the whole exchange, she took Lady Margaret's arm in her bony hand and squeezed it.

'Margaret . . . you alone bring balm to my hurts!' Then, with a simper, she turned to Doggett. 'You, and sweet Jack of course . . . he has been mortified at the way I've been moved about, like some old mare that must give way for a new thoroughbred. Come, let's inside . . . you too, girl. Make haste!'

The last order was aimed at Kat Jenkin, who picked up her skirts and followed her ladyship, seemingly untroubled by the slight. Thomas, standing by the mews, exchanged glances with Eleanor. But as the group began to move off towards the house, he froze. John Doggett, bringing up the rear, had turned deliberately – and the look on his face was one of jealous fury. Ignoring Eleanor, he was staring at Piotr. The young Russian, however, far from showing alarm, seemed flattered by the man's hostility. Seizing the chance he urged his horse alongside Eleanor's, tugged off his fur cap and made her a little half-bow, grinning through his beard. Eleanor, who to Thomas's thinking had enjoyed Piotr's attentions throughout the morning, lowered her eyes. Then despite herself she looked at Doggett, but the man would not return her gaze. Snapping his head round he hurried after his mistress, who was walking arm-in-arm with Lady Margaret. With a glance at her father, Eleanor shook the reins and rode to follow them.

Thomas sighed: his daughter turned the heads of many a young man nowadays, but never before had he seen such a marked rivalry for her attention spring up, and so abruptly. He was glad that Sir Robert, still leading his horse, had seen nothing of the little pageant. Suddenly the knight seemed to remember his guests, and forcing a smile, turned to wave cheerily to the ambassador. With a grunt His Excellency rode forward, his men following. Kovalenko the

falconer, whom Thomas had still had no time to converse
with, nodded to him as he moved off. In the rear was
Mikhailov, saddle-sore and in a poor temper. The man had
done little but scowl at everyone all morning.

Ned came out of the mews and stood beside Thomas, to
watch the party disappear round the wall of the stable yard.
Only then did the falconers breathe sighs of relief. After a
moment Thomas clapped the lad on the shoulder.

'It's my guess there'll be no further duties for us today,'
he said, glancing at the sky. 'Especially as the rain's on its
way again.'

Ned met his gaze with an expectant look. 'So, come
suppertime . . .'

'Come suppertime, we may as well walk into Chaddleworth
and take a mug.' Thomas raised an eyebrow. 'Would that suit
you?'

Ned grinned from ear to ear.

No sooner had the two falconers walked the mile into the
village, than the storm broke. Thankful for their good
fortune, they got themselves inside the welcoming door
of the Black Bear before the first drops fell against the
latticed windows. Within seconds rain was streaming
down, causing a few shaking heads from the assembled
drinkers. The harvest was doomed – everyone knew it. So
the best thing to do was call for another mug to steady
their nerves . . .

Thomas found his old friend Hugh Dillamore by the
barrels in the corner. While the landlord worked the spigot,
he bade Thomas spill the Petbury gossip. He had heard
about the men from Muscovy of course – who had not?
Was it true one of them weighed twenty stone, and needed
a carthorse to bear him?

'If you mean the ambassador's guard, he's a big fellow
all right,' Thomas told him. He accepted the mug of foaming
beer from Dillamore's fist, took a pull and lowered it with
a contented sigh. Looking round, he saw Ned across the
room in conversation with a pretty, fair-haired girl.

'Will you take one to the boy?' he asked, and finding a

coin, tossed it to Dillamore. The man caught it expertly, and took another mug from its peg.

'Hear that rain?' The landlord shook his head. 'Did you ever know such a summer? Save the last one, that is . . .'

Thomas nodded, then turned as the door flew open, and two sodden figures hurried in. He lowered his mug in surprise.

'You asked about Sir Robert's guests,' he murmured to Dillamore. 'I think you're about to serve a couple of them.'

The landlord followed his gaze to see the two bulky men shaking the rain from their heavy coats. They looked about them uncertainly, and seemed somewhat relieved to see Thomas.

Dillamore blinked. 'I hope they don't start any trouble,' he muttered. 'By the looks of that big ox, he could break the place in pieces!'

Thomas raised a hand to Kovalenko. The other man was indeed none other than Mikhailov, the soldier; for that was how Thomas thought of him. Having shouldered arms himself, albeit for a short while, he recognized a fighting man when he saw one. And he knew the bodyguard's ranting speech yesterday was no bluff: Mikhailov had shed blood in his time, and would not scruple to do so again. The conversation in the inn dropped, as folk turned to stare at the newcomers. Chaddleworth – indeed, the whole Berkshire Downs – had never seen the like.

Dillamore, however, was quick to recover. 'Welcome, masters!' he called, and gestured the pair to a bench by the wall. 'I'll attend you at once, or my wife will . . .' He looked round quickly. 'Where in the blazes is Ann?'

'I'll see them settled,' Thomas told him, and took a couple of mugs down. 'Bring a jug, and I'll pour the ale.' He jerked his head towards the Russians. 'From what I hear, these folk like to see from whose hand their meat and drink comes.'

Dillamore frowned. 'Do they fear they'll get poisoned?'

Thomas shrugged, recalling what Nell had told him when he and Ned dropped by the kitchens for their supper. 'They're a suspicious lot,' he answered. 'The big man tastes all his master's food. He'll not allow anyone else to touch it.'

Dillamore snorted. 'Small wonder he's so fat,' he snapped.

But it soon transpired that conversation with the Russians would be difficult. Having been eager to talk falconry with Kovalenko, Thomas found the man subdued, seemingly by the presence of the dour Mikhailov. After a muttered greeting in his own tongue the bodyguard barely looked at Thomas, but stared belligerently about the room, which was fast becoming crowded. He seemed to have no inkling that it was he and his companion who had drawn in half the village.

'The white hawk,' Thomas said, looking pointedly at Kovalenko. 'She flew well today . . . though I think our English pheasants and partridges are but small game to her.'

Kovalenko sipped his beer, which he seemed to find passable. 'She is proud bird,' he allowed. 'Comes from the steppes . . . she take wild cranes, twice the size of your herons.'

Thomas nodded. 'There's a bird as big on Salisbury Plain,' he said. 'The great bustard . . . to my mind, it might be best if Sir Robert sold Dushenka to his friend Sir Giles Buckridge, in Wiltshire. Such a mighty falcon would be happier hunting on the open plain—'

He broke off as Kovalenko stiffened. The man had a gentle face, but his brow had furrowed. 'Is unwise, my friend. If my master hear of it, he be offended.' He looked down at the floor. 'It take little to rouse his anger.'

Thomas said nothing, but was aware that Mikhailov, sitting on the other side of Kovalenko, was watching him. The man spoke rapidly in Russian, before looking away.

'What did your friend say?' Thomas asked, indicating Mikhailov. He was beginning to grow weary of the big man's hostility. It seemed to sit upon him like a mantle.

Kovalenko met his eye. 'Master Thomas, you know little of us,' he murmured finally. 'We come here not like travellers, as you think – but like slaves. Our leashes may be long, but they can be pulled tight, like this!' He raised a hand to his neck and gave a sharp tug as if drawing a noose about it. Thomas blinked.

'Is that why the – what's the word, the *sotnik* – comes here?' he asked. 'To keep a watch upon you?'

Kovalenko gave a short laugh, then took a proper pull from his mug. In fact, he almost emptied it. Then keeping his eyes on the floor, he spoke quietly to Thomas.

'Is not him I fear,' he replied. 'He but serves our *batsushka* . . . you may read him like a child reads his letters.' He sighed. 'Yet there are those at the court of our Tsar whom every man dreads . . . that place is a forest, Master Thomas. Only darker than any you saw – and you not know who is behind the trees!' The falconer gave a little shake of his head. Then he raised his mug and drained the last drop.

'Good!' He held up the mug and smiled. 'Is better than *brague* . . . our poor beer, made of oats. We drink another?'

Thomas hesitated, then finished his own drink. 'Gladly,' he said. 'But are you free to keep from your master, or must you return by nightfall?'

Kovalenko snorted, and turning to Mikhailov, spoke rapidly in Russian. Nearby drinkers exchanged baffled glances.

'Tonight, we drink!' the falconer said, and grinned at Thomas. 'Tomorrow, I get beaten – what matter?'

Thomas raised his eyebrows, whereupon not only Kovalenko, but Mikhailov too laughed aloud. To his surprise the big man stood up, drained his own mug, then threw it to the floor. The whole of the inn turned to look.

'*Pogano!*' Mikhailov shouted, and to general astonishment kicked his mug away with his great black boot. Hugh Dillamore, passing nearby, stopped in his tracks. But Thomas caught his eye.

'I'll be responsible,' he said. 'Give 'em another, then I'll take them somewhere . . .' He frowned. 'I'm not sure where.'

'The Dagger – where else?' Dillamore retorted, with a wary look at the two Muscovites. To his practised eye, they now looked like any other men who had decided to get drunk.

Thomas's frown deepened. The Dagger was the only other inn in the parish – a low, tumbledown tavern on the Welford Road, a short way out of the village. Here was

entertainment more suited to Chaddleworth's rowdier inhab-
itants; those in search of bowling or dicing, or someone to
share the noisome upstairs rooms which could be rented
by the hour. Though in the end they would likely find they
had lost not only their money, but their clothes too. Thomas
had not been there in years; but tonight . . .

He stood up. 'Tell Ned where I've gone, will you?' he
said to Dillamore. 'If I'm not home by morning, he'll know
where to look!'

The landlord nodded and moved off. With a sigh of resig-
nation, Thomas retrieved Mikhailov's mug from the floor.

Night had fallen, and the rain still fell in sheets, so that all
three men were soaked within minutes of leaving the Black
Bear. But seemingly untroubled by the weather, the Russians
followed Thomas south of the green and past the last
house in the village, before the glow of a lighted window
appeared in the lane ahead. A cracked sign above squealed
on its hinges, whatever painted device it had once borne
long faded. With a sense of foreboding Thomas shoved
open the heavy door.

The place was poorly lit, and thick with the pungent
smoke of cheap tobacco mixed with willow-bark. It was
also remarkably noisy, which took the two Muscovy men
aback. Here were folk of all ages and both sexes, some of
them singing a bawdy song to the accompaniment of an
out-of-tune hurdy-gurdy. Thomas, who was known to many,
was able to shoulder his way through the throng without
trouble. But his companions were at once the subject of
curiosity, if not suspicion.

'What are they, Scotsmen?' someone called out. 'Make
'em pay double!'

A few laughed, but others looked keenly at the newcomers
– and Thomas knew why. Already they were being sized
up as potential marks by those who practised dice-cogging
and other sorts of cozenage. Turning to Kovalenko, he spoke
in his ear.

'Watch your purse, my friend. And don't take up any man's
offer to play at dice or cards, for you will lose everything!'

Kovalenko listened. Then as Mikhailov drew near, he spoke to him in Russian. At once, those closest fell silent: any foreign tongue was suspect. In that respect there was no difference at all between these folk and the Black Bear's customers.

But to Thomas's eye, the Russians seemed more at home in the Dagger. They were fortified by a couple of mugs of Dillamore's strongest brew; yet it was also clear that these surroundings put them at their ease. Thomas found the drawer and called for sack, before plonking himself down on a stool and attempting to wring some of the water from his jerkin. His breeches and boots would have to stay wet until he got home. But the next moment, he forgot about his clothes. For as soon as the cups of sack arrived the two Muscovy men stood up, faced each other and drank them off in one gulp. Kovalenko then turned to Thomas, and urged him to stand too.

'Come, drink my health as I drink yours!' he cried. 'We falconers will be friends unto death!'

Thomas stood up in embarrassment, aware that he was the centre of attention. Facing Kovalenko he drank the sickly, watered wine, then inverted his cup to show that it was empty.

'Bravo!' Kovalenko clapped him on the back, then looked round for the drawer, waving his cup in the air. Thomas began to doubt whether he was going to get these men back to Petbury by morning, let alone tonight. The grinning drawer appeared with a jug, eager to fill the Russians' cups afresh and take their money. To Thomas's alarm Mikhailov, whose humour seemed to be improving by the minute, drained his at once and held it out for a further refill. Kovalenko promptly followed suit, laughing loudly. Some of the Dagger's customers laughed too, but others shook their heads. These two looked like trouble.

Then it was that a scrawny-looking man in a long-faded doublet materialized from somewhere, and moved up to the Russians with a crooked grin. And the hackles rose on Thomas's neck, for he knew Jem Latter, who ran the bowl-alley at the rear of the tavern, only too well.

'Your friends look like men who know how to enjoy themselves, falconer,' Latter murmured. 'They speak English?'

'No they don't,' Thomas answered. 'And we're not staying.' He turned to Kovalenko – but the next moment his heart sank.

'I speak English good!' the falconer cried. 'Name Pavel Illyich Kovalenko – your name?'

Latter's grin widened. 'My name?' He gave a mocking little bow. 'I'm the Earl of Berkshire, master . . . you want a game?' He stooped, mimed rolling a ball, then straightened. 'Bowl at skittles . . . easy as getting soused. You win money, eh?'

Kovalenko blinked, then turned to Mikhailov and translated for him. But quickly Thomas spoke in his ear.

'You'd be most unwise,' he said, and tried to signal with his eyes that Jem Latter was not to be trusted. Unfortunately his words had little effect. Either the Russians were becoming too drunk to care, or they were sorely tempted by the notion of gambling. With barely a glance at Thomas, Kovalenko turned to face Latter.

'Win money?' he echoed. 'We play for gold?'

Latter coughed, then nodded. 'Glad to, friend . . .' He jerked his head towards Mikhailov. 'Will the big fellow play too?'

Then he stiffened, as Thomas placed a hand on his arm. In a firm voice, he said: 'These men are servants of an ambassador, who's a guest at Petbury. If anything happens to them you'll answer to Sir Robert.'

Latter looked down at Thomas's hand and waited until he had removed it. Then with a glance towards the poniard at his belt, he said: 'The alley's legal, Finbow, and any man who plays takes his chances. Call Tertius Gale if you like.'

He named Chaddleworth's current holder of the office of constable, a standing joke in the parish. The man could barely lace his breeches, folk said, let alone enforce the law.

'I don't need to call anyone,' Thomas answered. 'These

two are with me – and if you cozen them I'll break your bowling arm.'

A light appeared in Latter's eye, and some who sat near caught the whiff of danger and glanced over. But beyond them the singers' voices soared in a chorus, and most of the Dagger's customers had noticed nothing.

'Are you their wet-nurse?' Latter sneered. 'Why not let them decide for themselves?'

Then Thomas saw that he had already lost the argument. For Kovalenko was grinning broadly and patting the pocket of his soaking-wet coat. 'We play, master!' he cried. 'We come – win all your money!'

Mikhailov too stepped forward eagerly. Thomas cursed under his breath at the gullibility of the two, whom he could not help but think of as his charges. It did not sit well with men of their station, he thought; nor with their characters, as far as he knew. Perhaps he had misjudged them . . . he sought to find a way to dissuade them from this action, but it was too late. The Muscovy men brushed past him, following Latter as he walked off towards a back door. Gloomily, Thomas trailed after them.

The bowl-alley was nothing but a lean-to stuck on the back of the inn, surrounded by a low fence of wattle. Above the fence its sides were open to the elements. Rain still fell, dripping from the thatch. As the small group appeared in the doorway, several men who were standing about glanced round. But unlike the drinkers inside, they showed no curiosity at the sight of the Russians. Thomas, tense as a wand, scanned the faces. As he expected, almost every rogue in Chaddleworth was present – among them one he had spoken with but a short time ago: Will Greve. Grimly Thomas met the poacher's watchful gaze, then moved over to Kovalenko.

'Will you not listen to me?' he said urgently. 'These men live by cheating. They work together – you are about to be shorn, like a spring lamb. Do you understand my words?'

But Kovalenko barely heard, for Mikhailov was speaking to him. The two of them conferred, taking in their surroundings with interest. The alley itself was no more than six yards long, with a row of pegs set up at the far end. On

the ground was a small bowling ball. It looked a simple
enough task to roll the ball at the pins. Thomas, of course,
knew better, but he was alone. With a sigh, he watched
Latter pick up the bowl and bring it to Kovalenko.

'The game's Cloish, master,' he smiled. 'We don't roll
at the jack here . . .' He nodded towards the strip of packed
earth. 'It's flat as a tabletop – no rubs. Clean course, see?'

And if the man heard Thomas's snort he gave no sign of
it. But as Kovalenko put out a hand to take the ball, he held
on to it.

'How much will you bet, my friend?'

Thomas opened his mouth, then closed it. It was hopeless, he decided. He was soaking wet, and already tired of
shepherding these fools about. Why not let them lose all
their money, since they seemed to need a rudimentary lesson
in judging character? With a sigh, he stood back and watched
Kovalenko dig into his pocket.

'*Kopeks!*' the falconer said, and showed a handful of small
coins to Latter, who blinked before deciding that money was
money, wherever it came from. With a smile he took the
coins, then handed the ball over. And watched by everyone,
especially by an eager Mikhailov, the Russian knelt down,
took careful aim and rolled the ball down the alley. But to
his dismay, it travelled barely two yards before veering aside
and thudding into the fence, where it came to an abrupt halt.
And why would it not, Thomas thought, since it was weighted
with a hidden piece of lead?

There was a moment's silence. Kovalenko remained on
one knee staring at the ball, and at the row of upright pegs.
Then very slowly he stood up and turned to gaze at Thomas,
who did not speak. He merely shrugged, letting the man
decide for himself how big a fool he had been.

Latter came forward, shaking his head. 'Your first time,
master,' he said with a rueful smile. 'It's a game of skill
rather than luck. No matter – will you play again, you or
your friend?'

Then he froze. For the Russians were staring at him as
if blindfolds had been torn from their eyes; or as if both
had sobered up very quickly. And too late, Jem Latter read

the signs. The bystanders stirred uneasily, but they were not in danger. And even as Thomas tensed himself to intervene, he knew he was too late. For with a bull-like bellow, Mikhailov the *sotnik* launched himself at the cozener, and threw him to the floor as if he was a puppy. Then a collective groan went up, as the giant fell upon Latter's chest, driving the air out of him like a bellows, and began to beat him. Kovalenko merely watched. But Thomas winced, hearing the terrible crack of a breaking jaw. Then as Mikhailov sat back astride his victim, breathing hard, Kovalenko walked up, stooped, and prising open Latter's clenched fist, retrieved his money without a word.

Thomas looked round to see that the three of them were suddenly alone. His heart thudding, he hurried forward and dropped to his knee beside the still form, while Mikhailov got up heavily. Both Russians stood in silence, looking down at the rogue who had tried to cheat them.

And who was now stone dead.

Four

'**Y**ou mean to tell me you stood there, and did nothing?' Sir Robert's voice rang out harshly in his small private chamber, where he sat frowning behind the oak table. Outside the rain had ceased, but ragged clouds sped by. Thomas stood before his master, trying to maintain an outward calm. His task was not made easier by Martin the steward, who was leaning on his staff of office and glaring at him.

'You've seen Mikhailov, sir,' Thomas answered unhappily. 'I'm thankful the fellow didn't draw that sabre of his and start hacking heads off . . .'

'A lame excuse, falconer!' Martin gave a shake of his white locks. 'The guard may be the servant of our important guest, yet he's subject to the laws of England like any other. As one of Sir Robert's most trusted men, you should have stayed him!'

'Enough!' Sir Robert looked uncomfortable. 'Thomas's courage is not in question.' Yet he looked grimly at his falconer. 'I gather the business was over with quickly?'

Thomas nodded. 'From what I saw, Latter died from a great blow that drove his jaw upwards, into his brain.' He looked away. 'I doubt if three men could have stopped someone of Mikhailov's strength.'

'Witnesses?'

Thomas shrugged. 'Several, though none that I'd trust.'

'So none that couldn't be bought?' From Sir Robert's expression, there was little doubt that he was in earnest.

Thomas managed a nod. 'I suppose so, sir. In any case, they only saw the start of it. They were all so quick to get themselves outside, there was no one left by the time—' With a sigh, he broke off.

There was a short silence. Despite his feelings about Jem Latter, Thomas was stunned by what had happened at the Dagger. He had barely slept, reliving the grisly scene many times over, knowing that somehow he should have tried to stop the enraged Mikhailov. Instead he had been wrong-footed by the speed of his attack. Afterwards he had found himself shoving both Russians out into the rain, away from the bowl-alley by a back gate and on to the Petbury road. In silence the three had returned to the manor, where Thomas left his charges to their own devices. Having sent word to Sir Robert, who was about to go to his bed, he had been told to present himself in the morning and tell his tale. What the consequences would be – for it was a matter of murder – he had not dared to think upon.

Sir Robert took a fortifying drink from a silver cup, and gave a sigh. 'Had the man any family?' he asked.

Thomas shook his head. 'He wasn't Chaddleworth-born. He'd dwelled here but a year or two.'

Sir Robert grunted. 'Well, one thing's plain: this is going to cost me dearly. I'll speak with the constable. There will be a burial at St Andrew's. As for the ambassador . . .' The knight wore a look of distaste. 'He refuses to admit any responsibility! His followers, he says, are all men of courage, who would die a thousand deaths for him. His Excellency bids me deal with the matter, as none of his concern – in fact, he deems it too trivial for his ears. And now he has gone riding with Lady Margaret, without so much as asking my leave!'

Martin coughed, signalling his desire to be heard. Sir Robert glanced up, saw the steward's brow creased in irritation. 'In God's name, sir, how long must Petbury house this rude company?' he asked. 'They've been here but two days, and already they behave like wild beasts! They eat and drink enough for a regiment of foot soldiers – even their gifts prove all but worthless! Furs, in the height of summer? Lamp oil when we least need it – not to mention that vile black jelly—' With a look of exasperation the old man broke off, shaking his head.

Thomas too had heard about the barrel of caviar. No one cared for the stuff – like black soap, some said. Instead of having it served in the great hall, Nell had quietly given it to the boy who fed the pigs.

'What would you have me do?' Sir Robert had calmed himself. 'It's the Privy Council's wish that Stanic's visit here be as pleasant as possible. The man wanted to stay in the best hawking country, yet not too distant from London. Hence the honour was all mine!'

The knight threw up his hands, and took another drink. Then he frowned again, glancing from Martin to Thomas. 'Yet it's not only for the sake of his office. The Tsar . . .' He hesitated. 'I know little of affairs in far-off Muscovy – it sounds a frightful place to me. I do know that our trade is under threat from the French and Dutch, who vie for the Tsar's favour. But it seems that Feodor himself is not the one we need fear – for he is not the real power. That lies in the hands of his brother-in-law, a man as clever as he is ruthless – and who, they say, will one day become famous throughout Europe. He's called Boris Godunov.'

If the name meant anything to Martin, it was new to Thomas's ears. Both men remained silent, as Sir Robert continued: 'I had not meant to speak of this now, however . . .' The knight looked intently at them. 'You will learn more today, when one of the council comes here. He is Sir Thomas Rivers, who is charged with presenting a most valuable gift from the Queen to the ambassador, to take back with him – yet this gift is not for the Tsar. It's for Godunov.'

Thomas met Sir Robert's eye, and understood. Glancing at Martin, he saw that the old steward knew nothing of any royal gift – let alone that it was already here, at Petbury. Now, he guessed the significance of the black case that Sir Robert had entrusted to him. He waited.

'You must not go far today,' Sir Robert told him. 'I will send for you at suppertime, and when I do, I wish you to bring the . . . to bring it with you. Though I need not ask that you conceal it from view.'

Martin cleared his throat, leaving Sir Robert in small doubt that he resented being kept in the dark about something that was clearly important. Quickly the knight raised a hand.

'We'll speak of it now, master steward. For when this prize – an emperor's gift, no less – comes into the house, it shall become your charge too. And you must guard it, as must I, as if our lives depended on it!'

Now Sir Robert signalled to Thomas that he was dismissed. Feeling highly relieved, Thomas made his bow and left the chamber. Within minutes he was outdoors, filling his lungs with rain-washed air.

Like his master, he too was beginning to wish that he had not set eyes on Ambassador Stanic or his men. And yet his curiosity was aroused: for it seemed that he was about to learn what was inside the mysterious black case that lay buried under a stone on the Ridgeway. An emperor's gift? He took a breath, and was soon striding away from the house.

The day passed slowly, but Thomas managed to busy himself with his work. He said little to Ned, who had clearly not heard of the events at the Dagger. And he saw nothing of the Russians save young Piotr, who appeared once with Eleanor, following her about the kitchen garden. Mercifully there was no sign of John Doggett.

In the late afternoon he sent Ned home, saying he would fly Lady Rooke's saker before supper. Then as soon as the lad had gone he hurried up to the Ridgeway to recover the case. There was no one in sight, and it was but the work of a minute to dig up the precious object. Concealing it in his jerkin he returned to his cottage and waited. And within the hour a servant came with the order: he should attend his master – not in the great hall as he expected, but once again in Sir Robert's private chamber. So Thomas took the case under his clothes, for what he hoped would be the last time, and walked down to the house.

The moment he was admitted to the room, which was curtained and candlelit even though sunset was hours away, he sensed a taut atmosphere. And he blinked at the sight of a dour-faced man seated at the table beside Sir Robert, who was regarding Thomas with suspicion. There seemed small doubt that this was Sir Thomas Rivers, newly come from London; and though Sir Robert was dressed in good clothes, there was also no disguising the fact that he was a country knight, while the visitor was one of the Queen's Council. The man was thin and grey-bearded, but appeared bulky in a richly faced gown and wide ruff. A single, armed servant in livery stood behind him. The only other person present was Martin the steward. Where, Thomas wondered, was the ambassador, whom he understood was to be custodian of the royal gift? He had imagined this was to be a formal presentation, with pomp and speeches. Instead there was a clandestine air about the whole business.

He made his bow, and Sir Robert waved him forward. Everyone looked at Thomas as he approached the table and, at a nod from his master, drew forth his precious charge. Carefully he set it down and stood back; and now the tension in the room doubled, as all eyes fell upon the black case. For a moment no one spoke; then Thomas realized that Rivers was waiting for him to depart. But when he looked to Sir Robert, the knight signalled with his eyes that he should stay.

'This is my falconer, sir,' he murmured, turning to his guest. 'He and my steward are our most loyal servants. I would have him see what it is that he has been entrusted with.'

After a moment Rivers nodded. In a flat, lawyer's voice, he said: 'As you wish, Sir Robert. I will leave it to you to impress upon him – and upon your steward – the grave importance of the chain.' He hesitated, then: 'Not until it has left our shores will I breathe easily again. After that, we can only pray that it reaches its destination safely. It is a long way from the port of Archangel to the Tsar's palace.'

The chain . . . ? Thomas glanced at the black case. Was that what it contained? He was familiar enough with the chains of office that men of wealth and power often wore across their chests. Some were indeed very valuable: gold or silver, often jewelled. He waited expectantly, noting that even Martin was showing signs of eagerness. Finally Rivers signalled to his servant to come forward. With a glance at the assembled company, the fellow pulled the case towards him and rotated it so that the clasp faced him. Taking a small key from his doublet, he fitted it to the lock. Then he opened the clasp, threw back the lid and stepped back.

There was no sound; no gasp of admiration or wonder. Each man remained still, letting his eyes feast upon the gleaming gold chain that sat in its indentation on a bed of scarlet velvet. Even Thomas, who cared little for such finery, felt his heart stir at the sight. For to call it a mere chain was not enough: this was no bauble, but indeed an emperor's gift.

It was made up of thirty or forty intricately worked gold bows, interspersed with Tudor roses of crimson enamel set with milk-white pearls. But suspended from its centre, where it would sit on the wearer's chest, was a great pendant, unlike anything Thomas had seen – and which put the value of the gift beyond any price he could imagine. It was made of a mass of clear sapphires, fashioned into the likeness of a loping white bear. Its eyes were perfectly cut rubies. It almost made him smile: Tudor roses and a bear, signifying the happy union of England and Muscovy. What gift could be more fitting, for the most powerful man in that land?

'Regard: the Muscovy chain.'

Even the dry-voiced Rivers could hardly keep emotion at bay as he gazed upon the mighty jewelled bear, beside which even the pearl roses looked commonplace. Meeting Sir Robert's eye, he said: 'Now you understand, sir, why so much secrecy has surrounded this royal gift . . . why the Queen herself was charmed, and loath to part with it. Yet she well understands that only a thing of such magnificence may move a man like Godunov, who's Tsar in everything but name – and who wields power in his own land the like of which any other ruler can but dream!'

Sir Robert nodded. 'Well . . . I can understand now why I was not permitted to see it at Richmond Palace.' He frowned. 'Might I enquire, sir, how many people know precisely what it is? Indeed – how many know *where* it is?'

'That need not concern you, Sir Robert,' Rivers answered shortly. 'Nor should the history of the jewel, which I understand is a lurid one indeed. Suffice it to say that in time this gift will repay Her Majesty well, in valuable trade for our nation. Our enemies will be filled with envy when they learn of it – for none can hope to match it.'

Sir Robert was silent, but Thomas guessed the cause of his discomfort. How long, the master of Petbury must have wondered, must this priceless, not to say dangerous, treasure remain under his roof?

Rivers was about to speak again – but without warning

there was a commotion outside the door. The next moment
it flew open to reveal a couple of nervous attendants, being
shoved aside by someone bent on coming in. Voices were
raised, both English and Russian – for the intruder was none
other than Ambassador Grigori Stanic, wearing an angry
expression. Behind him trailed an embarrassed Keril Yusupov,
whom Thomas had not seen for the past two days. With a
stamp of heavy boots, the ambassador strode into the room.

'Sir Robert . . .' The secretary hurried forward and made
a hasty bow. 'His Excellency has waited long hours for you
to call him – we heard the envoy from your Queen is come.'
Yusupov's gaze flew to Rivers, who was clearly irritated by
the intrusion. 'Should one of his station not have been
presented first—'

The man broke off as Stanic made another outburst. But
before Yusupov could interpret, Sir Robert had risen.

'Your master need not take offence, for none was intended,'
he said. 'We merely wished to inspect the gift and ascertain that all was in order before sending word to His
Excellency . . .' He looked at Rivers, who sighed and stood
up. Introductions were quickly made, and at a sign from Sir
Robert, Martin the steward moved stiffly to a sideboard
where a jug and cups stood. Thomas helped him pour the
wine, and acting as impromptu footman, took a cup to Stanic.
After a moment the ambassador accepted it, though his look
of resentment remained. He was about to make some further
remark when his eyes fell on the open case.

'This is the great gift from our Queen that we entrust to
His Excellency to take back to our esteemed friend Godunov,
the Tsar's kinsman. We trust that it will be in safe hands.'

Rivers had spoken in a voice of authority. Stanic looked
up and met the man's eye; and for the first time, Thomas
saw a look of uncertainty on the ambassador's face. Yusupov
moved closer to his master and translated in a low voice.
After a moment Stanic muttered an answer.

'His Excellency is pleased,' Yusupov said with some relief.
'He asks to examine the great chain.'

The tension was evaporating. With a glance at Sir Robert,
Rivers stood up. Both men then walked around the table to

join Stanic, who had stepped forward and was peering intently at the mighty jewelled bear. Cups of wine were passed around, as everyone waited to hear what they assumed would be words of approval. But when the ambassador looked up, every man stiffened. For the look of apparent wonder on his broad face had disappeared – to be replaced by a mirthless smile that bordered on contempt. The man spoke at some length, glancing from Rivers to Sir Robert and back. Then he turned to Yusupov and waited.

There was a silence – and the look on the secretary's features was plain. For if ever a man had been asked to convey something he did not like, it was Yusupov. Feeling all eyes upon him, the secretary coughed, then said: 'His Excellency admires the splendid gift.'

'Indeed?' Rivers exchanged glances with Sir Robert. 'Were those his very words?'

Yusupov nodded, then his face fell as Stanic spoke again. This time there was no mistaking His Excellency's scornful tone. By the time he had finished, the secretary was looking aghast.

'Interpret, please!' Rivers appeared to be enjoying himself. No doubt he had witnessed some of Queen Elizabeth's famous meetings with pompous ambassadors – and her equally famous triumphs over them.

'Translation is sometimes difficult from our tongue, sir.' The secretary put on a sickly smile. 'Yet you have seen how moved we are by your Queen's generosity . . .'

'I don't think I have.' Rivers looked to Sir Robert, keeping a straight face. 'Would you care to learn what it was the ambassador said, sir? I know I should.'

Sir Robert returned his gaze; and it seemed that the earlier brittleness between the two men had disappeared. He nodded and turned to Yusupov. 'Master secretary, I will not be insulted under my own roof. Will you tell me truthfully what your master said?'

Yusupov gulped, glanced at Stanic, and found no help in that quarter. Finally he answered: 'His Excellency says the chain is a pretty trifle . . . but you have not seen the palace of our Tsar. He is attended by a hundred *boyar*s dressed in

coats of gold – there are jewels everywhere. And more . . .'
The man hesitated, then added: 'Many years ago your Queen
Mary sent not only rich cloths, velvet and satin – but a lion
and a lioness too. Even your own Queen once sent an organ
and a pair of fine virginals to our Tsar's father, the great
Ivan . . .' The man gave a nervous shrug. 'We receive many
gifts. So you see that a chain with a bear upon it, no matter
how large, will not sway a man like Godunov. Nor does it
dismay His Excellency.'

Then, to the consternation of both Rivers and Sir Robert,
the ambassador drained his cup, tossed it to Thomas, who
managed to catch it, and turned away. And after waiting
only for his hapless secretary to hurry forward and open the
door, he swept out of the room without another word.

As the door closed, a stunned silence fell. Yusupov was
left alone, gazing at the floor in apparent dismay. But then
with an effort the man turned around, walked deliberately
back to Rivers and made a low bow.

'Sir, I ask a thousand pardons. His Excellency is—'

'In a poor humour; indeed, we have seen that for
ourselves!' Rivers interrupted in a sardonic tone. But the
secretary gave a quick shake of his head.

'You do not understand, sir . . .' His glance strayed to Sir
Robert, then back to Rivers. 'The ambassador is awed by
the magnificent chain. It is merely not in his nature to admit
it . . . indeed, it is a duty of his office that he does not.' The
man wet his lips. 'If you will take the word of one in my
humble position: be reassured that Her Majesty's gift will
be well received in Muscovy. And despite what he said, my
master will spare no effort to see it delivered.'

Yusupov paused, seemingly choosing his words with care.
'Trade is our future, sir,' he continued. 'All Russia knows
it. If relations have cooled since the days of our great Tsar
Ivan, who was a friend to your Queen, there are many who
wish to remedy this. It's merely . . .' Yusupov shrugged. 'It's
merely that those who are chosen by Tsar Feodor to be his
envoys are not always the best men.'

Then as if aware of the import of his speech, the secretary swallowed and added: 'I beg that you regard my last

words as a confidence, sirs . . . you cannot know what would happen to me were they reported to my master!'

The man fell silent. But Rivers favoured him with a nod of understanding. 'Your frankness does you credit, master secretary,' he murmured. 'And I am certain that under your watchful eye, the royal gift will reach its rightful destination.' With a glance at Sir Robert, he added: 'And you may be reassured that it will be secure under this roof until you leave. Sir Robert is as loyal a servant to our Queen as you will find anywhere in England.'

There was a moment, while Yusupov realized that all had been said. With a relieved look the man bowed, walked to the door and got himself outside.

The relief in Sir Robert's chamber, however, was more muted. First to speak was the indignant Martin.

'These folk dismay me, sir!' he cried. 'They know naught of how to conduct themselves, let alone how—'

'I know, master steward . . .' Sir Robert made an impatient gesture. After taking a pull from his cup he glanced at Rivers, who now spoke up.

'So trade's their future, is it?' the Privy Counsellor grunted. 'I wonder if they realize how important it is for us? Or indeed, how much they truly know about England's position . . .' He shook his head. 'Poor harvests, the state coffers all but empty . . . why, even fears of a Spanish invasion have surfaced all over again!'

No one spoke. Even here in the Downlands folk had heard of the great fleet under the command of Sir Walter Raleigh and the Earl of Essex that had gone to attack the Spanish in their own harbours. Would England ever be free of the old threat?

'And as for the great Tsar Ivan . . .' Rivers gave a snort. To Thomas's surprise the man's severe manner seemed to have disappeared. Perhaps Sir Robert's claret had loosened his tongue more than he knew. Taking a generous pull from his cup, Rivers went on: 'The whole world knows what a butcher Ivan the Terrible was! His court trembled for fear of offending him – and small wonder. Do you know the tale of the French Ambassador who refused to remove his cap in

Ivan's presence?' When Sir Robert signalled that he did not, Rivers said: 'Why, he had the fellow's hat nailed to his head!'

Sir Robert blinked. 'Fortunately, from what I hear, his son is unlike him in every respect . . .'

'True – and that is why we are in this position: having to sidestep Feodor and set our sights on Godunov. It's common knowledge that he overrules his feeble brother-in-law in everything!' Rivers frowned. 'Do you know what they call the Tsar? "Feodor the Bellringer". The man has no interest in affairs of state – travels about visiting churches and praying! They say when he lost his infant daughter, he lost his wits too. Now he has no heir – and shows no sign of producing one. It's plain enough who will succeed him. Hence . . .' Rivers looked keenly at Sir Robert.

'It's Godunov we need, sir, and he must be assured of our support! Which is why Her Majesty's Privy Council relies on you, not only to send his ambassador home content, but to safeguard the precious gift that he will take to the *boyar* Boris: the future Tsar of all the Russias!'

Everyone was silent. Finally Sir Robert murmured that the chain would be kept under close guard in his personal chest, which was iron-bound with a heavy lock upon it. Only he and his steward had keys. Rivers appeared satisfied, and nodded approvingly when Martin spoke of a late supper waiting in the great hall. Whether His Excellency the ambassador would be joining him and Sir Robert was now a matter for some doubt.

So at last the business was over, and Thomas, with many things to reflect upon, was dismissed. As he made his way out of the house, he felt relief that the priceless chain was off his hands. And yet he was uneasy – for like his master, he too would be unable to rest until the Muscovy chain had finally left Petbury, and was safely on its way.

Hence his disappointment the following morning, when a servant came to rouse him early. It seemed that His Excellency the ambassador, far from showing any sign of leaving, wished to go hawking once again.

Five

It was a day to remember, but not one to relish. In a
morning heavy with mist, Thomas emerged from his
cottage to see Ned Hawes arrive somewhat out of breath.
Instead of giving his usual greeting, the boy was frowning.

'You might have told me about that tussle you had at the
Dagger, Thomas – you and those Russians,' he said. 'On
account of it, I almost got into trouble myself.'

It was Thomas's turn to frown. 'What sort of trouble?'

'Last night, when I was leaving the Bear,' Ned answered.
'There were a few men on the green, waiting for me. They
let me know plain enough that Petbury folk weren't too
popular, since the killing of Jem Latter.'

Thomas sighed, berating himself for not confiding in Ned
about the grisly affair. The lad had earned his trust long
ago, and he in his turn trusted Thomas completely.

'I ask your pardon, Ned,' he said. 'I had much to think
on yesterday, after Sir Robert was done with me . . . I should
have told you the whole tale.'

'You should,' Ned agreed. 'For now it seems you and I
must look over our shoulders . . . there's some who did well
out of Latter's cozenage, are out for a bit of revenge.'

'Men like Will Greve?'

'He wasn't among them. But I'd say he's as likely to
pick a fight as any.'

Thomas nodded, and started towards the falcons' mews.
As Ned fell in step beside him he told the boy of the events
of the night before last, when he had been obliged to play
host to the two Russians. By the time he had finished Ned's
fresh face bore a look of mingled alarm and wonder.

'That big Mikhailov's a danger to himself, let alone to

the rest of us!' he said. 'But then, he'll likely be gone soon – we'll still have to live here.'

Thomas shrugged; he was not going to fret about a few bowl-alley rogues who would happily have relieved not only Mikhailov and Kovalenko but Thomas too of every penny he carried. His thoughts were on yesterday's gathering in Sir Robert's chamber – and on the precious Muscovy chain. Should he tell Ned about that? It occurred to him that several people now knew about the royal gift: not only Yusupov and his master, but perhaps the other Russians too. It seemed unlikely that the matter would remain secret. But even as he reflected on it, there came a shout from some distance away. He and Ned turned to see one of the wenches waving from the archway that led to the kitchen garden.

'Thomas – Master Martin needs help!' the girl called. 'There's two vagrom men at the gate making trouble!'

The falconers exchanged glances, then hurried off down the slope. In a moment they had skirted the house, crossed the front courtyard and reached the main gates.

It had been a rule, since the days of Sir Robert's father, that the Petbury gates were never shut save in times of pestilence. Yet in recent years, with gangs of hungry ex-soldiers tramping the roads, Martin the steward usually ordered them barred at sunset. Last night, however, the instruction seemed to have been ignored – or perhaps it was never given; Martin was forgetful nowadays. And as luck would have it, two travellers had seized the opportunity to come in demanding charity. On these occasions such folk would have been given a bit of bacon or cheese, which generally satisfied them. But as Thomas drew near the two men standing inside the gateway, he saw that these were of a bolder stamp. One appeared to be an Abraham man: an ex-inmate of Bedlam, released to wander the country and beg as he would. His shambling, savage appearance, coupled with the pitiful whining and the flecks of foam about his mouth, would have been enough to convince most people. But Thomas, who had been inside the fearful hospital of St Mary of Bethlehem, suspected a fake. He eyed the fellow grimly, knowing the foam was produced by a piece of soap concealed somewhere about him. Then he looked to the second man, a rough-bearded fellow in a wide-brimmed hat, who acted as the first one's keeper.

'Falconer . . . you at least came!' Martin looked relieved. 'I've called the grooms, yet none seem to hear me but kitchen folk!' The steward indicated a couple of nervous maids and the turnspit boy, who had seized a ladle as a weapon. Then, gesturing with his staff towards the incomers, Martin said: 'These two have been given cheese and a good loaf, yet they refuse to leave!'

Thomas eyed the keeper, who at once pointed to his sorry-looking companion.

'Have pity, master! Look upon poor Joshua, whom I raised up off the streets of Shoreditch, where he was cast out cruelly from Bedlam's door! Are ye not moved to weep for him, as I do? Have I not pledged my own life to protect him – to walk the roads with him in all weathers, putting our faith in the common charity of good folk like your-selves?' The fellow sniffed loudly, his eyes flicking to Ned and back to Thomas. 'Will ye send us out into the wet lanes with naught but bread and cheese? Joshua needs shelter, as he wants physic, as—'

'He wants a pint of wine, more likely!' Martin retorted. 'I've given you all I will – now be on your way, before we throw you out!'

At that Joshua the Abraham man gave a fearful cry, shaking his head wildly and pawing at the ground with his foot. Both feet were wrapped in filthy rags. His companion gripped him by the shoulder, murmuring words of comfort. When he had seemingly calmed his charge down, he turned back to Martin.

'Well, sir, it seems I was ill-informed!' he cried. 'For they told me in Chaddleworth that the weak and destitute would find sympathy at the manor of Petbury. Yet we are turned away, as beggars have always been, since the days of our saviour! For does it not say in the good book—'

'What's your name, my friend?'

Thomas's question was sharp, though he had not raised his voice. The ragged man broke off, and answered: 'My

name, which matters naught, is Swift. Tobias Swift . . .' He
thrust his hand into his patched jerkin, and showed the edge
of a tattered scroll. 'I have my licence to beg, signed by
two justices.'

'Forged, I'd guess,' Thomas said, breaking into a smile.
'Who was the jarkman – Fludd, from the Welsh Borders?'

The man blinked. 'Y'are cruel, master,' he muttered,
shifting his gaze from Thomas to Martin and back. 'I was
a sailor who fought for my queen upon the high seas, till
I was set ashore without a penny—'

'A freshwater mariner.' Thomas's smile widened. 'I've
met others.' He glanced at Joshua, who was staring about
wide-eyed. 'Where do you keep the soap to make his mouth
foam? On your back?'

He indicated Swift's pack, which looked somewhat bulky
for a beggar's. He knew that it contained the men's real
clothes. There would likely be a purse hidden in there too.

Swift did not answer. His charge Joshua stopped whining
and shaking, and threw a fearful glance at Thomas.

'I'll believe you're from Shoreditch,' Thomas said. 'I may
be a countryman, but I've been there myself and seen rogues
a-plenty, each with a practised tale to tell.'

But then he hesitated, and looked away. 'And yet, a man
must be in desperate straits to go to such lengths, and travel
so far from London . . .' He turned to Martin. 'Will you not
spare them enough for a supper and a night's lodging, master
steward? I doubt they'll trouble us again.'

Martin frowned. But the two kitchen maids, who had
hung back, exchanged relieved glances. Ned, too, relaxed.
Only the turnspit boy seemed disappointed that he was not
about to beat anyone with his ladle after all.

'Falconer . . .' The steward shook his head. 'You are a
closed book to me at times! Having exposed these men as
false rogues, you would now give them alms?'

Thomas did not answer. There was a moment, until feeling
all eyes upon him, Martin relented. 'God's mercy . . .'
Fumbling in his gown the old man found a well-worn purse,
and with a glare at the beggars drew out the coins. At the
glint of silver, the eyes of both men widened.

'Take it!' Martin threw down the money, which Tobias Swift lost no time in picking up. 'And you may thank our soft-hearted falconer for your good fortune. Now go your ways, before I change my mind. If you come again you will find the gates locked!'

Without a word, the two counterfeit beggars turned and shambled out of the gateway into the mist. Joshua did not look back; but at the bend in the lane, Swift turned about and cast a long look at Martin and the Petbury servants. And it seemed to Thomas that the man wore a little smile: partly of gratitude, partly of triumph. *We're but gamesters,* he seemed to say, *who were found cheating – yet you let us play on; and for that we thank you.*

Thomas watched them disappear, then walked off towards the falcons' mews. He had a hawking party to prepare for; and for now, that was enough to think on.

The party rode all morning, far from the manor, west beyond Greenhill Down where the open grassland rose. The mist lifted, and to Thomas's relief the sun broke through: his first sight of it in weeks. He rode a gelding from the Petbury stable, for it would be impossible to keep up with Sir Robert on foot. Today his master had a restless energy about him that belied his sixty years. Perhaps, Thomas thought, it was his intention to tire his guest the ambassador out. For the tension between Sir Robert and Grigori Stanic was now plain. With utter disregard for her husband, His Excellency had barely taken his eyes off Lady Margaret from the moment they arrived at the mews to take their falcons. Every chance he got, the man would ride alongside her, smiling and making some remark or other. And again, since Yusupov the secretary did not ride to hawking, it was left to Kovalenko to do his best as interpreter.

Thomas had made a curt greeting to the ambassador's falconer, though not to the stolid Mikhailov, when the two rode up behind their master. For their part both men remained impassive, as if the camaraderie that sprang up between them and Thomas back in Chaddleworth had never existed. Whether they had been punished by His Excellency, or merely been told to keep their mouths and their purses shut from now on, Thomas could only guess. There was a wariness about them as they followed Sir Robert, Lady Margaret and Stanic across the Downs. To Thomas's relief Eleanor did not accompany her mistress; hence there was no John Doggett, and no Piotr trailing along. Mikhailov as before carried no bird, but Kovalenko bore a tercel upon his wrist, as did the ambassador. Sir Robert again flew the great white falcon – and now he seemed determined to show how well he could handle her.

There were partridges and snipe on the Downs. And as the falcons soared and stooped, Thomas busied himself bagging the catch to take to the kitchens. Dismounting to pick up another bird, he saw that Sir Robert had drawn rein and was sitting on his horse some yards away. So shoving the limp partridge in his pouch he took up the gelding's rein and led it towards his master.

'He's not such a hawksman as he would have us think, is he?' Sir Robert nodded in the direction of the ambassador, who was urging his horse uphill, following a distant speck. His falcon had soared so high, it was almost out of view.

'Indeed he's not, sir,' Thomas smiled. 'One of those who enjoys eating his catch more than he does the getting of it.'

But if Sir Robert was glad of his falconer's loyalty, he did not show it. He was more preoccupied than Thomas had seen him in years. The chief reason he could think of – apart from the ambassador's brazen flirtation with Lady Margaret – was the presence of the Muscovy chain.

'I'd wager they will not stay more than another week, Sir Robert,' he said after a moment. 'I hear it's a mighty long voyage back to Muscovy – and one that must be made in summer.'

Sir Robert nodded absently. 'Never have I wished for a speedier departure from any guest at Petbury,' he murmured. He glanced at the white falcon, perched docilely upon his wrist, and frowned. 'I knew the Privy Council were relieved to palm the man off on me. Even Sir Thomas Rivers, whom I counted a friend, was swift to take his leave this morning. Now the royal gift is handed over, his duty's done.'

Thomas looked round, as there came the sound of hooves. Lady Margaret, carrying Lady Rooke's hooded saker upon her wrist, was cantering easily towards them. As she drew rein her husband bristled, but the mistress of Petbury did not appear to notice.

'Thomas . . .' Lady Margaret smiled at him, and as always his heart lifted.

'My lady . . .' He returned her smile. 'Do you not fly the saker? She has been short of exercise . . .'

'I will,' Lady Margaret replied, then turned deliberately to her husband. 'And will you ride with me, sir? Or must I make do with His Excellency's tedious small talk all day?'

There was a brief silence, before Sir Robert began to lose his frosty manner. Thomas too relaxed, though for his part he had no fears of any rift between his master and mistress. If some Petbury folk had started to wonder whether Lady Margaret was enjoying Grigori Stanic's attention, or even encouraging him, Thomas knew better. He knew how hard she worked to safeguard her husband's estate, as well as his reputation. Being the gracious hostess to an ambassador, however tiresome, was but a part of her duty.

'Well – shall we say another mile, then home?' Sir Robert asked, giving his rein a tug, and enjoying the way the big coursing horse responded. 'I've an appetite would match even that of our ravening guests.' He gave a wry smile. 'It's lucky His Excellency's falconer has caught some birds for the pot, Thomas – unlike his master the Duke of Nosgorod, Lord of Karelia and Warden of the Great Paunch. If we'd left it to him, we'd all go hungry!'

Lady Margaret kept a straight face. 'I think it's *Novgorod*,' she said mildly. But Thomas saw the tautness in her mouth and stifled a smile of his own. And to his relief, Sir Robert laughed aloud.

'I stand corrected. Yet for all his titles, I'd not change places with the fellow – not for twice his wealth!' As his horse leaped forward, he turned in the saddle. 'Who'd want to live in a country where black soap's counted a delicacy?'

And with that the master of Petbury rode off, guiding his mount expertly with his right hand. The left hand he raised with a smooth, bowling motion; and the great white falcon rose from his gauntlet, and soared into the sky.

But it was on the return to Petbury that matters took an unexpected turn, and a fine morning gave way to a dark afternoon.

Sir Robert, Lady Margaret and their guests rode into the stable yard, where grooms hurried to attend them. Yet there was an air of unease about the men which even Sir Robert noticed. Finally one fellow came forward and made his bow. 'Sir, something's happened . . . something fearful. Master Martin knows of it – it's best you hear it from him.'

'Something fearful? What do you mean, man? Speak!' Sir Robert had dismounted and was glaring at the groom, who flinched.

'It's . . . There's a poor soul been found dead, sir.'

Sir Robert froze. Lady Margaret, who was being helped down from the side saddle, overheard and gave a start. The Russians as always stood in a group, talking among themselves. But Thomas also heard, and took a step towards his master.

'Dead?' Sir Robert was slow to take in the information. 'Where . . . ?'

'In the gardens, sir,' the groom answered, then added quickly: 'He's not from here. A stranger . . . that's all we could tell. He was found an hour after you'd gone, though it looks like he's lain there all night.'

Sir Robert exchanged glances with Lady Margaret. 'Did no one think to ride out and find me?' the knight asked testily. 'I was but hawking on the Downs . . .'

'Indeed, sir,' the groom replied. 'Only, Master Martin said by the time they found you, you would likely be on your way back . . . He's sent word to Gale the constable.'

Sir Robert grunted. 'That's all I need . . .' He drew a breath, and turned grimly to Thomas. 'Will you come with me?'

Thomas nodded.

Moments later he stood between his master and Martin the steward, looking down at what was indeed a fearful sight.

The body was that of a man of middling height, blond-haired with a thin beard, aged perhaps twenty years. Otherwise there was little that could be said with certainty about him, for he had been stripped of every stitch of clothing. What could not be removed was the blood: a great patch of it, now dried to a dark mass. It covered much of the man's body and the grass upon which he lay, sprawled on his back beside a stone statue. The statue, of Diana the huntress holding a bow and arrow, was near the edge of Sir Robert's formal gardens, at the front of the house close to the Hungerford road. It was not an area people came to often, save the gardeners. Hence the late discovery of the body – by a milkmaid, who was taking a short cut home from Boxwell Farm, and had seen something lying on the grass.

Thomas glanced at Martin the steward, and saw how distressed he was. He could guess at one reason: his failure to ensure the gates were barred the previous night. With a kindly look at the old man, he spoke up.

'This was no brabble, master steward,' he said. 'Nor any robbery – there are too few folk upon the road to draw such rogues here. Besides . . .' Thomas hesitated and looked to his master, who signalled him to continue.

'The great loss of blood . . .' Thomas knelt down to take a closer look. 'It was a deep wound, straight to the heart. A sword-thrust, if you ask me.'

Sir Robert started. 'There's none here carry swords, save myself and . . . well, some of our guests. That oaf of a body-guard, for one.'

But Thomas shook his head. 'It was not a sabre . . .' He peered at the wound. 'A rapier, more like. I'd say it was a powerful upward blow – what fencers call a *montanto*.' He glanced up at his master. 'This murderer knew how to wield a blade.'

'Murder – at Petbury?' Martin looked bewildered. 'But who . . . and why here, in the knot garden?' He gestured lamely to the well-tended flower beds, from which came the scent of roses. 'It makes no sense!'

Thomas stood up and glanced about. The location, by

the great statue of the goddess, suggested one thing to him: a place of assignation. Quickly he voiced his thoughts to Sir Robert.

'Yet to strip the body . . . was it an attempt to make it look like robbery? Or was the villain afraid someone might tell who this man was from his clothing?' The knight shook his head. 'What a terrible waste of a young life!'

Neither of the others spoke. Finally Sir Robert turned to Martin and gave orders for the body to be taken away. 'The man died on my land,' he murmured. 'Hence he may lie in the Petbury chapel, and be buried as if he had been a guest here. Which in a way he was – but for a short while.' His brow furrowed. 'Besides, Chaddleworth already has one parish funeral on its hands, does it not?'

Thomas winced. It being high summer, it was likely the body of Jem Latter was already in the ground. 'Do you have any instruction for me, Sir Robert?' he asked quietly. 'I will do whatever I can – though I cannot bring Latter back to life.'

'Indeed you can't – any more than that Russian oaf can!' Sir Robert retorted, with a look of distaste. He turned to Martin. 'Now I gather that dolt of a constable will come?'

'This afternoon,' Martin answered. 'Though there's little for him to do as far as I can see but make report of the death. Whoever was responsible will surely have long fled.'

'No doubt!' Sir Robert was eager to be gone. With a nod to both his steward and his falconer he walked away towards the house. Nearby the gardeners stood in a silent group, but the knight seemed not to notice them. For a man who a short while ago had spoken of how hungry he was, he looked to Thomas like one who had suddenly lost his appetite.

Tertius Gale appeared mid-afternoon and was taken to see the body, lying in Petbury's small chapel. At the same time an order came from Sir Robert for Thomas, to see if he could assist the constable. When he arrived, he found the man peering at the corpse, which was lying on a board upon the altar. Now that the blood had been cleaned away the location of the single, fatal wound was obvious – even to Chaddleworth's constable, the most pedantic man in the parish.

'A sword-thrust you say, falconer?' The man rotated his long neck and regarded Thomas through watery eyes. His thin frame, clad in dusty grey, always suggested a heron to Thomas; though Gale had none of that bird's speed or grace.

Thomas nodded. 'A fencer's blow,' he agreed.

'So – might that have any bearing upon this mark here?'

The constable pointed to a puckered scar on the dead man's right side, below his ribs.

'You are perceptive, Master Gale,' Thomas said after a moment. 'It's an old scar by the look of it, but likely got from a sword. The blood had concealed it . . . it seems clear to me that the dead man was a fencer.'

Gale nodded sagely at him. 'But if so, what was this fencing fellow – a complete stranger – doing in Sir Robert's garden?'

Thomas hesitated. 'I'd say he was meeting someone,' he said. 'He was killed during the night. In the dark, in a place the size of Petbury, a stranger would need a landmark that was easily seen, like the big stone statue of the huntress. Someone else could have directed him to it.'

'Then whoever he was meeting killed him?'

'I don't know,' Thomas answered. 'But it would seem so.'

'Then why?'

Blackmail . . . The notion sprang to Thomas's mind. He drew a breath and told Gale.

The constable frowned, and made a show of stroking his thin grey beard. 'Might there have been some other reason for a night-time meeting? Between two men, that is?'

Thomas shrugged. 'Perhaps.'

The two of them looked down at the body in silence for a while. Finally the constable cleared his throat.

'I will make report of the death . . . its cause I leave to the coroner and his jury. Meanwhile I will ask folk about the parish – sightings of strangers and so forth.' The man stiffened suddenly. 'There are two who come to mind! A couple of beggars, one a madman—' Then seeing the expression on Thomas's face, he broke off.

'They came here today,' Thomas told him. 'Rogues, perhaps – but not murderers. And if they were, I can't think they'd present themselves the next morning at the Petbury gates, near to where the body was found.'

Gale was barely listening. 'Nevertheless, I will seek them out.' He turned his filmy eyes upon Thomas. 'A killing in our little parish is rare, as you know, Thomas Finbow. And two in the space of as many days beggars belief. Then I've small need to remind you – since you weren't only present at Jem Latter's death, but a party to it.'

Thomas met his gaze. 'As you say, you've small need to remind me,' he said.

The constable let the matter drop, and turned again to the body of the fair young man. 'You've been all your life at Petbury,' he muttered. 'Is there anyone here who you think could do such a deed?'

Thomas hesitated, then shook his head.

But as he and the constable left the chapel soon after, he could not help thinking of the Russians. He had seen Mikhailov kill a man – but that was in a rage, with his bare hands. And as he had told Sir Robert, the fatal wound was made by a narrow blade, not one like the big man carried. Might there be another among the ambassador's train who knew how to use a sword?

The business troubled him – as he now knew it would, until this murderer was found. But whoever it was had left no sign, and the trail was cold.

Six

That evening, after Ned had gone home and Thomas had seen the falcons settled for the night, he returned to the cottage to find Eleanor waiting for him. And one glance told him that she was angry.

'When did you plan to tell me what happened at the Dagger?' she demanded. 'Did you not think I would worry?' Before he could answer, she went on: 'And have you thought on Nell's feelings? She had to hear of it from a kitchen boy—'

'If you'll let me, I'll tell you,' Thomas broke in at last. 'Nell and I spoke this afternoon – she knows the whole sorry tale. I've been sent here and there from the moment I got up – and she's been so pressed, she slept the last two nights with the wenches. We're like distant relations, who must beg for news of each other!'

He turned away and bent to make up the fire. After watching him for a moment Eleanor found a stool and sat.

'Isn't it always so, when Petbury entertains important guests?' she asked in a calmer voice. 'Let alone ones who gorge themselves like our friends from Muscovy.'

He glanced round at her. 'Not to mention those who demand possets in the night, and spiced ale for their secretaries.'

Eleanor was silent. Lady Jane Rooke's sleeplessness was well known, as were the demands of her servant Master Doggett.

'I know how you dislike John,' she said finally. 'But if you mean to speak against him you may save your breath. Both he and Lady Jane were disturbed enough to learn that a murder has been done in Chaddleworth – and by a man who lodges under the same roof as they. Now that there's been this terrible killing in the gardens, Lady Jane is distraught. It's likely she and both her servants will return to London.'

Thomas was breaking twigs from the little stack by the fireplace and laying them crosswise. But Eleanor knew him too well not to sense his relief.

'I thought that would cheer you,' she said.

He knelt and turned his gaze upon her. 'And what of your other admirer?'

The faintest flush of embarrassment showed on her delicate face. 'Piotr could charm the larks from the skies,' she admitted. 'As I guess he has charmed many young women, back in his homeland.'

'But not you?'

When Eleanor shrugged, he went on: 'Since you know he cannot stay here . . .' Then he caught a look in her eye, and frowned. 'I hope he has not made any false promises.'

She hesitated. 'He talks of quitting his master. Seeking leave to remain in England, in the service of some nobleman.'

Thomas shook his head. 'From what I've learned of the ambassador, he would never permit it.'

Eleanor frowned. 'They hate him,' she said quietly. 'All of them . . . even that murderous Mikhailov, though he's sworn to protect his master. Only Yusupov the secretary is truly loyal, for he's of noble birth himself – a *boyar*'s son, or whatever it is.'

Thomas considered. His daughter's words chimed with what he had learned from Kovalenko and Mikhailov. Finally he said: 'Tread carefully, my duck. Piotr's a handsome, jolly young fellow right enough, but—'

'But what?' Eleanor's eyes flashed. 'You mean he's a foreigner, from a backward land? Or is it because he can't even fly a hawk that you despise him?'

Thomas blinked. 'I don't despise him. I've never even spoken to him.' He stared. 'And since he knows no English, how have you learned so much from him?'

'Master Yusupov sometimes translates for us,' Eleanor answered. 'At other times . . .' She lowered her eyes. 'Piotr is skilled at conveying his thoughts by different means.'

Thomas gave her a wry look. 'Is he indeed.'

She caught his gaze. 'Nothing improper!' she retorted. 'I thought you trusted me better than that!'

'I do,' he replied. He looked away, and began choosing logs from the stack. Try as he might, he could not help thinking of Eleanor's mother whenever he looked at her.

'All of Petbury have taken against these Muscovy men,' he said after a moment. 'And none wishes them to depart more than Sir Robert himself – yet he must hide his feelings, put on a false smile and pander to their every need. Even as far as looking the other way when Master Stanic rides up smirking beside his wife. That secretary of his is mighty skilled in finding other words for what the man really says!'

He thought of the tense gathering in Sir Robert's private chamber when the ambassador had spoken scornfully of the priceless Muscovy chain. But Eleanor knew nothing of the royal gift. He decided not to speak of it.

'I hope you don't mean that he translates in such fashion for Piotr,' she said sharply, 'for I don't believe he would be coarse or cruel in his speech!'

Thomas sighed. 'I do not say such,' he told her. 'I only urge you to have a care. We know little of these folk – Kovalenko told me himself.' He placed a log on the neatly laid fire and looked about for the tinderbox. But Eleanor stood up suddenly.

'You treat me as a child still!' she cried. 'Do you never wonder what passes between Lady Margaret and her women, in private, in her chamber? Do you not think she values me more than a simple maid, and confides in me—'

'Eleanor!'

At the look of exasperation on Thomas's face, she fell silent. Whereupon her father stood to his full height, almost cracking his head on a beam.

'Everyone knows how much Lady Margaret values you,' he said. 'And I've naught but pride in you . . .' He looked away again. 'I merely pray, as your mother would have, that when you find a match it's someone worthy of you. One who will make a life for you – give you something better than this . . .' He spread out his hands. 'This hut where you grew up, that was built for a man who must tend his master's falcons before he thought of his own flesh and blood.'

She was silent for a while; then she broke into a smile. 'But what harm has it done me?' she asked. 'Growing up here?'

And before he could answer she moved to the door, lifted the latch and went out.

That night, as Thomas was hoping Nell might be able to leave the kitchens for once and come home, he was surprised to receive a hasty message from one of the grooms. It seemed a torchlight party would be arriving soon from the house, to inspect the falcons. Foremost among them would be Sir Robert and the ambassador.

He and the groom stood outside the door of the cottage. A light breeze blew, but the air was warm. The man – the same one who had told Sir Robert of the discovery of a body – was ill at ease, and Thomas was quickly alert.

'A torchlight party?'

The fellow shrugged. 'The ambassador's soused,' he said. 'Drunk enough for two men! They say he's made some wager that the bird he brought – the big white hawk – is better than all of yours put together.'

Thomas sighed. 'And Sir Robert . . . ?'

'What can he do but humour him?' the man answered. Then he looked down the slope, as Thomas did. Lights showed at the windows of the great house. But closer to, figures bearing torches had appeared from the stable yard, heading towards them.

'If you need any help . . .' the groom began, but Thomas shook his head.

'Nay – let me head them off.' And as the relieved groom hurried away, he sighed and braced himself to meet his visitors.

The torch carriers were Kovalenko the falconer and Yusupov the secretary. Behind came a tense Sir Robert, walking beside his honoured guest Grigori Stanic, looking bearlike in his heavy fur-trimmed coat, and clearly unsteady on his feet. But there was an unexpected addition to the group: Kat Jenkin, Lady Rooke's young maid, who seemed to be supporting the ambassador. Then Thomas saw that the poor girl had no choice in the matter – for His Excellency's left arm was clamped firmly about her slender shoulders, binding her to him. As they drew near she caught Thomas's eye; and her look of helplessness made him bite his lip. He drew a breath and addressed himself deliberately to Sir Robert.

'The birds are settled for the night, sir. If they are disturbed they will be edgy in the morning . . .'

'I know it, Thomas.' Sidestepping the ambassador, who lurched to a halt, Sir Robert drew close. 'He insisted on this foolish jaunt,' he said in an undertone. 'Things were getting ugly in the great hall . . . it was best we bring him outside.' He threw a look of distaste at Stanic. 'I thought the walk would sober him – or at least wear him out.'

'And the maid . . . ?' Thomas began. But at that moment the ambassador roared something in Russian, swaying dangerously. Beside him poor Kat struggled to keep her balance.

Thomas kept a respectful tone. 'What would you have me do, sir?' he asked. 'You know I cannot fly the birds at night.'

'Then tell him so!' Sir Robert answered in a voice of exasperation. His glance strayed from Stanic to the two attendants, who were standing impassively with their torches. Quickly, Yusupov the secretary stepped forward.

'I will translate the falconer's speech, sir,' he said in his diplomatic voice. 'The night air will soon calm His Excellency . . . he is tired, and should go to his bed.'

'Tired isn't the word I'd use,' Thomas remarked. And as the secretary flinched, he added: 'Can't you at least get him to release the poor maid?'

Yusupov said nothing. Instead he glanced at Kovalenko, who now moved forward. 'Is unwise to refuse our *batsushka*—' he began in a phlegmatic voice, but Thomas interrupted.

'I don't care. Nor do I believe there was naught you could do.' Then catching Sir Robert's glance, he broke off.

'Speak to His Excellency, falconer. He respects men like you – he will listen.' Yusupov wore a faint smile, but there was a look in his eye that Thomas had not seen before: was it a warning? He glanced at Kovalenko, but saw no expression. So with a breath he turned towards the ambassador and made his bow. Yusupov hurried forward to do his office.

'Sir – the birds are tired and at their rest now,' Thomas said. 'Even your white hawk – the finest of them all – needs her privacy at night. As any great lady would.'

With a nod of approval at Thomas, Yusupov translated; a rapid flow of words. To Thomas's surprise the ambassador listened attentively. Then when Yusupov had finished, the man opened his large mouth, showing a set of blackened teeth, and gave a bellow of laughter. He spoke, gesturing wildly at Yusupov. The secretary's face fell; but this time, seeing Sir Robert's eye upon him, he made no attempt to dissemble.

'His Excellency understands,' he said flatly. 'Yet he wishes to know if the hawk *dushenka* is . . .' He hesitated. 'If she is being well served by the tercels. We Russians are people of passion.'

Thomas threw a glance at Sir Robert, who looked away. 'Tell him there is no comfort she lacks, master secretary,' Thomas answered. Then while Yusupov turned to interpret, he spoke low to Kovalenko.

'I thought better of you than this,' he said.

Kovalenko met his eye. 'What I can do?' he asked. 'Our *batsushka* rules in everything. He punish us if—'

'So you've said.' Thomas looked towards the ambassador, who was taking time to absorb his secretary's speech. Finally the man grinned, and spoke a few slurred sentences.

Yusupov hesitated. Then forcing himself to meet Sir Robert's frowning gaze, he said: 'His Excellency is pleased. He . . . he hopes the lady hawk gets enough for her needs. He in his turn intends to pleasure this young maid, and show her what Muscovy men can do.'

Sir Robert froze – then started. For on an impulse Thomas

moved quickly round to Stanic's side. There was a gasp
from his two attendants, but Thomas did not halt. He merely
lifted the befuddled ambassador's arm firmly off Kat
Jenkin's shoulder, and took it upon his. Then he smiled
apologetically.

'You are too heavy for this young girl, sir,' he said. 'I
was afraid you would fall.'

At once Yusupov translated. But Kat, her chest heaving,
tucked her loose hair under her cap and bent close to
Thomas. 'I thank you, master,' she whispered.

'For what?' Thomas asked.

But with a look of relief, Sir Robert came forward.

'Go back to the house, girl,' he muttered, not unkindly.
'I'm sure your mistress wonders where you are.' He paused,
then added: 'And try not to get within reach of the ambassador's hands again.'

The girl bobbed, and with a fleeting glance at Thomas,
hurried away.

'Well, sir . . .' To the alarm of the attendants, Sir Robert
turned and clapped Grigori Stanic hard on the back, making
him stagger. 'Now that we're all men here, what's your
pleasure? A sword-bout? Wrestling? Or a midnight swim
in the pond? You'll have to ignore our frogs, they're a noisy
lot.'

The ambassador was looking confused. Then, finally
noticing that Thomas had replaced the girl under his arm,
he frowned deeply. Quickly Yusupov spoke up.

'You mentioned some new colts that His Excellency might
like to see, Sir Robert,' he said.

'Did I?' Sir Robert appeared not to remember. 'Well then,
we'll take a stroll down to the paddock. If your master can
stay on his feet, that is.'

Yusupov wet his lips nervously. 'Once again I ask your
pardon, sir,' he said in an undertone. 'Your claret is so fine,
His Excellency has made too free with it . . .'

'As he does with the women,' Thomas could not help
putting in. Catching Sir Robert's glance, he looked away.

But the danger had passed. The ambassador, apparently
forgetting why he had chosen to come here, was looking

dazedly about. And at a glance from Yusupov, Kovalenko moved close to Thomas.

'You take torch, I take *batsushka*,' he muttered.

So Thomas lifted Grigori Stanic's arm, which was as heavy as a log, from his shoulder on to the falconer's. Taking the man's torch he moved away and joined his master.

'What a performance . . .' Sir Robert sighed and adjusted his narrow ruff. 'I'll get him to the paddock, let the grooms do their share.'

Thomas nodded. And holding the torch aloft, he stood before his cottage and watched the group move off down the slope. And though the ambassador lurched from side to side, the stolid Kovalenko was equal to the task of keeping him upright. Sir Robert fell in step on the other side, talking with a false heartiness that would have fooled no one – unless they were too drunk to notice. The hapless secretary trotted close by, his torch bobbing about.

Thomas watched until the light was but a faint glow, before thrusting the torch into the damp grass to quash the flame. Then he threw the stick a long way, towards the trees above the mews. Sparks flew into the darkness, then died.

The next day, a windy Saturday, Thomas set Ned to work cleaning out the falcons' mews. Confident that the ambassador would be in no condition to go hawking, he then went to the kitchens and spoke with Nell. After that he walked the mile into Chaddleworth. For Ned had brought news: that the inquest into the death of the young man found in the Petbury gardens would be held in the Black Bear this very morning.

The inn was full; a hot mass of bodies. Greeting folk by name, Thomas shouldered his way inside and saw Dillamore in a sweat by the barrels. His wife Ann hurried by, a pair of foaming mugs in each hand.

'Thomas! Did you know you're called as a witness?'

Thomas started. But before he could answer a tall figure caught his eye, beckoning to him. With a sigh he pushed through the throng towards Tertius Gale.

'The coroner wishes you to give evidence, in place of

Sir Robert's steward,' the constable said. 'You can tell of
the condition of the body, and so forth . . .' The man's watery
eyes swivelled towards a corner, where a long table had
been set up. Already a group of Chaddleworth's worthiest
men, selected as jurors, were taking their seats.

'Are there no other witnesses?' Thomas asked, scanning
the faces. Gale gave a shrug.

'I know only of the milkmaid, the finder of the body.'
He pointed out a nervous-looking girl sitting in her best
clothes with an older woman, likely her mother.

'Now – I expect your master wishes to know how my
enquiries have progressed,' Gale said, pursing his lips.

Thomas nodded absently, knowing that the matter was
unlikely to be uppermost in Sir Robert's mind today.

'I've not been idle,' the constable told him. 'I spoke to
the vagrom men – those two cheating rogues, who have now
swapped their rags for better attire. Would you believe they've
hired a room at the Dagger, and carouse there as bold as
brass? They must have stolen a purse somewhere—'

'They were given charity by the steward,' Thomas interrupted. 'He's a soft-hearted soul, at times.'

'Indeed?' Gale looked suspiciously at him. 'That's not
how I'd describe Master Martin . . .'

But with relief Thomas saw the grey, stooped figure of
the coroner Sir William Danby seating himself behind the
table. He turned to the constable. 'Shall we find a place?'

And before Gale could answer, he was pushing forward.

The inquest was short, for there was little evidence to
be heard apart from the milkmaid's testimony. The girl told
how she had been taking a cut through the field below the
Petbury gardens, making for the village lane, when she
saw the body lying beside a statue. It was the exposed
flesh that had caught her eye . . . that and a swarm of flies,
and the fearful swathe of blood. It distressed the maid even
to speak of it. Only after a reviving cup of sack was she
able to finish, by which time she seemed to be enjoying
the attention.

After that one of the Petbury gardeners told how the girl
had called him and his fellows and led them to the body.

Then it was Thomas's turn to give evidence, including what he had deduced about the wound. This caused a stir, not least from Sir William Danby.

'A fencer's blow – a *montanto*, you say?' He peered at Thomas through spectacles thick as bottle-ends. 'Then whoever used the sword followed the Italian school, rather than the Spanish?'

'I cannot say, sir,' Thomas answered. 'Only that it was a powerful thrust, well aimed.' Then he remembered the scar on the dead man's side, and spoke of that.

'So he too was a fencer?' The coroner looked perplexed. 'Do you mean to imply that these two men – let us assume two men – were having a sword-bout in the Petbury gardens, by night?'

'I know not, sir. It would seem a foolhardy venture.'

'Indeed . . .' Danby glanced at Tertius Gale, who stood to one side, rotating his scrawny neck as he followed the discourse.

'If you wish my opinion, Sir William,' Thomas went on, 'I can only think that the dead man may have arranged a meeting with someone. The statue is a good landmark.'

Danby nodded vaguely. 'There were no other distinguishing marks, beside this old fencing scar?'

Thomas replied in the negative. There was a lull, and conversation rose on all sides, for the entire company of the Black Bear were now spectators. It occurred to Thomas suddenly that there had been no inquest on Jem Latter. Thanks no doubt to his master's arrangements, that business had been speedily despatched – and so was this. For the coroner now marshalled what facts he had and addressed the jury, who retired into a huddle. And it was but a short time before they emerged to deliver their verdict: that the deceased, a man unknown to the parish, had suffered unlawful killing by the sword, wielded by a person unknown.

As if given permission, the company burst into conversation, prompting Danby to bang the table and call for silence. But clearly feeling dry himself, he soon brought the proceedings to an end. His obvious relief at seeing Ann

Dillamore approaching with a tankard of best brew caused some stifled laughs.

'I like this not, falconer!'

Thomas found Tertius Gale at his side, wearing a look of fierce disapproval.

'Surely it's what was expected?' Thomas countered, but the other shook his head.

'There's been scant respect for the Queen's law in Chaddleworth, these past days!' he said severely. 'And I speak not only of the way Latter's killing was dealt with . . . though you know more of that than most, Thomas Finbow. I mean the quick dismissal of this young man's death, so that certain folk can say they've done their duty, and get to the business of downing mugs of ale!'

Thomas shrugged. 'There was no more to be said . . .'

'And no more to be found out?' Gale was peering darkly at him. 'You of all people – who are famous throughout the Downlands for your skills of deduction – will you too let the matter drop so soon? A young man has been murdered, cut down in most untimely fashion . . .'

Thomas looked about helplessly. Gale was on his high horse – something for which he in his turn was quite famous. Unfortunately, as constable he was also famously unable to back up his righteous views with results. On these occasions folk would mutter their excuses and drift away.

'What would you have me do?' Thomas asked him. 'I've barely time to do my work, let alone start ferreting about . . .'

'Yet I need you to!'

The man spoke low, but his tone was more than urgent: it bordered on desperation. Thomas showed his surprise – never before had Gale asked for his help; in fact to his knowledge, he had never asked for anyone's.

He met the constable's gaze. 'Well then, I can but try,' he said. 'But I won't make promises I cannot keep—'

'I know,' Gale replied. 'I also know how you helped Will Ragg in Lambourn three summers back, after the murder of Stubbs the churchwarden. My wife's from Lambourn—' He broke off, then added: 'It was you who guessed how

this young fellow's wound was made. All I ask is that you
seek to uncover whatever you can.'

'I'll try,' Thomas repeated. Whereupon the constable,
recovering his usual manner, nodded gravely.

'Then I thank you,' he said, and moved away.

Finding that he too had a powerful thirst, Thomas looked
around for Dillamore. But someone else had been waiting
to waylay him. As he began easing through the crowd, there
came a tug at his elbow. He looked round to find himself
gazing into the unwashed face of Will Greve.

'I said I'd stand you a mug,' the poacher said in a sly
voice. 'Only I heard you and Gale talking, so I've information instead. Mayhap it's you should treat me.'

Thomas frowned. 'I never knew a man who stretched his
luck as you do,' he said. 'And I dislike folk who eavesdrop
on me—'

'The dead man,' Greve broke in. His breath stank, as did
his old jerkin, thick with ancient grease and dirt. 'He was
in Chaddleworth, before he went and got himself killed.'

Thomas stiffened. 'You saw him?'

Greve gave a nod, whereupon Thomas leaned forward
and gripped his arm. 'So why didn't you speak up? And
why haven't you told Gale—' Then he broke off. This man
never gave away anything – and certainly not information.
'Where did you see him?' he went on. 'And who else—'

'Easy!' Greve pulled his arm free of Thomas's grip. 'I'll
tell you what I know. In turn you can—'

'The devil I can!' Thomas's patience was disappearing.
'You tell me what you know and I tell Gale – and that's
all! If it's useful, the best I'll do is not say where I heard
it.'

Greve eyed him. 'I'll wager it's useful, falconer,' he said
softly. 'And what you can do, next time you hear one of
my arrows, is walk off in the other direction.'

Thomas exhaled. 'I said you'd be the ruin of me,' he
muttered. 'Well – spin your tale and let me judge its worth.'

But Greve shook his head. 'Not here . . .' He glanced
towards the rear door. 'I'll be emptying my bladder.' And
at once he disappeared into the throng.

Thomas waited a moment, then made his way out by the front door. He walked round the back of the inn, loosening his breeches. There was Will Greve, making water cheerfully on Ann Dillamore's flower bed.

'Well?' Thomas stood beside him. The two of them were alone.

'He must have arrived by night,' Greve said. 'Took a chamber at the Dagger, and left it near dawn. Few would have seen him – not even Chalke.'

Matthew Chalke was the landlord of the Dagger – a man Thomas would trust no further than he had trusted Jem Latter.

'Who else saw him go out?' he asked.

Greve threw him a wry grin. The poacher, on one of his nocturnal jaunts, had likely been the only one.

'Can you describe him?'

Greve shrugged. 'Good clothes . . . a travelling cloak, feathered hat. No pauper, so . . .'

'So why stay at the Dagger, unless he wished not to draw attention to himself.' Thomas hesitated. 'Anything more?'

Greve was lacing up his breeches. 'Is't not enough?'

Thomas was frowning. 'How can you be sure it was the same man?'

'Young, fair, scant beard . . . how many other strangers are about? Save your friends from Muscovy, that is.'

Thomas gave him a sour look. But he knew Greve, and he knew the truth when he heard it. 'An arrow, you said . . .' He drew a breath. 'Well, then: if I hear one, I might walk away. But if I hear two . . .'

Greve sniffed. 'One is all I'd need, falconer,' he said. 'And you'd best take care it's not aimed at you!'

Seven

That evening, after his work was done, Thomas returned to Chaddleworth. But instead of taking the lane from Petbury, he crossed the fields until he struck the deserted Welford road and headed for the Dagger.

He had told no one of his intention, not even Nell. Secrecy seemed best – not least because if he was expected there might be a reception party, bent on revenge for the killing of Jem Latter. Tense in every sinew, he entered the noisome inn as dusk was falling, and looked about for its notorious landlord, Matthew Chalke.

At first no one paid him much attention. But there were soon eyes upon him, peering through the haze. Seeing an empty booth in one corner, Thomas made his way towards it. But as he slid sideways on to the bench a head appeared, directly opposite him. The man had apparently been fumbling under the rickety table. Seeing Thomas he almost leaped out of his skin.

'Jesu! What do you mean, coming up on me like that . . .' Then recognition dawned on both men. And it was hard to say who was the more surprised: Thomas or Tobias Swift, the false rogue who had come begging the day before, at the Petbury gates.

With a muttered oath Thomas rose to go; he had no desire for conversation with the man. But at once Swift stayed him.

'Wait! Take a mug with me, won't you? I owe you that much.'

After a moment, Thomas sat down. 'Where's your friend the Abraham man?' he asked drily. 'Taken his act somewhere else?'

The other's face clouded. 'No call to be cruel, master,' he muttered. Quickly he stowed away what he had dropped, though not before Thomas had seen the glint of a coin. But at that moment the drawer appeared, asking what they lacked. Swift called for small beer, and waited until the fellow had gone.

'I heard you were lodging here,' Thomas said. 'Minding false madmen looks like a profitable trade.'

Swift frowned. 'Who are you to preach?' he demanded. 'This isn't Paul's Cross. You're but a hired man who serves a rich knight, friend.'

Thomas said nothing, whereupon the other went on: 'Joshua's not what you think. He's a poor simple soul—'

'Who never saw the inside of Bedlam,' Thomas put in.

Swift was about to answer, then thought better of it. Already Thomas regretted accepting a drink from the fellow. He intended to down it and move off, when he felt the hairs rise on his neck. And without looking round, he knew he had company of the worst sort . . . worse than a plain rogue like Swift; worse even than Jem Latter. Slowly he turned, to find a short man with a wide mouth and staring eyes standing beside the table.

'Small beer, wasn't it?' The landlord plonked two battered mugs down.

'We thank you,' Swift muttered, looking uneasy. But Thomas met the sheep-like eyes calmly, though he knew enough of Matthew Chalke to heed the warning therein.

'You're a brave man, Finbow.' Chalke began massaging his cheeks above his black woolly beard; a well-known habit. 'It's a mite soon to come here after what happened in the bowl-alley, wouldn't you say?'

Unhurriedly, Thomas picked up his mug and took a sip. 'Your beer's no better than it used to be,' he said.

Chalke went on rubbing his beard. Swift picked up his own mug and gulped his beer, then set it down nervously. 'If there's bad blood between you and this man, master,' he began, 'I need no part of it—'

'The ale all right with you, is it?' Chalke enquired. 'I wouldn't want to disappoint.'

'It's a good brew,' Swift answered quickly. 'Best I've had in weeks . . .'

'That's well.' Chalke had never taken his eyes off Thomas. 'I'll watch your friend drink his, then I'll see him out.'

Thomas looked into his mug. Inwardly he was cursing himself: this was a poor start, for a man who had come here seeking information. He took a further sip.

'Supposing I want another?' he asked.

Chalke's great round eyes – the man was never known to blink – regarded him unflinchingly. 'I'd say you were stretching your good fortune somewhat.'

'A pity,' Thomas said. 'I came thinking you and I might do business.'

The landlord made no reply.

'A simple matter of information, about a customer of yours,' Thomas went on. 'Stayed here the night before last . . .'

There was a sudden movement from Tobias Swift. Having drained his mug, the fellow rose and started to ease himself through the narrow space between his bench and the table. 'I leave you to it, masters,' he said. 'I've matters of my own to—'

'Sit down!' Chalke almost spat the words. He turned his alarming eyes upon Swift, who blinked and sat.

'Your credit's done,' the landlord said harshly. 'One night's food and lodging you and your cripple friend bought. So now you'd best take your old rags out and get back on the road. You'll not stay here tonight.'

Swift reddened. 'You said two nights!' he cried. 'It's near dark, and—'

'And you'll sleep in the ditch, where you belong!' the other threw back. Then he turned his gaze upon Thomas.

'No one stayed here that night,' he said. 'So take your business and shove it down your throat. And if I were you, I'd not ask for another. You've been noticed.'

He jerked his thumb over his shoulder, but Thomas did not need to look. The inn had become silent, as all eyes and ears were turned towards him.

Without further word, Chalke rotated his squat body and moved off through the tobacco smoke.

Tobias Swift let out a breath. 'A pox on you!' he muttered.
'You've got me and Joshua thrown out!'

'I thank you for the drink,' Thomas said, and got up. He
glanced across the room, saw his way clear to the door. As
he went, he threw a glance at the other. 'I ask your pardon,'
he murmured. 'But for my part, I'd rather sleep under the
stars than in this rat-hole.'

'Wait.' Swift half-rose from his seat. 'You said you—'

'I'll make myself scarce,' Thomas said. And without
looking around he walked across the dimly lit room, between
tables where men watched him pass. But no one moved,
and soon he had reached the door and got himself outside.

There was nobody in the lane. It was indeed almost dark,
and night birds called from the nearby woods. With a mixture
of relief and disappointment – for he had learned nothing
– Thomas began walking towards Chaddleworth green. He
had half a mind to seek Gale in the Black Bear . . . he quickened his pace, as a light from the nearest cottage showed
in the distance. The turning to Petbury was beyond.

Then they came, without warning.

There were two of them, from the bushes to his left –
and he berated himself for his carelessness. They must have
slipped out of the back of the Dagger and run ahead through
the trees . . . but what did it matter? Heart pounding, Thomas
turned to face his doom.

He heard the cudgel before he saw it, whirling through
the air. Ducking aside, he managed to avoid the weapon.
But the second man was closing on his right, and this one
caught him a heavy blow on his side with a billet. Feeling
no pain yet – that would come soon enough – he lashed
out in the near-darkness, taking some small comfort when
his fist connected with a head. There was a grunt, but the
other man was swinging his cudgel again . . .

If I could see their faces, he thought, ducking again and
trying to grab the cudgel man. But the fellow was ready:
avoiding Thomas's grasp he cracked him hard on the knee.

The pain arrived, with a rush that made him stagger. His
legs threatened to fold. But knowing that if he fell he was
finished, he fought the harder, grabbing the other man's

arm and twisting it, while kicking out. The fellow yelped, but the other merely uttered an oath and struck Thomas again – hard, across his shoulder, making him let go.

'That's for Jem Latter!' he shouted.

The crack alarmed Thomas. Fighting dizziness, he struck out with both fists, wildly now, but the men stepped back, avoiding the blows. They knew it was only a matter of time.

Then, voices . . . another two – or was it three men? Shapes, dimly glimpsed as they emerged from the bushes . . . then shouts. Someone screamed horribly . . . grimly Thomas fought on, knowing it was hopeless. He had been hit again – on the arms and thighs, and on his mouth . . . he was losing track of events, and tasting blood. He managed to catch someone by the hair, tearing desperately at it, hearing a yell. But there were more screams, closer – then running feet . . . he sagged, feeling dizziness envelop him. It would be easy, too easy, to sink into unconsciousness . . .

He was on his knees, but no one was hitting him. In fact, his assailants were running off . . . hope sprang inside him, as he peered into the gloom. The screaming had stopped. He heard someone crashing through the bushes . . . and caught his breath. There were still two of them, standing over him. Weakly he looked up . . . whereupon someone struck a flame from a tinderbox, and thrust it towards him.

'They've gone.' The man bent and stared into Thomas's face. 'You can rest . . .' He turned to his companion, who also leaned forward. But the first one's voice, he knew at once.

'Chalke said you were brave,' Tobias Swift muttered. 'Foolish, more like. Did you not think you'd be followed?'

Breathlessly Thomas focussed on the face of the man he had drunk with but a short while before. Then he saw the other: Joshua the Abraham man. He swayed and opened his mouth, but only a grunt came out.

'Best sit yourself, until it clears,' Swift said.

Thomas sat down in the lane, grateful for the damp grass that soaked through his breeches. He risked a feel of his collarbone, wincing at the pain. But there was no break . . . relieved, he looked up at the vagrom men: the unlikeliest pair of rescuers he could have imagined.

'Was it you doing the screaming?' he asked.

Swift jerked his thumb. 'Joshua has his uses,' he said. 'He can't talk, but he can screech like an owl.'

It was becoming clearer: these two had scared the others off. Thomas looked gratefully at them both.

'It's my turn to offer thanks,' he said.

Swift shifted on his feet. Thomas now saw that the man bore his heavy pack. Though neither of them had yet changed into their beggars' rags. And Joshua was agitated. Bending close to his friend, he whined something incomprehensible.

'We must be gone,' Swift said. 'Put some miles between us and this place, before those two come back with a few friends.'

Thomas managed a nod. Swift snuffed out the light and stowed away his tinderbox. 'You'll get help, won't you, being a local man?'

'I will . . .' Thomas was recovering his breath. 'If you'll stay a moment, I've money. They didn't take my purse . . .'

At that, the other two exchanged glances. And they waited as, with difficulty, Thomas found his purse and emptied out the contents. It wasn't much, but . . .

'Take it,' he said, holding out his hand. Swift took the money. Beside him Joshua gave a whine to convey his approval.

'Well now, Master Finbow – if I heard your name aright . . .' Swift adjusted his pack and glanced along the lane. 'If you'd stayed a mite longer in the Dagger and let me speak, you'd have heard me say what I'll say now. What I wouldn't tell that whoreson constable when he came poking about – talking to us like we were dirt!' He sniffed. 'You asked Chalke about a fellow that stayed under his roof, the night before last. He said there was no one – well, he lied.'

Thomas paused. 'Did you know this man had been killed?'

'Aye, the constable said . . .' Swift turned and spat heavily. Beside him Joshua hopped about, eager to be gone.

'He was a young man,' Thomas said. 'Good clothes . . .' He peered intently at the other. 'You saw him?'

'I not only saw him,' Swift said, 'I knew him!'

Thomas started. But Joshua was becoming very anxious now. He tugged at his keeper's coat.

'Hold, will you? I'll tell him what I know . . .' Swift bent low to Thomas. 'There were no other strangers about that night, aside from us,' he said, and gave a short laugh. 'Only, it looks to me now as if half of Shoreditch had come to Chaddleworth . . . must be the Downland air that draws them!'

'Shoreditch . . . ?' Thomas did not understand.

'The cove you're interested in hailed from without Bishopsgate – the same dirty tenements I do,' Swift told him. 'Though he's done a mite better for himself than me. That's what swordsmanship can do – that, and a winning smile.'

'Then he was a fencer . . .' Despite his hurts, Thomas was intrigued. 'Will you tell me his name?'

'Richard Cutler. A honey-tongued rogue, if ever there was. Spent his days at the old fencing school by Moorfields, teaching young city men. Having bouts for money. Only he wasn't too particular how he came by his glimmer.'

'Would blackmail be one way?'

'Very like . . . he had a sharp eye for men's weaknesses, did Cutler,' Swift replied. 'And he'll not be missed!'

'Did you speak with him?'

'Nay . . . we were bedding down near the road. Saw him go to the Dagger . . . looked like he was bent on business.'

Joshua, having decided he could wait no longer, stamped on the ground and gave a yelp. Swift laid a hand on his arm. 'That's all I can tell ye, master Finbow,' he said. 'Now we'll take our leave. Likely we shan't meet again.'

Joshua was dancing about like a child. Swift murmured to him, and at once the two turned and walked off. In seconds they had vanished.

Thomas sat for a while, listening to the night birds. Then, slowly, he hauled himself to his feet. There would be bruises – blood too; but he knew how lucky he was. Had the two false rogues not come to his aid, he would not have got up. His body would have been dragged into the trees, to be found later, after the foxes had taken their share of him . . .

Wondering how grim he must look, he began to walk stiffly towards Chaddleworth green. Never had he been so glad to see the lights; already he heard the din from the open windows of the Black Bear . . .

But he never got inside the inn. For on the green, only moments later, he was waylaid by an anxious servingman from Petbury who had been sent to look for him. Thomas must present himself before Sir Robert at once, on a matter of grave urgency.

An hour later he entered Sir Robert's private chamber, to hear tidings that drove every other thought from his head.

The Muscovy chain had been stolen.

He had changed his clothes and cleaned himself hastily, but he knew he was a sorry sight. However, the attention of both Sir Robert and Martin – the room's only occupants – was elsewhere: upon the iron-bound chest that stood near the wall, its lid wide open. Thomas made his bow stiffly and waited while his master delivered the news, his face haggard in the candlelight.

'The lock was picked,' he said hoarsely. 'It's gone!'

Without thinking Thomas glanced at the ring of heavy keys that hung from Martin's belt – and at once regretted it. For the old man's eyes blazed.

'Aye, look well!' the steward cried. 'But as you see, the key is still there – and it has not left my person!'

'For pity's sake!' Sir Robert waved a hand irritably. 'None will suspect you—'

'Will they not?' Martin's anger gave way to helplessness. ' 'Tis known that you and I alone have keys, sir. Do we ask folk to believe that a common thief gained access to this room so easily, when both door and casement were locked . . .'

'Enough!' Sir Robert sank into a chair. At last, he noticed Thomas's bruises and frowned. 'What's happened to you?'

' 'Tis naught, sir,' Thomas answered, still taking in the news. 'May I see?' When no refusal followed, he took a step towards the chest and looked inside it. Apart from some papers, there was nothing.

'I've said the lock was picked,' Sir Robert repeated. 'You know Martin and I have the only keys . . .' He put a hand to his forehead. 'I did not even place a guard outside, for I did not wish to draw attention. And besides – I believed the chain was safe! I wouldn't have known of the theft before morning, if I hadn't chanced to come in here. The rogue left the lid wide open, to show me my folly!'

'If a man's skilled enough to pick such a sturdy lock, then he's skilled enough to open the window,' Thomas ventured. 'It would not have taken long . . .'

Sir Robert looked around for a fortifying drink. But there was none to hand.

'Was there money in the chest too?' Thomas asked.

His master nodded. 'A bag with twenty or thirty angels . . . a trifle, compared with the Muscovy chain.' He smote the table with his fist. 'Why did the ambassador have to stay?' he cried. 'If he'd gone yesterday, and taken the wretched thing with him—'

He broke off, knowing words were fruitless. Martin hovered about, looking forlorn. Both men were so dismayed by the theft, Thomas tried to rally them.

'Have you ordered a search of the grounds, sir?' he asked. 'We could call for aid from Chaddleworth . . .'

'Of course not!' Sir Robert snapped. 'No one must know! If word gets out . . .' He turned a haggard face towards Martin. 'God in heaven, supposing the Privy Council get wind of it . . .'

'They shall not!' Martin found his voice at last. 'We can throw a cordon about the whole of the East Downs, comb them from Shefford to the Ridgeway—'

'No!' Sir Robert was on his feet suddenly. 'Any search must be carried out in utter secrecy! Don't you see what's at stake? If the Queen learns of it—' He glanced at Thomas. 'Where were you this night?' he asked abruptly.

'I was doing a little searching of my own, sir,' Thomas replied. 'For what it's worth, I found out who the dead man in the gardens was.'

Sir Robert blinked. 'Well – who was he?'

Thomas drew a breath, and told him all that he had learned from Tobias Swift.

'And you think that has any bearing on this . . . ?' Sir Robert gestured vaguely towards the chest.

Thomas shrugged. 'It's hard to see how, sir.' He glanced at Martin, who was trying to summon his reserves along with his dignity. Giving one of his coughs, the old man gained Sir Robert's attention.

'With your leave, sir – I'm of no use here. I will go and try to mount some sort of search myself.'

'Wait.' Sir Robert too seemed to collect himself. 'Let me think . . .' then pointedly, he turned to Thomas. There was a short silence.

'I will do what I can, sir,' Thomas said finally. 'But it's hard to know where to start. Whoever was cunning enough to steal the chain will have moved quickly . . .'

'I know,' Sir Robert answered. 'But we must spare no effort.' He hesitated. 'You will need help. Perhaps there are others we might trust – tell them merely that a case of jewels is stolen . . .'

'Is that wise?' Martin looked anxious. 'If our Muscovy guests hear that, they will know full well what it means.'

'Yes . . .' Sir Robert sighed. 'Whatever happens, the ambassador and his people must not learn of this – at least, not until I have no choice but to tell them.'

He gave a bark of laughter. 'Last night I couldn't wait to be rid of the man – now it looks as if I must contrive to keep him here as long as possible!'

Thomas and Martin exchanged glances, but there was no more to be said. And a short while later, Thomas left the chamber to begin the most impossible task he had ever undertaken: to find the Muscovy chain.

He would have laughed, as he left the house and saw the dawn's fingers streaking the sky. But his jaw hurt too much.

Eight

The next day was the Sabbath, but Thomas was not at morning prayers with the rest of the household. Instead he found an excuse to be at the front of the house, outside the window of Sir Robert's private chamber.

There were footprints of course, in the damp earth of the flower bed. But they told him little he had not already guessed. The old Petbury casements with their cracks and crannies would have presented only a slight challenge for any accomplished housebreaker. The thief had simply slipped a dagger into the gap and forced the catch. He would have been inside within a moment.

The iron-bound chest, however, was another matter. With Martin's knowledge but no one else's, Thomas re-entered the house and went to Sir Robert's chamber. Here too he learned little that was new, though there were traces of earth on the floor by the window, where the fellow had climbed in. After his work was done he had simply let himself out, closing it behind him. Though he had not bothered to close the chest, which suggested two possibilities to Thomas. Either the man was in haste to be gone and afraid someone would hear – or he knew he would get clean away, and did not care. Or perhaps he was arrogant, and wanted to make a show of his success.

Sir Robert had re-locked the chest, but Thomas knelt and examined it anyway. There were old scratches about the heavy lock, but no recent markings. He knew there were men with the skills, and the tools, to pick any such device – the Black Art, as it was known in thieves' cant – though this particular theft troubled him. For who apart from Sir Robert, Martin and himself, and perhaps Lady Margaret,

knew where the Muscovy chain was? Sir Thomas Rivers
had known, but he would be back in London by now, along
with his servant. And besides, they were above suspicion.
That left the Russians: Stanic and Yusupov had been in this
room, and seen the chain. They would have seen the chest
too; it was the obvious place to secure something so valuable – indeed, the only place. It was conceivable that Stanic's
other servants knew of it too – but they served their master,
and feared him. Though Eleanor's words came back to
Thomas: *They hate him – all of them* . . .

He stood up, knowing he was wasting time. There was
nothing for it but to try and follow the chain from Petbury.
Where would the thief go? He sighed: though strangers
were easily recognized in the Downland villages, there were
many folk on the roads this summer. Of late there had been
Swift and Joshua – and the man Swift recognized, Richard
Cutler. He frowned, staring through the latticed window.
Surely that man's killing had no link with the theft?

Eager to be outdoors, he left the chamber. As always
when he wished to think matters through, he would fly one
of the falcons; try to view the ground from above, as they
did. And an hour later on the Downs, with the great white
hawk soaring above him, he made a resolve.

He would risk Sir Robert's wrath, and seek some help
– for his task was impossible. The chain could be
anywhere . . . halfway to London by now. Though he did
not know the hour when it was stolen, it was quite early
in the night, for Sir Robert was still up. He grimaced;
the chain might be nowhere near London. It could even
have left the country . . .

He drew a breath: he could but do his best. He was no
conjuror, to seek the chain by divination. But he could do
some poking about, as could others. And though he had
little faith in Tertius Gale, he was a man he could trust. By
the afternoon he was back in Chaddleworth, knocking on
the constable's door.

Gale heard him out in silence, sitting in his small front
parlour. The cottage stood north of the green, by St Andrew's

church, from where the bell clanged at times. Thomas finished his tale – of the theft of a black case containing some valuable jewels – and waited. But if the constable was startled, he would not show it. He merely raised his pale eyes from the rush-strewn floor and fixed them on Thomas.

'I fail to understand the secrecy, falconer,' he said. 'Why does Sir Robert not raise hue and cry? The theft of such gems is a grave felony, punishable by death. The sheriff of Berkshire should be told—'

'My master has ordered discretion in this matter,' Thomas told him. 'I know he would be most grateful for your help, if the goods are recovered. But then and only then will I tell him of your involvement. That is, if you are willing to help me?'

Gale frowned. 'I like not the sound of it. Are these jewels of which you speak—'

'They're not my master's,' Thomas broke in. 'They are a gift, destined for an important personage. Hence they must be found before their absence is noted, and restored to their proper ownership. It's a matter of some delicacy.'

'Then you ask me to risk my office as well as my reputation,' Gale said. 'For if we fail . . .'

'None shall even know that I told you of it,' Thomas said. 'But I'm charged with hunting for the . . .' He stopped himself in time. 'For the case. All I ask is that you walk the roads as I will, find out who has passed by Petbury in the past few days.'

Gale stiffened. 'I know of two!' he snapped. 'Those counterfeit rogues whom you chose to overlook. Now perhaps you will revise your opinion of them.' He broke off, seeing the expression on Thomas's face. And only then did he appear to notice the cut on Thomas's lip.

'Is there aught else you wish to tell me?' he asked in a dry voice.

Thomas drew a breath and told Gale, as he had told Sir Robert, about his visit to the Dagger and all that followed. But now the constable was dumbfounded.

'This Richard Cutler is another rogue, you say? Then

I cannot believe he is not bound up in the theft in some way! Perhaps there were two thieves, who fell out over the prize . . . ?'

Thomas explained patiently that the case was still in Sir Robert's chest two days before, when Cutler was already dead.

Gale fell to pursing his lips. 'I will tell the coroner,' he said finally. 'Now we know the dead man's name, and whence he came. His body should be returned to his own parish.'

Thomas nodded. 'Master Martin the steward will help you make arrangements . . . and likely Sir Robert will bear the expense.' When Gale looked relieved, Thomas steered him to another matter.

'There is one man I'd like to speak with again,' he said. 'One who's already lied to me – and who might well shed some light on Cutler's death.'

Gale looked up. 'Matthew Chalke?'

'Indeed . . . only I'd prefer someone with me this time.' Thomas raised his eyebrows expectantly.

'He's lied to me, many a time,' the constable said darkly. 'And I'd pay him a visit in any case. Shall we say, at sunset?'

They met on the Welford road a few hours later. Thomas had been back to Petbury, and after seeing to the falcons, sent word to Nell. He had seen nothing of her, but knowing that his bruised appearance was noted, he had a feeling he would have some explaining to do. But a restless urgency was upon him, and he could not wait. Seeing Gale with a stout billet in his hand, he wondered whether he should have armed himself beyond the poniard at his belt. But there was no time now. Wordlessly the two men walked the short distance to the Dagger, and without preamble stepped inside.

The reaction was instantaneous: a hush, followed by muttering and one or two groans. The constable was as popular here as the measles. But Gale, at his most righteous, ignored his reception and moved through the stuffy room.

'Matthew Chalke!' His voice could be sonorous when he chose. 'I would speak with you!'

Nobody moved and nobody spoke, until at last the drawer in his dirty apron appeared. 'Landlord's away,' he began, spreading his hands – then gulped. For Gale had grabbed him by the collar.

'I'm in a poor humour,' he said. 'So test not my patience. Point me to your master, or I'll crack your nose.'

The fellow squirmed. 'You know me, Gale! I but do my work . . . I an't seen Matthew for an hour or more . . .'

Gale raised his billet, while Thomas looked round. He had begun to wonder which of the men staring at him were the ones who had attacked him on the road. Then, looking back at the frightened drawer, he caught the man's eye and saw it flick in the direction of the rickety staircase in the far corner. To the man's dismay, he smiled.

'Save your breath,' he told Gale. 'I've an idea our friend Chalke's too busy to have noticed the commotion.'

Gale looked round, whereupon Thomas nodded towards the stairs. In a moment they were climbing, two steps at a time. Below them an angry hum of voices broke out. Someone – the drawer? – banged on the ceiling with an empty mug. But if this was a signal, the warning came too late for Matthew Chalke. Tertius Gale threw open a door at the top of the stairs and strode into the tiny room. Thomas followed – to find the landlord half-dressed upon his knees, his eyes almost popped from their sockets. Below him on a noisome pallet lay a young girl, her smock pulled up to her neck, who cried out in alarm. Chalke swung round to stare at the incomers, and a look of fury appeared on his face.

'Get out, you whoreson javel! I'll break your head!'

He scrambled to his feet, fumbling with his hose. The young girl, eyes wide with fear, lay still.

'Like you sent someone to break the falconer's?' Gale gestured to Thomas. 'That alone could put you in the stocks. As for harbouring felons . . .' He shook his head. 'I'd need to get a sheriff's escort up here, take you down to Reading Gaol.'

Chalke's pop-eyes blazed. He glanced at the billet in Gale's hand, then reached to the floor and found his breeches. As he pulled them on, he began talking rapidly.

'I know naught of any felons! Any man who pays the tariff can stay here – I ask no questions, and no names. And if you mean those two beggars, I sent them away. Finbow saw me—'

'I speak not of them,' Gale snapped. 'I speak of the man who stayed here the night of Thursday last – and who fetched up dead next morning in the gardens of Petbury Manor!'

Chalke fell silent. There was a sudden movement from the pallet. Thomas and Gale glanced round to see the young girl sitting up, covering herself. Her frightened eyes swung from one man to another.

'Take yourself off,' the constable said irritably. 'Or I might remember the penalty for whoring on the Sabbath!'

The girl needed no further bidding. She grabbed her shoes from near the wall and got herself outside. Thomas closed the door after her.

'See now – I don't know who that cove was!' The land-lord was glaring at Gale. 'He came after dark, paid for a night's stay – he gave no name. His business was his own!'

'His name was Cutler. He came up from London – and he came to do blackmail.' Thomas spoke, forcing Chalke to turn his eyes upon him. 'Is there more you can tell?'

Chalke gave him a baleful look. But eager to be rid of the two of them, he would cooperate. 'I've a notion he got a message,' he muttered. 'A boy came asking for him, late . . . he stepped outside with him, then came back in. He must have gone out after, towards dawn. I never saw him. The inn was dark, and we were all abed.'

'Did you know the boy?' Gale asked.

A sneer spread across Chalke's sweaty face. 'I believe I did: he was one of yours – one of the Petbury folk.' He fixed his gaze upon Thomas. 'So if this Cutler fetched up dead, mayhap you should be talking to those closer to home!'

Thomas's pulse quickened. He knew everyone at Petbury

well enough, but an image of the cocky kitchen boy had sprung to his mind: the one who had been so keen to crack heads with his ladle, when Swift and Joshua came begging at the gates. He glanced at Gale.

But the constable was not done. 'I'll lay a sovereign you know more than you tell,' he said in his severe voice. 'Like who it was set on Finbow and near killed him—'

'I don't know!' Gale made a dismissive gesture. 'You can ask downstairs – ask who you like!' His sneer was back. 'Only I doubt you'll learn much. The falconer's not that popular hereabouts!'

Gale opened his mouth, but Thomas laid a hand on his arm.

'I'm leaving,' he said. 'There's a bad smell in this place – then, there always was.'

And without looking at Matthew Chalke he tugged open the door. Gale followed him outside. The two did not speak again until they stood in the lane, with the dusk falling.

'I must go back,' Thomas said. 'I'll seek out this boy. Then tomorrow I'll be out at first light.'

'As will I,' Gale said. 'We must both do what we can ...' He looked helpless. 'One felony here is rare enough ... now I seem to have two on my hands: a murder and a robbery!'

Thomas nodded and gave the man his thanks, then walked off through the trees, cutting through to the Petbury road. He had much to think on. But uppermost in his mind now was a confrontation with Nell. Beside that, even Sir Robert's wrath shrank to insignificance.

He was at the cottage and had lit the fire, after which he meant to walk down to the kitchens. But his wife had other ideas. He turned as the door opened, and blanched as she strode in, looking her most majestic.

' 'Twas kind of you to send word at suppertime,' she said. 'Else from all the gossip I've heard, I might have thought you were laid out in the chapel with sprigs of yew about your head!'

He put out a hand, but she was in no mood to listen. 'Then you disappear until nightfall, and the only sign I get of your return is a glow from that fire!' She pointed to the blaze now leaping about the logs. 'Were you thinking of staying, or—'

'The kitchen boy,' he said flatly, knowing from experience that only a surprise would deflect her. 'The cocksure lad with the tousled hair . . . Will, isn't it?'

She blinked. 'Will Corder – what of him?'

'How well do you know him?'

Nell frowned. 'Why – what's he done?'

Thomas shrugged. 'Maybe nothing but carry a message. Only the man he took it to is the one found dead in the gardens.'

He waited as Nell took in the news. And she hesitated long enough to observe his bruises. 'Well . . . I've seen you look worse,' she muttered. 'Are you hurting?'

He shrugged. 'I'll heal . . .'

'I can't bear this!' she cried suddenly. 'Hearing tidings of you from others, while you roam far and wide . . . what in Heaven's name has been going on?'

He took both her hands. 'If you'll sit a while now,' he said, 'I'll tell you.'

With Nell, at least, he could relate the whole tale and know it would go no further. But when she learned how much had been kept from her and the rest of the household – about the Muscovy chain, and its disappearance – she was hurt.

'So many secrets,' she said. 'Does Sir Robert not trust any of us?'

Thomas shrugged. 'I doubt if he thought much upon it. He's been like a man possessed ever since he brought the chain here that night—'

'So that's what it was about! Could you not have told me?'

'It seemed best not to tell anyone,' he answered tiredly. 'I hoped, as Sir Robert did, that the ambassador would be gone soon, taking the chain with him . . .' He frowned at the floor. 'It's as if there's something evil about the thing. There's been naught but trouble since it arrived!'

She nodded, then her face clouded. 'Well, perhaps Sir Robert was right. I love my kitchen folk: the wenches are like sisters to me, even if I shout at them sometimes . . . the boy I regard as a little brother. Now you tell me he carries messages by night – to the Dagger, of all places. What am I to think?'

Thomas looked up. 'We'd best ask him,' he said.

Will Corder, barely twelve years of age, was a Chaddleworth boy through and through: of hardy Downland stock, short but sturdy. He turned the spit for the roast, took scraps to the pigs and poultry and swept the kitchen floor. He also ran errands. And it was about one particular errand that he found himself being questioned a short time later: by Nell, of whom he was often wary but never frightened, since the worst he got from her was a cuff on the head. But her husband the tall falconer, who had once been a soldier and was close with the master and mistress – he was a different matter. The boy stood in the kitchen by the chimney corner looking nervous. Nell had sent everyone else out, so he was feeling very alone.

'I an't done wrong, mistress,' he said. 'I was given a penny to take a message, is all.'

'By whom?' Nell began, but at a glance from Thomas, she quietened.

'You took it to the Dagger, late at night, to a man who lodged there,' he said, not unkindly. 'Were you told to ask for him by name?' The boy blanched and did not answer, but Thomas seemed unperturbed. 'His name was Cutler, wasn't it?' He went on. 'Richard Cutler. He's the same man the gardeners found the next morning, run through with a sword in the garden.'

The boy gasped. 'Jesu . . . you won't tell Sir Robert, will you, master Thomas? I don't want to go to prison! They starve you and put hot irons on you – I beg!'

Nell looked away. Will's fear was so great he was starting to shake. But Thomas raised a hand. The boy jerked in alarm, then fell silent as the hand fell on his shoulder.

'I don't think prison's likely,' Thomas said. 'If you tell us all that happened.'

Will looked from Thomas to Nell and back. Then he began to talk – so eagerly that it would have been hard to stop him.

'Three days back – Thursday,' he said. 'I was by the pigsty, and he came upon me so quick I near dropped the pail. But he smiled, like he always does – told me to fear naught. Said I could earn a penny if I went very late – after midnight. I could steal out the back door as it's not locked. I had to go to the Dagger and ask for Cutler, only he might not call himself that, so he told me what he looked like . . . blond hair and such. All I had to do was say he'd to meet him just before it got light, in the gardens by the statue of the maid with the bow and arrow. That was all – I swear!'

Nell was looking impatient, and this time she would not be stayed. 'You haven't told us who sent you!' she snapped. 'Who came up by the pig-pens, and gave you a penny?'

The boy caught his breath. 'Did I not say? 'Twas Lady Jane's servant. Master Doggett.'

Thomas did not bother to hide his astonishment. He merely sat down on a nearby stool. But Nell's impatience only increased.

'What else did he say?' she cried. 'Speak, or I'll—'

'He said there'd be another penny to follow, if I kept silent,' Will answered. 'Only he's never given it me!'

Doggett . . . Thomas was staring at the boy. 'Did you not think it strange – not to say dangerous?' he asked. 'You know what the Dagger's like, as the rest of Chaddleworth does.'

The boy shrugged. 'My father drinks there, so I know folk . . .' He gulped. 'I did want they two pennies, falconer. For Father drinks so much, and Mother and me shift poorly . . . a penny buys a loaf still! Only what'll happen if the wheat price do soar like they say, I don't want to think on!'

Thomas stood up, making the boy flinch. 'I'll speak for you,' he said gently. 'Sir Robert or Master Martin may want to talk to you . . .'

The boy's jaw dropped, but Thomas stayed him. 'Your fault was in not telling of it,' he said.

The boy was close to tears. 'I know . . .' He looked miserably at Nell. 'I'll lose my place, will I not?'

Nell said nothing. But Thomas caught her eye, before moving away towards the door. He knew the soft heart that she kept well hidden would win. As he went he heard her throw open the back door and call the wenches in.

Then his thoughts turned to Master John Doggett . . . and try as he might, he could not help feeling a sense of grim satisfaction. He had never trusted the man, but even he would not have thought him a murderer. Yet . . . it did not add up. Surely Doggett was no swordsman?

He pushed that aside; first he must tell Sir Robert. Though how the knight was going to break the news to his sister Lady Jane, he could not imagine. That at least was one task Thomas was not charged with. Though he would have to tell Eleanor . . .

And there was still one small matter to deal with: that of finding the Muscovy chain.

Nine

The hour was late, but Sir Robert had not yet gone to bed. After sending word Thomas was ordered to wait in the great hall, where the remains of a fire still smouldered. The room was deserted. Finding a taper, he lit a couple of candles and was carrying them to the high table when Sir Robert hurried in. And there was such hope on the knight's face that Thomas was loath to impart his discovery. Quickly he told all that he had learned.

Sir Robert was at first disappointed that the news did not concern the Muscovy chain. But when he heard what Thomas had discovered about Richard Cutler, he was astounded. And predictably enough, his manner soon changed to anger.

'The kitchen boy will be cast out of my service!' he cried. 'I'll have none at Petbury who cannot be trusted!' He took a few paces before the great fireplace. 'As for Doggett . . . I've detested the man since I set eyes on him – but murder? And what of the manner of that death . . . the fencing stroke? There's something odd here, isn't there?'

Thomas nodded. 'And the only one who can explain it is Doggett. Perhaps if his chamber was also searched?'

'Indeed!' Sir Robert strode to the door and shouted. A startled servingman appeared a few moments later, and was told to carry a message to Lady Rooke's secretary, rousing him from his bed if necessary.

'And if the fellow doesn't present himself within a quarter of the hour,' Sir Robert added, 'tell him he'll be brought here by force!'

The man made his bow and hurried out. Whereupon Thomas seized the moment. 'About Will Corder, sir,' he murmured. 'He's sorely chastened by what he did. He's a village lad with a drunken father . . .'

'You may save your pretty sentiments, Thomas.' The knight gave him a dry look. 'Corder knew who the dead man was – he could even have guessed who killed him! He should have spoken up.'

'He knows it,' Thomas replied. 'Yet I still ask your mercy. The boy fears not merely poverty, but beggary . . .'

But seeing Sir Robert's expression, he held his tongue: at such times his master would brook no argument. So the two of them waited in silence, while the embers in the fireplace slowly dimmed. Finally the door opened, and both men looked round – to see not John Doggett entering the room, but Lady Rooke's servant, Kat Jenkin.

Sir Robert frowned as the girl hurried forward and bobbed. 'Your pardon, sir, but we can find no sign of Master Doggett. His chamber is empty – and now I think on it, I haven't seen him since last night. My lady has not called for him, being abed all day . . .' The girl hesitated. 'I think he's gone, sir.'

John Doggett had occupied a small chamber next to his mistress's, in the eastern arm of the great house where Lady Jane had stayed since she begged to be moved. The west side was occupied by Ambassador Stanic and his followers. Sir Robert and Thomas entered the darkened room a short time later, bearing lights. Kat Jenkin followed them. And it was but the work of a moment to confirm the girl's tale: Doggett had departed, seemingly in haste. Many of his fine clothes still lay about the room, and more hung in the closet. Though the cloak that Thomas remembered was gone. He threw back the covers on the small trundle bed, and found the sheet cold. Watched by his master, he went to the window and drew back the curtain. The casement was locked.

Sir Robert turned a fierce eye upon Kat, who blanched. 'You say your mistress has not risen all day?' he enquired. 'Why – is she ill?'

Kat was uncertain. 'I took her breakfast in early, sir,' she answered, 'yet she did not wake. 'Tis not uncommon, for

you know she tires easily . . .' The girl bit her lip. 'She'll
be beside herself when she hears of this,' she said. 'She
adores her secretary . . . she could not bear him to leave
her!'

Sir Robert let out an exasperated breath. 'In God's name,
I cannot imagine why!' he cried.

He turned to look at Thomas. 'With your leave sir, I'll have
a poke about,' Thomas said. 'There may be some sign . . .'

His master nodded. 'Search all you like.' He glanced at
Kat. 'This is not the hour to break such news to my sister.
We'll wait until morning . . .' He thought for a moment.
'Say nothing of the matter to Lady Rooke until I have
spoken with her,' he ordered. 'Indeed, say nothing to anyone!
Go to your bed now.'

The girl made her curtsey and went out. Sir Robert
followed, with a brief nod at Thomas. His candle he left
on a small table, before closing the door behind him.

Thomas sat on the bed and looked round the room.
Everything he saw suggested flight on the part of Lady
Rooke's secretary: the way the clothes were scattered about
showed the man had taken only what was essential. And
for a vain man like Doggett, to leave such finery behind
spoke of desperation. If further proof were needed, the man
had even left his lute. It stood in a corner, looking somewhat forlorn.

Thomas stood up, took the candle and began to move
slowly about. There were no papers, nothing that spoke of
messages. From what Kat Jenkin had said, it seemed likely
Doggett had indeed left the previous night, Saturday. Why
was that? Then the answer came to him: it was the day of
the inquest. The death of the man Thomas later discovered
to be Richard Cutler was noised abroad; the coroner was
here, and gossip was rife . . . if Doggett had indeed murdered
the man, then perhaps he felt the Downland air was
becoming a little too warm for him.

He began going through the man's clothes, examining
pockets and linings, moving quickly now. But if there were
clues, they eluded him. In fact the more he searched, the
less he felt he knew about Master John Doggett. It nettled

him, not only because of the persistent way the fellow had
pursued Eleanor, displaying such jealousy – but because
he had always believed himself a fair judge of character.
Now, thinking upon what Nell had said about the man's
reputation in London, he began to form a different view
of him. A vain peacock Doggett may have been, but he
was no fool . . . and if he harboured secrets, then perhaps
he had been a mark for a blackmailer like Cutler, after all.

He had worked his way round the room, and found nothing.
He was by the tiny fireplace, bearing the candle . . . then he
frowned. The flame was still, when it should have flickered:
there was no draught from the chimney. It also struck him
how stuffy the little room was. And in a moment he was on
his knees by the grate, thrusting the candle into the chimney,
peering upwards – whereupon a little sigh of satisfaction
escaped his lips: something bulky was blocking the shaft.
And it was but the work of a few seconds to pull it down,
along with a small cloud of soot. His pulse quickened at the
sight of a bundle of dark clothing. Sitting on the floor he
raised the candle again, and started: the clothes were stained
with blood.

He set the candle down, and began to separate the
garments carefully. And in a short time, he knew that Tobias
Swift had spoken the truth: this was the attire of the dead
Richard Cutler. A travelling cloak, a pair of good boots,
breeches, hose and a dark-blue padded doublet, the last stiff
with congealed blood. Grimly Thomas spread it out . . . and
found what he sought: a hole above where the wearer's
heart would have been.

He stood up, the stench of the blood-soaked clothes in
his nostrils. The evidence was strong enough, he knew, for
a manhunt to be mounted for John Doggett: the murderer
of Richard Cutler. Yet he could not help but feel a pang of
disappointment. Where was the sword, assuming Doggett
knew how to use one? And if there had been a scrap of
paper bearing a message . . . but at that, he almost laughed.
Now he was clutching at straws.

He would go to Sir Robert's body-servant and ask him
to rouse his master; the discovery was too important to wait.

The clothing he folded again, into a bundle. The cloak was last, as it had been the first thing he opened. He had to admire the workmanship: the lining was of goose-green silk, which crackled suddenly beneath his fingers . . . and then he started. For peering close, he saw the tiny stitches where a pocket was hidden . . . and in a few seconds he had torn it open, and drawn out the paper.

But it was no message. Kneeling, holding the document close to the candle, Thomas made out the words easily – for they were in a clear, scholarly hand. Then when he had read, he sat back on his haunches and let out a sigh: for he had learned John Doggett's secret. Perhaps it should wait until morning after all; for it was so simple, that he berated himself for not guessing it sooner. And this time he did laugh, if in somewhat hollow fashion.

The man was married.

Having slept on the matter, Sir Robert was adamant: the news must be broken gently to Lady Jane Rooke, and he would not do it. The only one who had sufficient delicacy for such a task was Lady Margaret.

Thomas stood before his master, his mistress and Martin in Sir Robert's private chamber. The morning was misty, with no breeze to disperse it. A silence had fallen, as the knight read the paper Thomas had given him for what seemed like the fifth time. Finally he sat back and threw it on the table.

'So – he's a married man. Here's the testimony from the parson who performed the ceremony!' The knight glowered and turned to his wife, but Lady Margaret said nothing.

'Small wonder the wretch wished to keep it a secret!' Sir Robert went on. 'For to gain Lady Jane's affections, let alone flirt with her, he must appear a bachelor . . . which also allowed him to pursue others. Including your daughter, I hear, Thomas!'

Thomas made no reply. But Martin coughed pointedly.

'Surely what's most important, sir, is the fact that he was wed to the daughter of a fencing master!' the old man exclaimed. 'From this, all else follows.'

No one needed reminding. The document Thomas had read by candlelight in Doggett's chamber was plain enough: a testimony bearing the name of the parson of St Helen's church in Bishopsgate ward, London, proving the marriage two years ago of John Doggett to Emilia Saviolo, the daughter of Baptista Saviolo, fencing master. It fitted: Cutler's acquaintance with Doggett, through the fencing school . . . he must have learned that Doggett had left his wife and joined the household of a rich widow. The man was indeed ripe for blackmail . . . and another thought struck Thomas. Had it been Doggett's suggestion that Lady Jane quit London for the summer? Perhaps Cutler had already threatened him, then found out where he was and followed him all the way to Petbury. The man was persistent, if nothing else . . . He looked up to see Lady Margaret's eyes upon him. Taking a breath, he told his thoughts.

'I believe you are right,' Lady Margaret said, and turned to her husband. 'It was Doggett's idea that Lady Rooke should take the Downland air – for her health, he said. She spoke of it herself.'

Sir Robert shook his head. 'The boldness of the fellow! But what's worse is that when this rogue Cutler catches up with him, he sends word to meet him in the Petbury gardens – by one of my own servants – then kills him in cold blood!' The knight was fuming. 'I'll have the county scoured from border to border! And if the sheriff can't catch the devil, I'll hunt him down myself!'

So a manhunt began for Master John Doggett; the unlikeliest fugitive most folk would have imagined. Messages were sent to the sheriff of Berkshire, even to the Lord Lieutenant. In every town and village constables were put on the alert, and watches were set upon the roads; but it proved to no avail. Though the man was presumably on foot, and dressed like a city gallant, he seemed to have vanished into thin air.

At Petbury that day, tempers were somewhat frayed. Sir Robert rode about the countryside, visiting farms and outlying hamlets. Some said he had seized the opportunity to escape from his tiresome guest, the Russian ambassador. But it was clear to many in the household that his absence was due more to a desire to avoid his fragile sister. Lady Jane Rooke, having risen from her bed at last, was taken aside by Lady Margaret and told of her secretary's disappearance. And when the woman had bewailed that loss at some length, the remainder of what was now known about Doggett was broken to her, as sympathetically as only Lady Margaret could do it. Whereupon the distraught woman took once again to her bed, threatening never to leave it. Only Kat Jenkin was allowed to enter the room, bearing possets.

Thomas tried to busy himself, all the while answering Ned Hawes's questions. The boy was as excited as anyone about the unmasking of John Doggett as a swordsman, let alone a murderer. On that subject, Thomas was willing enough to talk. The other matter, which weighed upon him hourly – the whereabouts of a certain black case containing a priceless jewelled chain – he kept to himself.

'You were right about the cove,' Ned said for the third time as the falconers walked back to the manor with birds on their gauntlets. 'You never liked Doggett – nor did I! Always struck me as the sort who'd take a swig from your mug while your back's turned.'

Seeing Thomas preoccupied, the lad fell silent. But a short while later, as the Petbury rooftops came into view, Thomas slowed his pace and turned to him. 'I've business in the village,' he said. 'Can you see to the birds this afternoon, till I get back?'

Ned hesitated. 'Suppose those Russians want to ride out? I'm a mite uneasy handling the big white hawk . . .'

'Tell them there's a falcon with the frounce,' Thomas told him, 'and I've gone to get physic. That should stall them.'

The boy nodded. And a half-hour later Thomas was back in Chaddleworth, looking for Tertius Gale.

He found the constable on the green, emerging from the Black Bear. But when Thomas suggested they talk privately over a mug, the man shook his head. Indeed, he now seemed to want to put some distance between the two of them.

'I'm obliged for your helping me find out about this Richard Cutler,' he said stiffly, 'only now I've my hands full hunting down his killer. And when I ask for fellows to serve as under-constables, every man's too busy with the harvest all of a sudden. What harvest? Everyone knows the wheat's ruined . . .' He turned a gloomy face to the sky. 'And more rain coming, if you care for my opinion.'

Thomas curbed his impatience. 'I'll help if I can,' he said. 'But Doggett's not my concern. What I'm charged with by my master—'

'Aye, that's the nub of it!' Gale gave him one of his severe looks. 'The case of jewels, that no one must know about . . .' He hesitated. 'Your pardon, Finbow, but I can't concern myself with it any longer. It's beyond my powers, as it's likely beyond my borders. I'm constable of this parish, and of the hundred souls that dwell here. What happens outside, I must leave to others.'

Thomas saw his discomfort. But who could blame the man? He sighed. 'Then I'll not trouble you further,' he said. 'But if you hear anything that might have a bearing upon my search . . .'

Gale nodded, and the two parted. Thomas walked back to Petbury, wondering how he could possibly hunt for the Muscovy chain when nobody was even supposed to know it was missing.

That afternoon, however, his attention was diverted. For a short while after he had found Ned at the mews, a groom hurried up with a message: His Excellency Grigori Stanic wished to go hawking. And since Sir Robert had chosen to absent himself, Lady Margaret would be obliged to host the party.

It was a tense excursion. For not only did the ambassador continue his clumsy flirtation with Lady Margaret, Eleanor too was there, with young Piotr riding close by. Stanic's other servants also attended: Mikhailov, stolid as ever; Kovalenko, who greeted Thomas with a nod; and to his surprise, Keril Yusupov. The secretary, who had clearly been ordered to come along, looked uneasy on a frisky gelding.

The man was a poor horseman; at least, to Thomas's relief, he was excused from attempting to carry a falcon.

The party rode under a cloudy sky, crossing the Ridgeway and drifting northwards, following the birds. Thomas and Ned came behind on foot, bagging up the catch. The day waned slowly, and they were several miles from Petbury before Thomas at last had the chance to speak with his daughter.

Eleanor had reined in her mare, and was watching Lady Margaret use all her charm to keep the ambassador entertained. As Thomas walked up she turned to him. 'See how she keeps her smile!' she exclaimed. 'It would take all my control not to kick the man!' Then seeing her father looking at her, she flushed. 'If you wish to speak of John Doggett,' she began – but he shook his head.

'What need is there? You know as much as I do of the fellow. Have you now changed your view of him?'

Her chest rose. 'Yes – you're right as always, and I was wrong! Does that flatter you?'

But seeing his expression, she relented. 'Your pardon, father . . .' She lowered her gaze. 'What might have happened, if . . .' She was almost tearful. 'He . . . he had such a fine voice!'

Thomas would have spoken, but at that moment hooves sounded, and both of them turned as Piotr rode up. Seeing Thomas in conversation with his daughter, the young man reined in and gave a polite nod. Then he smiled at Eleanor and said some words in his own language. Thomas raised his brows, but Eleanor threw him a quick glance.

'He speaks of the hunting, I think,' she said. 'We've had the best of the day, or some such.'

Thomas watched Piotr carefully, but he detected no mischief in the young man. In fact, he saw how at ease he looked. And small wonder, he thought wryly – since his only rival was now found to be a murderer, and was being sought the length and breadth of the county!

'I'll leave you,' he said. 'If you wish to talk . . .'

Eleanor nodded. She shook the reins, and with a glance at Piotr urged her horse forward, towards Lady Margaret.

No doubt her ladyship would welcome the diversion, Thomas thought. With a sigh he walked away, his mind turning to other matters.

But on the journey back to Petbury he was given further cause for reflection. For Kovalenko – who though Stanic's falconer, never seemed to come to the mews – came riding up to him. The man dismounted and, leading his horse, fell into step beside Thomas. On his wrist he carried a hooded tercel.

'We go home soon, back to our country,' he said. 'His Excellency getting little bored, I think.'

Thomas stiffened. 'So soon? It's been less than a week . . .' Though to some, he thought ruefully, it already seemed like a month.

Kovalenko gave a shrug. 'Is long voyage. And His Excellency knows not what happen there, while he is away!' The man gave a grim smile. 'Trust is rare bird in our Tsar's court, Master Thomas,' he said. 'Like golden eagle, maybe.'

'Is there none to watch out for the ambassador's interests?' Thomas asked. 'A wife, perhaps . . . ?'

Kovalenko frowned. 'No wife.'

Suddenly the man was on his guard. Allowing his curiosity free rein, Thomas decided to do a little digging. 'No wife?' he echoed. 'Is that not rare for a man of his age?'

Kovalenko hesitated. 'There was a woman, betrothed to him,' he said finally. 'She is dead.'

Thomas raised his brows.

'But please, not speak of this,' the other added quickly. 'His Excellency get angry—' He broke off, as if regretting having said this much. But Thomas was in no mood for delicacy. Sensing an opportunity, he pressed his advantage.

'His Excellency seems to get angry a great deal,' he said. 'He certainly has you scared, does he not?'

Kovalenko's frown deepened. 'I speak to you from my heart, that night in the alehouse,' he said. 'We are like slaves—'

'The night your friend the *sotnik* beat a man to death?' Thomas broke in gently. 'I'd almost forgotten it.'

Kovalenko stopped. His horse stopped too, and bent to nibble at the lush grass. The two falconers faced each other.

'I thought *you* my friend,' Kovalenko said.

Thomas met his eye, and gave the other a brief account of his being beaten in revenge for the killing of Jem Latter. Kovalenko listened; and only now did he notice the yellowing bruise on Thomas's cheek, and the cut on his mouth which was now healing. When Thomas finished, the man appeared chastened.

'I ask forgiveness,' he said. 'Maybe we go back to that place, find those men – you and me and Mikhailov. We pay them good!'

But Thomas shook his head. 'I've other matters to think on,' he said. 'We hunt for a murderer, have you not heard?'

Kovalenko hesitated. 'My master say this English business,' he said finally. 'We not part of it.'

Thomas let his gaze wander across the treeless Downs. In the distance Lady Margaret and the ambassador were riding together, with Eleanor and Piotr some way behind. The great bulk of Mikhailov was also visible, astride his exhausted mount. Behind him Yusupov struggled to keep up.

'Supposing some other crime had been committed, that *did* concern you?'

It was pure instinct that made Thomas speak the words. But his gaze stayed on Kovalenko, watching his reaction. He waited.

The Russian stared; and if a tiny point of light flickered in his eyes, it was extinguished at once. Abruptly he looked to the falcon on his gauntlet, busied himself checking the hood and tightening the leash. To Thomas, it looked like a guileless bit of diversion.

'You know, don't you?' he said, bending closer to the man. 'You know about the royal gift – as you know it has been stolen!'

Kovalenko did not answer.

'The gift for Boris Godunov,' Thomas persisted. 'That your master must take back to Muscovy—'

'*Nyet!*' Kovalenko turned suddenly. 'We not talk of this . . .'

'Why not?' Thomas matched the man's gaze. 'Are you afraid of that, too?' When the other made no reply, he added: 'I think you know all about the chain. And if you know, then your master knows—'

'You stop!' Kovalenko put out his hand and gripped Thomas's arm. On his other wrist, the falcon shifted beneath the hood. With a swift glance towards the ambassador's party, who were still some way off, the man spoke rapidly, stumbling over his limited English. 'I tell before – you know little of us, Master Thomas. And if wise, you step back now – or you get big trouble. I know what I speak!' Deliberately the Russian nodded towards the distant figures.

'What shall I take that to mean?' Thomas asked. 'Will the big man crush the life out of me, too?'

But Kovalenko was not angry – quite the reverse. There was sadness in his gaze as well as fear. Letting go of Thomas's arm, he drew a long breath.

'Master Thomas, you friend of Pavel Kovalenko unto death,' he said. 'And if . . .' He sought for the words. 'If I could do different, I would do. But this is how we are, you and me: we tend hawks for our masters, do their bidding. Like I say: maybe we Russians go home soon, which is best for everyone. You understand?'

Thomas did not understand. But sensing that this was all the other would say, he let the matter drop. He was about to walk off and look for Ned when there came rapid hoof-beats. In some surprise he turned to see Yusupov trotting towards him. Clumsily the man drew his horse up, so sharply that he fell forward across its neck. Righting himself with difficulty, he gazed down at Thomas.

'Master Finbow . . . I wondered if you required my serv-ices.' The man smiled – but at once Thomas read the warning in his eye.

'I would not want there to be any misunderstandings,' the secretary went on. He looked pointedly at Kovalenko, who tried to appear unconcerned. But if ever a man was nervous, Thomas thought, it was he.

'There's no misunderstanding,' Thomas answered, summoning a polite smile. 'Master Kovalenko and I, as always, speak in praise of our birds. What else do falconers talk of?'

Yusupov nodded. 'That's well.' Gingerly he patted his horse's neck. 'We all have our duties. And if we do not keep to them, who knows what disorder may follow?'

Thomas returned the man's gaze; but the moment had passed. Kovalenko remounted his horse, and bearing his falcon rode quickly away. With another smile at Thomas, Yusupov shook the reins and managed to turn his own mount. He looked round as if about to speak, then apparently thought better of it and stared ahead.

Thomas watched him go, then glanced down. For some reason he found he had clenched his fist so that the knuckles showed, as white as the great hawk.

Ten

That night, there was an incident at Petbury that seemed of little consequence – but which, Thomas thought later, heralded a spate of disorder not even Yusupov could have imagined. For the train of events that followed threw a shadow not only over the manor, but over the whole of the Downlands. And it began with Lady Jane Rooke.

By now, Lady Jane's difficulties in sleeping had become such a commonplace that few bothered to mention them. Though her occasional sleepwalking still caused amusement; the tale of her wandering into Sir Robert's chamber and upsetting his bedside pot being a favourite. So when there was a commotion on the upper floor in the small hours, no one took much notice. But the screaming persisted, giving way to hysterical sobbing. Whereupon several people gathered outside Lady Jane's chamber, among them an angry Sir Robert.

'In God's name, will no one go in to her?' The knight looked about irritably. 'Where's her servant?' He broke off as the door opened, and an anxious Kat Jenkin appeared in her shift.

'Sir – I cannot console her,' the girl said. 'She has seen something fearful . . .'

Muttering an oath, Sir Robert pushed past her into the room, where candles burned. Other servants were arriving. As he went the knight called over his shoulder.

'Wake Lady Margaret! And you – ' he pointed at Kat – 'bring your mistress a drink. None of your possets – make it hot brandy!'

Lady Jane was not in bed, but standing before her window, which looked eastwards towards the Petbury gates. The curtains were pulled back, and as Sir Robert entered the room, his sister turned theatrically and pointed.

'He was down there – plain as a pikestaff!' Her hand was trembling. Summoning some words of comfort Sir Robert drew close to his sister, but she flinched away.

'Clad in black, from head to foot! Clothes, hood . . . it hid his face. He was wickedness personified, brother . . . like in the old plays—'

'Jane, in God's name!' Sir Robert cried. 'Have you not alarmed the servants enough? You were but dreaming again, or walking in your sleep—'

'I was not!' Lady Jane wore a distracted look. 'I saw a man, Robert! Fleetingly, I will allow. He climbed the gate – he must have! Then he darted away, towards the kitchen gardens . . .' She shuddered. 'He moved like a snake . . . or like a hound, perhaps – a great black hound that lopes!'

She broke off, burying her face in her hands. Helplessly Sir Robert gazed upon her, until a sound at the door caused him to turn. With relief he gestured Lady Margaret into the room.

'You speak with her . . .' The anguish in his voice was such that for once even his wife was lost for words. With a nod, Lady Margaret signalled him to leave. Outside, servants made their bows, but the knight seemed not to see them. With eyes downcast he walked back along the passage to his own chamber. The slam of the door was audible throughout the entire house.

Thomas heard the tale in the morning, when he walked to the kitchens for an early breakfast. Nell, having stayed in the house again the previous night, took a few minutes to share bread and pottage with him.

'If it had been anyone else, the maids might have taken fright,' she said drily. 'But being Her Ladyship . . .'

Thomas nodded. He had spent a restless night himself, turning over the events of past days. Something was working away at him, he knew; something besides the theft of the Muscovy chain, or the hunt for John Doggett – as if those matters were not troubling enough. Now, the prospect of the ambassador's departure filled him with apprehension.

No longer could the theft of the chain be kept secret –
assuming it was still a secret . . .

'Do you listen to aught I say?' Nell was glaring at him.
Thomas blinked, and nodded.

'Nay . . .' She gave a sigh. 'You play the intelligencer
again, Thomas. And you will not share your troubles!'

'You've enough to fret about, haven't you?' he answered.
'Without my adding my pennyworth.'

Nell made no reply; merely turned away to look about
her busy domain. Lady Margaret's maid was hurrying out,
bearing her mistress's morning drink. As she went Kat
Jenkin came in. The girl looked about, then seeing Thomas
and Nell seated in the corner, came over to them. She threw
a shy glance at Thomas, reminding him of the night he had
rescued her from the grip of the drunken ambassador. But
it was soon apparent that her mind was on other matters.

'Forgive me,' Kat said, 'but I must speak with those I
trust. I'm sore troubled, yet none will listen . . .' She trailed
off.

Nell stood up. 'You may tell Thomas,' she said. 'He's the
repository of everyone's secrets.' And without further word
she moved off to her duties. Thomas watched her ordering
the youngest kitchen wench to sweep the floor. Since Will
Corder had been sent away, there was no one to perform
the task . . . He looked at Kat, and summoned a smile.

'I hear your mistress has disturbed everyone's sleep
again.'

But the girl lowered her voice. 'It was no fancy, falconer,'
she said. 'For I believe I saw him too!'

A short while later Thomas and Kat stood near the Petbury
gates. Grey clouds drifted overhead, and already there were
raindrops, but the girl paid them no mind. She merely did
as Thomas bade her, and took him to the place where she
and her mistress claimed to have seen the running man.
Thomas squinted up at the great house: Lady Jane's window
indeed overlooked the spot. This morning it was curtained,
since the woman again kept to her bed.

'Which way did he go?' Thomas asked.

The girl led him round the side of the house. The wall of the kitchen garden was ahead, before it turned away to the left, the side with the archway. To their right were the pig and poultry pens.

He looked about. Like everyone else he had been inclined to dismiss Lady Jane's hysterical tale. But he believed Kat. And if her account was accurate, then this was a matter of import.

'Is there anything more you can tell?' he asked.

The girl gave a shrug. 'Lady Jane was up, for she could not sleep. She looked out of the window – that's when she screamed. I came at once, and saw him: a dark cloak and hood . . .'

'Do you think he knew he had been seen?'

'I cannot say. He did not turn, and he was soon gone. It was too dark to see more.'

Thomas favoured the girl with a kindly look. 'I'll search, and if I find anything Sir Robert will hear of it.'

Kat showed her relief: at least someone believed her. With a shy smile, she went back to the house.

Thomas was thoughtful. He doubted there would be anything to see – this man, whoever he was and whatever his reason for being here, had no doubt long departed. Yet he found himself walking along the garden wall, peering about. There was mown grass at the side of the house, stretching to a border of trees beyond which lay Sir Robert's fence, and beyond that the road to Wantage. There would be no footprints on the turf . . . he glanced towards the poultry pens, but saw nothing untoward. From the sties came a chorus of angry squeals: this spring's litter had been a prodigious one.

He sighed. There was nothing to see, and no reason to trouble Sir Robert . . . thinking of his work, he was about to walk off towards the mews, when his glance fell upon the tall flowering weeds that grew against the wall. The gardeners had been remiss here, he thought . . . then he stopped.

There was a break in the row that looked unnatural. And in a moment he was crouching, parting the stems – to reveal a patch of disturbed turf against the wall that had been clumsily replaced. Taking his poniard from his belt, he lifted the turf . . . then excitement took hold of him. And though the rain began to fall steadily, he did not notice: he was digging eagerly, throwing up an untidy pile of earth . . . and he almost cried out as the dagger's point struck something hard. The next moment he had thrown it aside and, hands caked with black soil, was tugging free a square case, its covering slippery with mud. And without caring whether or not he was observed, he was fumbling with the clasp. Suddenly he remembered the lock – but it did not matter, for the case was not locked at all. And at once he saw why, and his heart sank.

The lid opened . . . to reveal only a lining of scarlet velvet, ruined by damp and mildew.

The chain was gone.

Sir Robert sat in silence, staring down at the table. Apart from Thomas, Martin the steward was the only one present in his chamber. On the table lay the empty case which had held the Muscovy chain.

'How long do you think it was buried there?' Sir Robert asked finally.

'By the look of it, since the night it was taken.' Thomas glanced from his master to Martin, but the old man was gazing at the floor. The discovery seemed to have shaken him even more than it had Sir Robert, for its implications were plain: the chain was lost. And now the consequences must be faced.

'The lock was forced,' Thomas added. 'And if the hiding place tells us aught, it appears our thief was unfamiliar with the gardens. I would not have hidden the case so close to the house, where any gardener might find it.'

'Perhaps he was merely in haste – not unlikely, is it?' Sir Robert's voice was heavy with sarcasm. When Thomas made no reply, the knight turned to Martin. 'Well . . . in view of the rumours about our guest's imminent departure, I say we have no choice but to tell the man everything. What do you say, master steward?'

Martin met his master's gaze. 'I see no other course,' he admitted.

Thomas had intended to speak of Kat Jenkin's tale of the hooded man seen during the night. What bearing that matter might have upon his discovery of the case, he did not know. But now another thought struck him. When his master glanced at him again, he voiced it.

'I confess I hold out little hope of finding the chain, sir,' he said. 'Yet if we might buy a little more time . . . ?' He drew a breath. The matter looked beyond saving, yet something inside him refused to give up. Seeing the other two gazing at him, he went on: 'If you can keep the ambassador entertained a while longer, and I place the birds in Ned's care, I will search further afield. Indeed, I have had little chance to look anywhere, yet.' He made no mention of Tertius Gale's short-lived promise to help him. In fact it was better this way, for the man was a plodding fool. If Thomas took a good horse he could scour the estate as well as the roads. Even if it was somewhat late in the day, at least he would have tried. And now Sir Robert seized upon the notion, as eagerly as any man would who clutched at straws.

'Very well! You have free rein to go where you will – out on the London road, if necessary. Surely someone must know something!' The knight got suddenly to his feet. 'As for the ambassador, I will speak with Lady Margaret, see what might be done. Perhaps a feast in his honour, to be held tonight – no, tomorrow night! Knowing the fellow's drinking habits, that should tie him up for another few days – what say you?'

The last question was directed at Martin, who looked taken aback. 'I suppose no effort should be spared, sir,' he answered. His face clouded. 'A few days back I harboured expectations that His Excellency and his train would be gone by now,' he said forlornly. 'I only hope the kitchen stores are not exhausted!'

Thomas began his search within the hour. Despite the rain, it cheered him to ride a chestnut gelding from the Petbury stables, far across the Downs to the lonely village of Lambourn. He did not expect a fugitive to take that direction, yet he would leave nothing to chance. From there he intended to work his way downriver, asking at every farm and hamlet. He did not seek the chain – that task seemed impossible – but news of anyone who might have taken it. In fact the matter was made easier for him, since the whole county knew of the continuing hunt for John Doggett. The Petbury falconer's joining that search did not seem untoward.

Hearing nothing of note in Lambourn, he re-crossed the old packhorse bridge and rode along the swollen river, where he had stood a little over a week ago, lamenting the flood. Even that seemed unimportant now, when he thought of what might befall his master if the chain was not found. Knowing something of the machinations of the Queen's Privy Council, he knew the blame would be placed fully upon Sir Robert, who would be left to face Elizabeth's wrath. And the consequences of that, Thomas did not like to dwell upon.

The rain fell all day, yet he took little heed of it. From Lambourn he rode downstream, past the manor of Bickington, skirting the borders of Sir Robert's tenant farms. There was no need for enquiry here, since any news would have been conveyed to Petbury with speed. So Thomas next dismounted in East Garston, where a few sodden villagers gathered in the tiny square to hear him out. Yes, he was told, there had been travellers passing through: a couple of vagrom men, one a Bedlam cast-out . . . apart from them? The men scratched their heads. There were beggars a fortnight ago, but that was a family group seeking harvest work. Though what hopes such folk might have this wet summer, none could fathom.

The afternoon came and went. Thomas had eaten nothing, and barely dismounted save to water the horse and snatch a mouthful for himself. He had stopped at farms and cottages, spoken to shepherds and wood-cutters, haywards and housewives come from market; all to no avail. Finally he walked the tired animal into the larger village of Great Shefford, and drew rein in the street. The bridge lay ahead, to the south, giving on to the crossroads where the east highway met the road coming north from Hungerford. The same road passed between Petbury and Chaddleworth. And Thomas, soaked and saddle-sore, knew now that he would have to take that way homewards. His hopes were flagging at last.

Mercifully the downpour had eased, though great puddles stood in the street. He dismounted stiffly and led the horse to a trough, but the animal drank little. A good supper was what it needed, Thomas thought: that and a comfortable bed . . . He turned to retrace his steps, when he was startled by a shout. He looked round to see a tall brown-haired figure hurrying towards him, and at once relaxed. He knew John Hodge, the Shefford constable, by sight as well as by reputation. This was a shrewd, perceptive man. Would that Chaddleworth boasted such an officer, just now . . .

'Master Finbow, is't not?' Hodge offered his hand, and Thomas gripped it.

'It is, Master Hodge.'

'I heard about your bit of trouble at Petbury,' the man said. 'And about your fugitive. I've poked around here, but there was nothing to tell. Until now, that is.' Hodge glanced briefly up the road, towards the bridge. 'The fact is, I'm in a bit of a quandary.'

Thomas raised his brows. 'How's that?'

The other looked uncomfortable. 'It's my daughter . . . she only told me this morning, I swear to you. And I was mighty angry, I can tell you!' He hesitated, then: 'It seems she's been seeing this young fellow in secret – been going on for weeks. Fair turned her head, he has.'

Thomas started. 'He wouldn't be a city man, would he? A charmer, well dressed . . .'

'I believe he would.' Hodge nodded grimly. 'Only I swear to you I knew naught of it until now.' He gestured up the street. 'If you'll come to my house, you may question Alice. Mayhap you can get more out of her than I can!'

She was a pretty, spirited girl of eighteen years, bold and defiant. And she barely flinched when the falconer from

Petbury Manor, who was known across the Downlands for his skills as a seeker and a finder, came into her home. She sat in the small kitchen under the stern gaze of her father, and at first responded to Thomas's questions with a brazen silence. But when he told her of the murdered Richard Cutler, choosing not to spare the bloody details, she burst out angrily.

'John would never do such! He's a gentleman!'

'He's a rogue, mistress,' Thomas told her. 'What more shall I tell you? Of the marriage he kept secret from everyone – even from my own daughter, when he pursued her? Of the child – at least one that's known – that he fathered by a woman in London, and made her get rid of—'

'I'll not hear it!' Alice Hodge had paled. Springing to her feet, she glared at her father. 'You seek to fence me like one of your hens!' she cried. 'Do you wonder that when a handsome man cares for me, and shows it, I would fain keep it a secret?'

Hodge too stood up angrily, father and daughter locking horns. The man was a widower, like Thomas had been; and to him, the scene was familiar enough.

'So how did the cove show his care?' Hodge demanded. 'Do you wish to be talked of like Mary Jeap – a target for every man's lust?' The name of Mary Jeap, Shefford's professional woman, was known to Thomas as it was across the entire East Downs.

'I'm no harlot!' Alice threw back. 'I did love John – and he took naught from me that was not freely given!'

She broke off, but her father had seen the signs, as had Thomas. The dam broke, and in a moment the poor girl had slumped, dissolving in floods of tears. The two men exchanged glances. Hodge sat down heavily, eyes downcast.

Thomas waited before choosing his moment.

'When did you see him last?'

Alice plucked a kerchief from her sleeve and wiped her eyes. Finally she looked up. 'Not since last week . . . he said he had duties at Petbury.'

'Will you tell me where you used to go, you and he?'

There would have been a trysting place. With difficulty,

Thomas retained his calm. He knew that he might be
clutching at straws like Sir Robert, but . . .

'Outside the village,' Alice answered tearfully. Her resistance seemed to have ebbed away. 'Near where I first met
him, walking the old path by the river.'

Thomas glanced at Hodge, who stood up again. 'Then
you'll take us there – now!' he ordered. Slowly his daughter
raised her eyes to meet his, and gave a nod.

The three of them walked in silence along the muddy
pathway, eastwards from Great Shefford, until there were
only fields about them. Sheep dotted the hills, and more
were bunched under the trees close to the river. Finally
Alice stopped and pointed. There stood an old hut which
the shepherds used to store their folds. With John Hodge
behind, Thomas walked swiftly to the little hut and looked
inside. But the place was empty, save for a few fences made
of withies, leaning against the far wall. He came out again
and faced Hodge.

'No sign . . . ?' The constable sighed. 'Well, I won't
pretend I'm sorry for it.'

Thomas said nothing. He walked back to Alice, who was
watching them both. Her defiance seemed to have returned.
'You think he would hide here?' she asked. 'John's nobody's
fool. He'll be in London by now – or even further away.'

Thomas did not bother to hide his tiredness; a doleful
ride home loomed ahead of him. 'Was there anywhere else
you used to go?' he enquired, without much hope. 'Or
anywhere you can think of, where a man who's being hunted
would try to hide himself?'

The girl shook her head. But Hodge spoke up. 'There's
one place, though I believe the sheriff's men already went
there . . .' He hesitated. 'Then, they don't know Mary Jeap
like we do.' When Thomas turned to him, he added: 'I
should have thought of it sooner. The woman's been known
to hide men before – for a price.'

A scornful look appeared on Alice's face. 'A man like
John Doggett has no need to consort with whores!' she
cried.

But to Thomas, it was worth a last throw of the dice. He and Hodge walked back to Shefford, where the constable sent his daughter home. Then he led Thomas as far as the old wooden bridge, on the edge of the village. The last house was surprisingly large; but it was an unwholesome place, built too close to the river, so that the high waters now lapped its walls. The doorway on the side they approached had been piled with bags of sand, but the oak door was solid enough. Indeed it reminded Thomas of many such barriers, studded with nails, in noisome streets in other towns. He waited while the constable knocked loudly. And he was not surprised when a heavy man with scowling features opened the door; Great Shefford's bawdy-house had its own Cerberus, as did any in London.

'I would speak with Mary,' Hodge said. 'It's business. And if you try and thwart me I'll be back with a couple of bailiffs.'

The fellow glared, but stood aside. Thomas followed the constable into a low passageway. At the end was a door, from whence came the sound of a lute, played skilfully enough. Thomas started – surely it could not be . . . ? And in his eagerness he almost pushed John Hodge before him as he entered the room – to stop short. For there was only a gaunt middle-aged woman sitting by a window, her fingers plucking the strings of an old lute. As the two men came in she stopped playing, and broke into a thin smile.

'Master constable . . .' Her eyes strayed from Hodge towards Thomas, whom she favoured with a sly look. 'Who's this? Do you bring me a new customer?'

Thomas sighed, but Hodge stepped forward irritably.

'Do you harbour a fugitive?' he asked harshly. 'For if you do, this time you may hang for it!'

Mary Jeap barely flinched – but Thomas caught a wary look. And though a hard expression at once spread over the woman's painted features, he felt a stirring of hope. Even when she rose to protest, the feeling stayed with him.

'You've threatened me before, you long streak of mould!' Holding the lute by its neck, she brandished it like a weapon. 'Search all you like – you'll find nothing!'

They did search. But as the bawd had prophesied it was a fruitless undertaking. She was as sharp and as knowing as any such woman Thomas had encountered. She knew her territory and she knew her customers, as she knew the law. And though the two of them, their disappointment increasing by the minute, scoured the house from the attic down, they found no one who was not known to Hodge. Mary Jeap kept several girls in her house. Between them the women served the needs of the entire village, and those further afield. Several startled men, whose fear quickly turned to indignation, were found in various rooms; but there was no sign of John Doggett. As indeed, Thomas thought ruefully, there never would have been. As Alice had said, the fellow was no fool.

He stood in Mary Jeap's hallway beside Hodge, with the scowling doorkeeper looming over them. The mistress of the house, a bland smile on her face, took the trouble to see them out. 'Come back any time, master,' she said to Thomas. 'We'll find sweet work for you – and my prices are fair.'

They walked to the door, which the Cerberus threw wide. As daylight flooded in, Thomas's gaze fell upon another closed doorway he had not noticed earlier.

'What's in there?'

The doorkeeper bristled, but mistress Mary spoke up. 'Stairs to the cellar,' she answered. 'It's flooded – but pray look, if you wish.'

At her signal the servant reached forward and thrust the door open. There were indeed stairs – and below them a ripple of reflected light. There was also a dank, stale smell, and the unmistakable sloshing of water.

Without a word Thomas went out heavily, Hodge following. Behind them the heavy door banged shut. The two men retraced their steps along the river to the bridge. Hodge began climbing the steep path to the road, but for some reason Thomas halted.

On the far bank of the swollen Lambourn a heron stood motionless, watching the swirling water pass by. Thomas's gaze wandered, taking in the reeds, the floating twigs and debris carried down by the flood. It strayed under the little bridge . . .

Then he shouted, so loudly that Hodge swung round, to see him sliding down the muddy bank, fetching up knee-deep in the shallows. The constable sensed his excitement, and soon he too was slipping down the bank into the water, cursing as he lost his balance. He peered ahead, past Thomas's back . . . saw him stoop – and froze. Then bending low, he waded forward to stand at his side, the two of them gazing down at the grisly sight: a grey-white, bloated corpse, almost naked, caught fast in the tangled reeds under the bridge.

It was Doggett; but he was barely recognizable. For he had been gashed from head to foot with a hundred cuts, a nightmarish web of lacerations, now puckered and livid. Thomas turned, saw the constable's face, pale in the evening light. Hodge backed away, his head barely clearing the timbers above his head. Soon Thomas joined him, the two of them taking great gulps of air, while the cold water flowed about their legs.

From the far bank, the heron watched them without expression.

Eleven

The body had been placed in the Petbury chapel, where not many days ago that of Richard Cutler had lain. And to Thomas's mind, there seemed a harsh justice in the fact that the man's killer now lay in his place. The cause of Cutler's death, however, was but a single, well-aimed sword thrust. John Doggett, Thomas knew, would have died as slowly and as painfully as any man who had been unlucky enough to fall into the hands of an accomplished torturer.

The night had passed quickly, and early morning light now lanced through the old stained-glass windows. He had not slept. After riding to Petbury to break the news, he had been obliged to return to Great Shefford to help bring the body back. Word of Doggett's death had already spread. Indeed by now, the only person who had not heard the tale was Lady Jane Rooke. Nobody seemed in a hurry to tell her, just yet.

As he had done repeatedly, Thomas again surveyed the fearful mass of cuts on Doggett's body, made by a very sharp knife. He had looked at the man's wrists, and deduced that they had been tied. Then the interrogator – for there was no other word for him – had begun to work systematically upon his victim, apparently from the chest downwards. For to Thomas's eye there was a pattern: the wounds higher up were closer together, and made without haste. Whereas those lower down . . . he shook his head, knowing he was viewing the work of a truly terrible inquisitor. For it seemed that, perhaps not receiving the answers he sought, the man had begun to get angry. And as his anger grew, so the cuts on the body – on the abdomen and thighs, even the legs – had become longer and deeper, as the blade was wielded with increasing force. Finally the fellow had given full vent to his rage, and committed the most savage act of all. Evidence of that indignity had been hidden from Thomas and Hodge when they found the body. But when it was dragged from the water, the sight made several stout men turn away in horror. A *peotomy*, surgeons called it: the cutting off of a man's most private organ.

Gazing down at Doggett's remains, Thomas found his own anger towards the man had evaporated. He had disliked him, yes – as others had. And the more he had learned, the more his contempt for the fellow had grown. But no one, whatever his crime, even the slaying of another man by the sword – for Richard Cutler had been a fencer himself, as well as a blackmailing rogue – no one deserved such treatment as had been meted out to Lady Rooke's secretary.

He turned away, and took a few paces along the nave of the little chapel. What was he to think now? Cutler's death was no longer a mystery . . . but this? What could Doggett have done to merit such treatment? Or rather, what was it that someone wanted to know so badly that he would employ such methods?

The scrape of the latch startled him. He looked round to see Sir Robert enter, muffled in a heavy gown. His master too looked as if he had barely slept. Wordlessly the knight walked towards the altar where the body lay, to look down with distaste, which soon turned to disgust. After a moment Thomas moved up beside his master, who turned with a haggard expression.

'In Heaven's name, who would do this?'

Thomas returned his gaze frankly. Sir Robert had his faults, but cruelty was not one of them. He was numbed by this stark display of it.

'An interrogator,' Thomas answered. 'And if I know one thing, it's that whoever got hold of Doggett wrung every scrap of information he could from him before finishing him off. Though he would have been so weak from pain and loss of blood by then, it wouldn't take much.'

Sir Robert shook his head. 'A crude means of torture – yet effective enough, no doubt. I've heard of such practices in the East . . .' He shrugged. 'I thought those were merely old Crusaders' tales.'

'I think those means were used by someone who had no

access to an interrogation chamber, or its tools,' Thomas said. He would voice his theories, if only to save his master from despair. For the fact was that the search Thomas had begun in earnest had not only failed to produce any sign of the Muscovy chain – it had led to a gruesome discovery that drove the other matter almost to insignificance.

Sir Robert looked sharply at him. 'Do you mean that this . . . this dreadful act was carried out in the open?' he asked. 'Perhaps near where the body was found?'

Thomas shook his head. 'He could have been seen, or disturbed. And there would have been a great deal of blood – though the rain could have washed that away.' He thought for a moment. 'I cannot say with certainty, but by the condition of the body, Doggett died soon after he fled from Petbury – perhaps that same night. He took the road south – where someone saw him, and caught him. Whoever it was seems to have had no difficulty overpowering him, and taking him to some place he could question him. Later he dumped the corpse in the river, thinking the flood would carry it off. He's clearly a stranger, or he would know how the reeds choke the stream, under the old bridge.'

'So he threw it in upstream, west of Shefford?' Sir Robert was frowning. 'There's nothing there but fields.'

Thomas gave him a wry look. 'And Mistress Jeap's house; but the constable and I searched that. Besides, whatever else the woman is, I'm certain she would want no part of this.'

Sir Robert nodded briefly, then turned to go. As he went the knight laid a hand upon Thomas's shoulder.

'Take some rest,' he said. 'Martin will order the arrangements . . .' He sighed. 'And I must prevail on Lady Margaret once again, to break bad news to my sister. We will spare her the details – I only hope I can rely on everyone else to keep them from her.'

Thomas watched his master go out. Then after a last look at the ruined body of what had once been a handsome man, he too left the chapel.

Lady Rooke was inconsolable to the point of distraction – but on one matter she was clear, as well as resolute. She and her maid would leave Petbury at once for London, likely never to return. Her childhood home, she declared, had become a place of woe. Indeed, she now expressed tearful regret that she had come here for the summer. Neither her brother nor her sister-in-law Lady Margaret chose to remind her that it was John Doggett who had persuaded Lady Jane to come. The man had paid too high a price for his scheming.

A gloom hung over the manor that day that not even the appearance of the sun could dissipate. On Lady Margaret's orders Nell spurred the kitchen folk into activity, to prepare a feast in honour of the ambassador. Though it was plain there was little enthusiasm for the task. Not even the departure towards midday of Lady Rooke and Kat Jenkin, escorted by two of Sir Robert's men, aroused much attention. Perhaps only the Russians' taking their leave would have raised a few spirits, especially Martin's. The old steward was now obliged to busy himself with the disposal of a second body.

Around midday, having snatched a few hours' rest and spoken with Ned, Thomas took the chestnut gelding again and rode down to Great Shefford. He found an air of high excitement in the village, since the grisly discovery of the previous evening. And to his embarrassment, he was soon recognized. Folk clustered about him as he walked the horse through the street to John Hodge's house, shouting questions. But to their disappointment he would say little; only that the dead man was being returned to his family in London. He did not mention the fact, as was now well known at Petbury, that Doggett had left a widow. How that unfortunate woman would receive the news of her husband's last misadventure, he could not know.

He found the constable in his kitchen, struggling to write a report for the sheriff of Berkshire. Hodge was no scribe, and admitted that the task was almost beyond him. But his relief when Thomas offered to help was tempered by other concerns. It seemed his daughter Alice had shut herself in her chamber since the previous night, and would not come out.

'She refuses even to eat,' he complained. 'Well, so be it!

She'll show her face when she's hungry enough . . . though I cannot blame the girl for giving way to her grief.' The man sighed and gestured to Thomas to seat himself. 'Well now,' he added in a brisker tone, 'what's the word from Petbury?'

Thomas told him. And finding a sympathetic ear, he went on to say more: not about John Doggett, for Hodge knew enough of that man's story. Instead he found himself telling his other troubles: of the tiresome ambassador, and of a treasure that he was supposed to be searching for . . . only this time, in contrast to what he had told Tertius Gale, Thomas went even further. For he trusted Hodge more. Perhaps if they could work together . . . finally, and with a sense of relief, Thomas made a decision. Throwing caution aside he confided in this man as he had confided in no one else apart from Nell: he told him of the theft of the Muscovy chain.

Hodge listened with growing interest, if not alarm. By the time Thomas had finished he was frowning deeply. But what followed was unexpected. For it was this plain village constable who voiced the notion that, Thomas now realized, had been at the back of his mind for the past few days.

'What if someone else is looking for it too?'

Thomas frowned at him.

'If this jewelled chain's as valuable as you say,' Hodge went on, 'and as important . . . what if someone else has learned it's been stolen?'

Thomas gazed down at the scrubbed table, and at the evidence of Hodge's tortured attempts at letter-writing; the sheets of paper, ink-pot and broken quills. Finally he looked up.

'There was a man seen running near the manor, the night before last,' he began – whereupon Hodge drew a sharp breath.

'Was he hooded? Moving fast, with an odd gait like a dog's?'

Thomas sat back. 'He's been seen here?'

The other nodded. 'Twice! But I didn't pay the tales any mind. The first time it was a sot, come out of the Fox with a bellyful of ale – he sees devils jumping out of the bushes and whatnot, so I didn't listen to him. The second time . . .' The constable put a hand to his beard and rubbed. 'I should have listened . . . and it irks me now that it slipped my mind. For it was the night before we found the body!'

'Who saw him that time?' Thomas asked. But whatever the answer, it was unimportant. In his mind, things were falling into place . . . and he too was irked with himself. For the picture was becoming clearer by the moment.

'A fellow walking home, late,' Hodge told him. 'I was about to go to my bed when he stopped by. Told me he'd seen this figure, near the river . . . he didn't like the look of him. But it was dark, and there'd been no burglary or aught . . .' He shrugged. 'In fact nothing untoward has happened here for a long while, until now.' He broke off, not needing to remind Thomas of it. But Thomas startled him by getting abruptly to his feet.

'He doesn't know it's stolen!'

Hodge stared.

'He doesn't know it's missing . . . he only knows it was taken to Petbury!'

Pacing about the tiny kitchen, Thomas pieced the matter together, reasoning as he spoke. 'He didn't steal it – or he'd be long gone by now. He knows it was brought here, so he's searching – but he doesn't know the manor, or the country. So . . .' He stopped, frowning. 'He caught Doggett when he ran away from Petbury, and tortured him – but Doggett couldn't tell what he didn't know. Which is why the fellow became enraged, and—'

'Enough!' Hodge looked grimly at him. 'I saw what had been done to the man.'

Thomas sat down again, and met Hodge's troubled gaze. 'I would swear that this man – whoever he is – is still here,' he said. 'And more, he will not leave until he gets what he wants.'

After a moment, Hodge nodded. 'Then we'd better find him – before he gets hold of anyone else!'

Having left the horse in the care of a neighbour, Thomas and the constable walked the bounds of Great Shefford all afternoon. Those who saw them kept their distance: neither Hodge nor the Petbury falconer looked as if they would welcome interruption. The two skirted the village on all sides, examining every thicket and hollow. They followed the river once again, down to the shepherd's hut where Alice Hodge and her fickle lover had met in secret, and a mile beyond that, until the rooftops of Welford village rose in the distance. But they found nothing; nor did those they encountered have word of any strangers. Finally the two men walked back to Shefford and revisited the spot where they had found John Doggett.

'The other sighting of the hooded man . . . you said it was near the river.' Thomas stood on the path by the bridge, and gestured upstream. 'Yet there's nowhere to run to, is there? Not even an empty barn.'

Then he lowered his eyes, remembering. Four years ago a barn had stood nearby, across the lane from where they were now. Along with others Thomas had been forced to watch it burn to the ground, taking the life of a man who had sought refuge inside it . . . He sighed, then glanced up. Hodge was watching him.

'No barn,' the constable said, with a look of understanding. 'Not even a hut.' Then he frowned. 'That is, except . . .'

Thomas looked sharply at him.

'There's the old monk's cell, upriver. Where Elijah the Anchorite is said to have lived, a hundred years or more back. It's only a ruin . . .'

But Thomas seized upon the suggestion. So the two men began walking again, upstream along the bank of the swollen Lambourn. They passed Mary Jeap's house, which caused Thomas to halt and glance back at it.

'It's a mite close for comfort, isn't it?' he murmured. 'I mean to where the body was?'

Hodge grunted. 'Nothing would please me more than to arrest that old bawd,' he said. 'But I don't believe she knows aught of this . . . it'd be bad for business!' He nodded towards the house. 'Besides, she seems as shocked as anyone by what's happened. She's even closed the place up today – as a mark of respect, she says.'

With a wry look, he resumed his steps. But Thomas gazed thoughtfully at the big house. There was indeed a forlorn look about it. Some upstairs windows were open, but no sound came from within. Dismissing the matter, he turned to follow Hodge.

After a short walk they came to a slight bend in the river. The ground rose here, and the rooftops of Great Shefford were now behind. And Thomas was surprised when the constable stopped and pointed, for at first he could see nothing. Then he made out a tumbledown structure in the long grass ahead. In fact the ruined hut was so overgrown, it would have been possible to miss it entirely.

Despite the futility of their search thus far, he felt a surge of excitement. But as he and Hodge walked towards the stone hut, this gave way to a sense of foreboding. And by the time they had reached it, Thomas knew he had at last found what he sought. But there was no sense of triumph: merely one of grim realization. He stepped through the doorway – much of the wall, as well as the roof, being long vanished – and saw the flattened grass, dark with dried blood. Hodge peered through a gap in the crumbling wall, and took in the grim sight without a word: they had found the killer's interrogation chamber.

'Doggett's wrists were tied behind him – and he was thrown down in that corner,' Thomas said briskly. 'Likely his feet were tied as well . . . I didn't trouble to look for marks. There would have been a gag to stifle his cries . . . with no one to hear for a mile in any direction, our man could take all the time he needed. Indeed, I think where I'm standing is where he knelt, bending over his victim.'

Hodge gazed at him in silence. Though he knew the Petbury falconer's reputation, he had never been a part of any of his investigations. But he was surprised by Thomas's dispassionate tone; as if he had set aside his feelings. It occurred to Hodge that this was the way the man got his results.

'But then he lost patience,' Hodge put in grimly. When Thomas turned to him, he went on: 'He stopped cutting, and started slashing. That's why as you said, the scars were deeper and further apart, as he worked his way down . . . he must have known by then that he was wasting his time. Doggett didn't know anything about the Muscovy chain.'

Thomas nodded, his gaze straying eastwards, back the way they had walked. 'But where has this man been hiding all this time?' he mused. 'Even murderers have to sleep and eat. He's only been seen at night – indeed, he only works by night. With the cloak and hood, even if he's spotted he can't be recognized. But where is he during daylight hours?'

Hodge frowned. 'You want me to search every house in Shefford? The place has already been stirred to boiling—'

But Thomas shook his head. 'I wager you'd find nothing. This one's too clever . . .' He glanced again at the fearful spot where the hooded man who ran with a dog-like gait had done his terrible work. He had faced wicked people before, of both sexes; but this time . . .

'Have we seen all there is, d'you think?' Hodge's tone made Thomas snap out of his reverie. He saw the man's look of distaste, and managed a faint smile.

'I do, master constable,' he said. 'We may not have our man, but we know a little more about him – thanks to you.'

Hodge shrugged. Even praise from the celebrated Thomas Finbow could barely lift his spirits. Both men were turning to go, when Thomas stiffened.

'Wait!' Pointing to a spot near the doorway, he hurried forward. Hodge followed his gaze, and started. For something bright gleamed at them, lying among the weeds along the wall . . . and in a moment Thomas had bent to retrieve it. Straightening up, he lifted the object with an air of triumph.

How John Doggett had kept it hidden from Lady Rooke and Kat all this time, he did not know. But one small mystery at least had been solved: the whereabouts of the man's sword.

That night the great hall at Petbury was filled with the noise of revelry, as if nothing unpleasant had happened. Indeed, as far as His Excellency Grigori Stanic was concerned, that seemed to be the case. The ambassador glowed with pleasure as well as drink, seated as he was on the high table beside Lady Margaret. On her right, a tense Sir Robert struggled to keep his smile intact. Other guests, neighbouring landowners and hunting friends, had been invited to swell the occasion. Servants were kept busy, maintaining a continuous flow of delicacies from the steamy kitchen. And there, amid the bustle yet apart from it, a very tired Thomas the falconer sat taking a late supper.

He had returned from Shefford, having parted from John Hodge with promises to help in any way he could. But the constable was so preoccupied with the terrible events so close to his quiet village, the man barely seemed to hear him. Thomas had watched him go to his cottage with eyes downcast. With a heavy heart he had turned the horse homewards.

He was still deep in thought, as he had been throughout his ride back. He had sought an audience with Sir Robert, but the knight was already entertaining guests. Nothing, it seemed, must be allowed to interfere with that – nor to challenge the illusion that despite two recent deaths in the vicinity, all was well. And as far as Thomas knew, the ambassador still believed the royal gift that he was to convey to Muscovy was safe in Sir Robert's keeping. Though how many now knew the truth was something that troubled him greatly.

He had spoken with Nell, and though he was sparing with details she saw how burdened he was. Since the discovery of Doggett's violent death, she too was on edge. He watched her move about her domain, snapping at a servingman who almost upset a dish heaped with roasted larks. The little birds had been supplied by Ned Hawes, who had had a productive day on the Downs in Thomas's absence. A wry smile stole across his face; at this rate the boy would soon manage without him.

He rose and drained his mug of weak beer, intending to go to the mews. Glancing across the room he caught Nell's eye, and they exchanged nods. He sighed as he walked to the door: another night when he would sleep alone . . .

The light was fading as he stepped outside. A wench hurried past him from the well, water slopping over the sides of her pail. Unhurriedly he walked through the kitchen gardens and turned along the wall of the stable yard. From the pigsties behind him came a chorus of bad-tempered grunts, which in turn startled the hens. Then the household noises faded as he began to climb the slope above the great house. In the paddock, horses snickered, their numbers swelled by those of Sir Robert's guests. Thomas strode uphill, sniffing the air which was humid and heavy. The thin line of trees above his cottage rose faintly on the horizon. He was almost at the mews, his mind already on the falcons. Then he stopped, at first unsure of what he had heard. But after a moment it came again: a woman's voice, distant and muffled. And at once he turned with a frown, and started downhill towards the paddock. For he knew that voice as well as he knew his own: it was his daughter's.

He skirted the stable yard, gaining pace – but now, the closer he drew to the spot whence the sound had come, the more uncomfortable he became. And to his surprise another voice rose in his memory – that of the last person he expected. It was John Doggett as he remembered him, smiling defiantly at Thomas: *Surely you would not have Eleanor – a grown woman of twenty-one years, who knows her own mind – mewed up like your falcons . . . ?*

He slowed, biting his lip. Eleanor had left the hall and come outside – and clearly she was not alone. Further, Thomas had a shrewd enough idea who she was with . . . He halted. What if his daughter was in the long grass with Piotr? What then should he do?

He stood in the damp, clammy air, feeling foolish. She was not a child, and he must stop thinking of her as one. He had told her he trusted her, and believed her capable of ordering her own behaviour. Yet something tugged at him, tried to force him forward. He trusted Eleanor, but should he trust the young Russian?

He turned and made himself walk away, back up the slope. Tomorrow he would seek her out, try to talk to her. Then in a second everything changed, as a scream stopped him in his tracks. Eleanor had screamed – and he did not need to ask himself why! He simply swung round, and ran like the devil. And now, from the paddock, he heard horses whinny . . .

The fence was ahead. He vaulted it and ran through the wet grass, and as he ran he shouted. 'Eleanor – it's your father! Show yourself – now!'

A figure, far off to his right, running . . . He peered through the gloom and drew a sharp breath. There was no mistaking the stubby arms, the unkempt locks – he even made out the shape of a bow. Hoarsely, he cried out.

'I see you, Will Greve! You're meat for the hangman this time . . . stop, or I'll get a horse and ride you down!'

But he could not do that. For another voice, unmistakable, called out in panic from another direction. 'Father! In Heaven's name – quickly!'

He veered towards it and ran, his pulse racing. The south fence of the paddock loomed, and he sailed over that as he had the other. He was in the deer park – and now, there were two voices: one his daughter's, the other . . . Out of breath he raced forward, and at last they loomed up before him: Eleanor and Piotr, standing facing him. And now he saw that he had been mistaken. For as he drew near, the young man beckoned him forward urgently. And as he came to a breathless halt, he saw the frightened looks on both faces.

'Over there!' Eleanor pointed to something Thomas could not see. Piotr put out his arms and drew her to him. And to Thomas's dismay the girl fell against him, weeping.

'Eleanor!' he cried. 'What's happened?'

There was a moment, before she managed to control herself. Then pushing herself away from Piotr, she faced her father. 'The boy – Will Corder.'

Thomas's heart thumped. He followed her gaze. Then without further word he walked the few yards, to one of the small trees that dotted the park. His heart sank, for somehow he knew what he would find. And when the pitifully small body appeared, lying motionless in the grass at the foot of the tree, he could only stop and gaze dumbly at it.

His first emotion was relief: the boy was not a mass of terrible scars, as he had half expected. But his head lay at a wild angle, for the neck was broken. And there was blood on the chest and arms . . .

He let out a bitter oath, and his fists clenched as he dropped to one knee, to peer down at the poor kitchen boy who had lost his place; and had now lost his life.

The hooded man had claimed another victim.

Twelve

Sir Robert lit the candles himself, somewhat hurriedly. As the flames sprang up he motioned Thomas to close the door behind him. They were alone in his private chamber. As far as his guests knew, the knight had been called away to deal with some minor matter. Only Lady Margaret suspected something more grave. But in the great hall the mistress of Petbury kept her counsel, as she did her hostess's smile.

'Well?' Sir Robert faced him with an anxious look. And at last Thomas was able to tell him all he had discovered since they spoke that morning, in the chapel. That much was easy: more difficult was telling of the death of Will Corder.

Sir Robert sat down heavily. By the time Thomas had finished, he was gazing at the floor in disbelief. 'This is beyond me,' he said at last. Then quickly, fiercely, he looked up. 'Nor can I keep this . . . these cheap theatricals up any longer!' He hesitated, then: 'I'll send word to Sir Thomas Rivers. I'll tell him all, let him deal with it. I no longer care what follows.' When Thomas frowned, the knight added: 'What can they do – imprison me? I think not. I didn't steal the accursed chain – nor did I ask for it to come here, any more than I asked to play host to that oaf of an ambassador! Let them impose what penalties they will – if I must sell my silverware to make good the loss, so be it!'

Then seeing Thomas's expression, Sir Robert had the grace to look ashamed. 'As for the murders – we'll deal with those ourselves, Thomas. They were our people: even Doggett, in a way. And the boy died on Petbury soil, within shouting distance of my own hall!' The knight got angrily to his feet. 'To the devil with the precious chain – let the Privy Council mount their own search. We will find this murderous savage – and avenge the dead!'

Thomas watched his master with mixed feelings: relief – for with Sir Robert, anger had always been a spur to action – was tempered with regret at the evil that had befallen Will Corder. He had carried the lifeless body uphill to his own cottage, accompanied by Eleanor and Piotr. There he had counselled his daughter to say nothing until he had spoken with Sir Robert. The young Russian, clearly shaken by the event, had soon made himself scarce. And to Thomas's mind, it would not be long before Piotr spoke of what had happened. Now he told Sir Robert that, too – but the knight no longer seemed troubled by the matter.

'So His Excellency will hear of it – well, I hope it shakes him out of his complacency, along with his drunken stupor!' he exclaimed. 'Him and that great ox Mikhailov, and that weasel of a secretary – I'm weary of the whole pack of them! Let the Duke of Novgorod and Lord of Wherever-it-is pack up and leave – and let him take his oil and furs and his barrel of vile fish-eggs with him!'

Thomas blinked and would have spoken, but Sir Robert waved a hand irritably. 'Save your breath, Thomas! Now send one of the grooms to me – one who can ride all night! Meanwhile you'd better let that fool of a constable know what's happened. Not that I have much faith in him, but he should be able to get some men together.' The knight looked up. 'I mean Gale, not your friend from Shefford. He sounds like a man of keener wit.'

Thomas nodded absently. 'He is . . . and with your leave I will tell him, too. For he's as eager as I am to find this . . .' He trailed off. He no longer had a word for the hooded man, for none was adequate.

'Very well.' Sir Robert snuffed the candles out and moved to the door. 'I'll speak with Martin.' He frowned. 'This death will be hardest for him to bear. It was he who took it upon himself to dismiss the boy from my service.'

They parted in the passageway. Thomas watched his

master walk away towards the great hall. From that direction, the cheerful noise of revelry rolled on.

After the messenger had been despatched to distant Ewell
in Surrey, the home of Sir Thomas Rivers, the rest of the
night passed without incident. Sir Robert's guests departed
in the small hours, unaware that a brutal murder had taken
place close to where their horses were penned. The Russians
too had gone to their beds, though what conversations might
be taking place in the west rooms of Petbury, Thomas did
not trouble to guess at. He had other matters to deal with.

He had brought a pallet, and lain the body of Will Corder
down near the fireside. Here by lantern light he made his
brief examination. When day came he would take the boy
to Chaddleworth, to his family. Of all his tasks, that one
weighed most heavily upon him.

He pushed the thought away, forcing himself to become
the intelligencer again. He went out, filled a pail and brought
it inside. Methodically he began to wash the corpse, examining the wounds as he did so. And if any doubts existed
that Will Corder had died by the same hand as John Doggett,
they soon disappeared. There were indeed lacerations – only
a few and quite shallow, about the chest, upper arms and
shoulders. Looking inside the boy's mouth, Thomas found
blood there too. For Will had been gagged as Doggett had,
and in his pain he had bitten hard . . . Grimly, Thomas went
on to examine the cuts, made without doubt by the same
knife. They were neat, and skilfully made to exact the
maximum of pain. This time the interrogator had not needed
long to ascertain that the boy too knew nothing of the prize:
the chain that Thomas had come to loathe. Already it had
been the cause of two deaths. What astounded him now
was the boldness of the foe he faced: the inquisitor had
seemingly caught Will Corder in Petbury park and questioned him there and then – within sight of the house.
Though, mercifully, this time he had not lost his control.
The boy at least was spared the greater agonies that had
been meted out to Doggett – including the final, most
barbarous act. Instead he had been strangled – and that too

was done neatly and efficiently. In one sense Thomas was relieved: he could tell the boy's parents their son died quickly. He would leave out details of what had happened to him before that. What puzzled him was what the boy was doing in the deer park . . . but the answer to that came with a flash of memory: Will Greve running away, bow in hand. For what else would a plucky young Chaddleworth boy do, who had lost his means of livelihood? He would not be the first to try his hand at poaching; and if experience counted for anything, Greve was the best teacher for miles.

Thomas stood up and went outside. Already dawn was near. Standing by the cottage door, he gazed southwards into the gloom, across the manor and beyond. Somewhere the hooded man was abroad . . . though he did not know where, he could almost sense him. Breathing in the cool air, he resolved to find this murderer somehow, whatever it took; just to look him in the face would be some reward. He nodded to himself, thinking of Sir Robert's words. He too cared nothing about the Muscovy chain now; nor about the ambassador, nor the threats to English trade, nor even the Queen's displeasure. What did a bauble, even one of sapphires and rubies, matter when set beside the death of a young boy?

A resolve formed: he would start with Will Greve. Though the poacher was a bad lot, he was no torturer . . . but what had he seen? Thomas would seek him out in the morning . . . He sighed. It was morning already.

Stifling a yawn, he turned to go inside; to keep vigil beside the cold body, which he had covered with a shepherd's cape. Sleep seemed impossible: a distant prospect, like the departure of the ambassador. Though perhaps that event might not be so far off now, after all.

But Will Greve had gone to ground, like the wily fox he was.

Thomas found that out soon after he went to Tertius Gale's house and woke the startled man up. As soon as he had dressed, the constable listened to Thomas's tale with amazement. Finally he followed Thomas out on to Chaddleworth green. Smoke rose from a few chimneys, but some folk were still abed. Wordlessly the two men walked eastwards, crossing Poughley brook by the old stepping stones. There, where the trees began, stood Greve's tiny cottage with its sagging thatch. Without bothering to knock they shoved open the door and went in. One glance told them the place was empty.

'I'll do your master's bidding, and raise a party,' Gale muttered. 'But who am I to seek first? Will Greve, or this hooded murderer, or—'

'Whomever you will,' Thomas broke in harshly. 'And if you find aught, let Sir Robert know. I've a corpse to deliver.'

Then without further word he turned and went out.

An hour later he was sat outside the Black Bear collecting his thoughts. The short time spent at the home of Will Corder had been worse than he expected. The father was still drunk from the night before, and could not be roused. The boy's mother, a hollow-eyed mouse of a woman, had at first taken the news calmly. Then, as if the meaning had only now sunk home, she shot up like an arrow, so sharply that her head hit on a beam. Eyes wide, she had flown into a frenzy and attacked Thomas as if he had been her son's murderer himself. Screaming, arms flailing, she had driven him back against the wall before he knew what was happening. There she proceeded to kick him and beat him on the chest, screeching like an owl. And Thomas had no heart to do anything but wrap his arms about her, until at last a neighbour, alarmed by the noise, came hurrying in. After some words of explanation Thomas had got himself outside, to stand bruised and breathless in the misty morning. Then he had walked away, and kept walking until the frenzied screams of mother Corder did not follow him any more.

Beside him the door of the inn opened, startling him out of his reverie. There stood the solid figure of Ann Dillamore with her sleeves rolled. And one look at the man slumped outside her window was all she needed. 'You'd best come inside and take a mug, Thomas,' she said. 'It may be early, but if any man needs a bracer I'd say it's you.'

Thomas got to his feet. 'I'm sorely tempted, my duck,' he said. 'But I must get back.'

And he was gone, quickening his pace as he crossed the green. Ann sighed as she watched him go. If ever a man looked bowed with care, it was Thomas Finbow.

To the alarm of all at Petbury, Sir Thomas Rivers arrived in the afternoon in a smouldering temper. Having received the news at daybreak from an exhausted groom, the Privy Councellor and his servant had ridden hard all morning, crossing two counties without respite. And the man was in no humour to listen to what he regarded as feeble excuses. He faced Sir Robert across the floor of his chamber, both men on their feet. And it was the master of Petbury who was now growing angry in his turn.

'I've said I am doing all I can, sir,' he snapped. 'Parties are out in all directions, searching every corner of the Downs. The moment we hear—'

'But from what *I* hear you have already searched – and to no avail!' Rivers threw back. 'Indeed, what is hardest to bear, sir, is that I now learn the chain was stolen no less than five days ago – the night after I left Petbury. Yet in fear of the consequences – for it was entrusted to you, as a loyal servant of the Queen – you chose to keep the matter from everyone, including me! Do you forget that I'm one of your oldest friends? Indeed – ' Rivers snorted – 'after this, you may find I'm the only friend you have!'

Sir Robert bit back a reply, and looked at Martin, who was standing nearby. But the old steward seemed unable to voice any word of support. Since learning of the death of Will Corder, he had barely spoken to anyone. So it was Thomas, who had been summoned to the house the moment Rivers arrived, who now came to his master's defence.

'Your pardon, sir – it was I who prevailed upon Sir Robert to keep the theft secret, at least for a while,' he said. 'I know the country, and if anyone suspicious had been seen I believed I could track him down—' He broke off, knowing how weak his explanations sounded. But Rivers turned to him, his eyes narrowing.

'I remember you, falconer,' he said. 'By sight as well as reputation. Perhaps you will give me a fuller account of events than I have received thus far!'

If Sir Robert felt the rebuke, he managed to control his anger. He merely nodded to Thomas, signifying that he should tell his tale. So Thomas drew breath and told it, leaving nothing out. And phrase it as he would, he could not disguise the fact that both Sir Robert and his steward now appeared very lax in safeguarding the Muscovy chain. By the time Thomas had spoken of the brutal murders done nearby, Rivers was almost speechless.

'You confound me!' was all he could say. With a bleak look at Sir Robert, he sat down heavily. His close-mouthed servant, the only other man present, poured a cup of wine and handed it to him. Rivers drained it in a gulp, then set it down on the table with a thud.

'So you have been seeking two felons,' he said grimly. 'One is seemingly a common thief, who climbs through this very window, picks the lock of your chest with ease and makes off with the chain – the empty case of which then turns up in a flower bed!' Rivers let out a sigh of exasperation. 'While the other is a murderous fiend, who seems able to roam your lands with impunity, torturing anyone he finds as to the whereabouts of the chain – which is in all likelihood nowhere near here! If, indeed, it is still in England at all! But what is worse . . .' The man was scornful. 'What is worse – this person knows that the chain was here, and is seeking it himself! Who in Christ's name can he be? . . . No!' Seeing Sir Robert about to make a reply, Rivers held up a hand. 'Spare me any further explanations, sir. Or I might begin to suspect some of your own household – of tongue-wagging, if naught else!'

Thomas glanced at Sir Robert, expecting a furious riposte. But the fight seemed to have drained from him. He too sat down, and reached for the wine jug. Finding something to do at last, Martin came forward and poured him a cup.

'It was for the good of England, and of our Queen, that I have tried to order the matter, Sir Thomas,' the knight said tiredly. 'Indeed, I have used every means at my disposal

– even to pandering my own wife . . .' A bitterness came into his tone. 'All of it to buy time, so that every effort be made to find the chain before the ambassador learns of its loss!' Sir Robert took a drink, and met Rivers' eye. 'Yet I fear that by now, even as dull-witted a fellow as Grigori Stanic may have an inkling that all isn't well.'

Thomas spoke up again. 'If not him, then his servants, sir. Yet how much they tell the ambassador, I don't know.' He faced Sir Thomas Rivers. 'I'm told that with the exception of his secretary Yusupov, they despise him to a man.'

Rivers frowned. 'Well – the one your daughter was entertaining in the park certainly knows all isn't well, falconer!' he snapped. Ignoring Thomas's struggle to keep his composure, he added: 'Who else do you think might know?'

Thomas drew a calming breath, then recounted the conversation he had had two days back with Kovalenko the falconer. He went on to mention the veiled threat from Yusupov that had followed, but, impatiently, Sir Robert broke in.

'This gets us nowhere,' he said. 'With the murder of the kitchen boy, and all the rumours now flying about, it's too late for further deception.' He turned deliberately to Rivers. 'With your approval, sir, I will invite the ambassador to join us, and tell him the Muscovy chain is lost.'

Rivers gave him a long look. 'It would seem the only solution,' he said.

There was a silence. All eyes were upon Rivers, for as a Privy Councellor and the one who had presented the chain to the ambassador, it was his decision. After a moment, the man's brow puckered.

'Unless . . .'

Sir Robert met his eye, then bristled; the other seemed to enjoy baiting him. Perhaps, Thomas thought, it was Rivers' means of punishing his master, for being the cause of what was now a diplomatic disaster.

'Unless, that is, you can think of a way of keeping His Excellency occupied, while we speak privately with his chief servants?'

Sir Robert frowned. 'That's impossible. His guard goes

everywhere with him. So does the secretary, as a rule. Otherwise the man can't understand a word that's said.'

'Not *everywhere*, surely?' Rivers raised his eyebrow. And at last, Sir Robert grasped his meaning. Furiously the knight sprang to his feet.

'What do you mean, sir?' he demanded. 'Speak! For if you dare to suggest that I would allow my wife—'

'Sir Robert – rein yourself!' Rivers met the other's look of outrage calmly. 'I was merely about to propose a little hawking trip. That's His Excellency's favourite sport, is it not?' When Sir Robert let out a sigh of exasperation, he gave a faint smile. 'Why – what on earth did you think I meant?'

That same afternoon the scheme was put into practice. And Ned Hawes found himself promoted suddenly from falconer's helper to falconer's deputy: for it was he who must manage the hastily arranged excursion. Fortunately the ambassador, who had slept late, welcomed the suggestion once he learned that Lady Margaret would host the party. Though she would also take Eleanor along: upon that, Sir Robert had been insistent. Mikhailov would accompany his master, and Piotr too would go. The two who would not were Kovalenko and Yusupov.

The secretary was surprised when he was asked to attend Sir Robert and his guest, the Queen's envoy who had presented the chain to the ambassador a week ago. And he soon became uneasy – especially when he was told that the presence of His Excellency's falconer was also required. Nor did the brief explanation – that it was a matter touching upon the ambassador's well-being – appear to satisfy him. So it was a tense gathering that took place, again in Sir Robert's private chamber. And both Yusupov and Kovalenko were on their guard as they entered the room, to find themselves under the scrutiny not only of Sir Robert and Sir Thomas Rivers, but Martin the steward, Thomas the falconer and Rivers' sharp-eyed servant, who never spoke. Warily the two Russians made their bows. And even Yusupov's composure was dented when, after a perfunctory greeting, Sir

Robert eyed him and said: 'Well, master secretary, I think it's time we aired a matter that no doubt troubles us both. You are of course aware that the priceless chain with the jewelled bear upon it has been stolen from this very room?'

Yusupov blinked, and did not answer. But Kovalenko, who was no diplomat, drew a sharp breath. Then at a swift glance from the secretary he fell silent.

The other men also remained silent, and waited. It was a bold strategy they had adopted, but to Thomas's relief it appeared to be working. Especially when the secretary, forcing a weak smile, spoke up. 'Is this some trick, or a test of my loyalty, Sir Robert?' he asked. 'I see no other explanation . . .'

Sir Robert raised his brows. 'You credit me with more guile than I have, Master Yusupov,' he answered. 'We country folk speak as we find . . .' He gave a smile of his own. 'Why, do you think I should have cause to test your loyalty?'

Yusupov flushed slightly. 'Then if the chain is truly stolen, sir, this is a matter of grave import,' he said. 'I must tell His Excellency at once.'

'His Excellency will be a long way off by now,' Sir Robert told him. 'And my falconer has given instructions to his helper to keep the party out until evening. They will have good sport, I am sure.'

Yusupov retained his calm with difficulty. But Thomas was watching Kovalenko, who was clearly afraid. He glanced up and caught Thomas's eye upon him, then immediately looked away.

'This is some strategy you have prepared, sir – to what purpose, I cannot know.' Yusupov was frowning at Sir Robert. Whereupon Sir Thomas Rivers chose the moment to add his weight.

'You'd best have a care, fellow,' he snapped. 'Our Queen takes any slight against her loyal followers as a slight upon herself.'

Yusupov's tongue darted out. He wet his lip, then said: 'I think you know I mean no slight, sir. Yet I do not understand what is done here . . . if the chain is stolen as you say, why have you not told my master?'

'We were hoping you might be able to answer that.'

Sir Robert, Thomas saw, was starting to enjoy himself. After ten tiresome days of playing the genial host to Grigori Stanic and his men, the knight now found himself with the upper hand. The others in the room also saw the secretary's discomfort. And abruptly, the man's composure broke.

'I know not what you speak of!' he said sharply. 'And I ask you in turn to remember that any slight upon His Excellency's servants is a slight on him too – and on the great Tsar whom he serves!'

But to the man's dismay, Sir Robert rose to his feet. 'Then you swear that your master does not know of the theft?' he demanded.

'I do swear it!' Yusupov cried. 'And this is an outrage! For if it is so, His Excellency will . . . he will be . . .'

'Ruined?'

The word was out before Thomas could stop himself. But catching Sir Robert's eye, he took his master's silence for assent to continue. For something, though he knew not what, was about to come out: he sensed it, as he sensed deception on the part of Yusupov; as he smelled fear, seeping from every pore of Kovalenko's skin. And the secretary, who now knew that he had walked into some sort of trap, began to work his fingers nervously.

'You know the chain is missing, don't you, Master Yusupov?' Thomas asked him. 'As my friend Kovalenko here knows – I saw it in his eyes that day on the Downs when you rode up and warned me to keep to my place.'

Yusupov's gaze flew from Thomas to Sir Robert, to Rivers and back. Even Martin the steward had brightened now, and was watching the man fiercely from under his white brows.

'I repeat, this is an outrage,' Yusupov said. 'I will go now, and await my master's return. His anger will be immense – you cannot know what will follow . . .' Then he stopped. For Kovalenko suddenly turned to him and said something in his own language. Yusupov countered with a sharp reply, the meaning of which seemed clear enough to Thomas: the man was being told to hold his peace.

But Kovalenko would not be stilled. He uttered a harsh response, which provoked an even harsher one from the other man. Then the next moment everyone started – for without warning, Kovalenko grabbed Yusupov by the collar of his black coat and shouted at the top of his voice.

'*Nyet – Pogano!* Is finished – broken! You see and you know – yet you keep doing! And now, you lose!'

And to general alarm the falconer fell upon the hapless secretary, beating him about the head while keeping up a stream of invective in his own language. And all Yusupov could do was cry out as he backed away, shouting and struggling to fend off a man who was physically stronger. If Thomas and Rivers' servant had not both leaped forward to separate the two men, the consequences for the secretary could have been grave. As it was he merely slumped to the floor and put his head in his hands. Kovalenko, held by the arms and driven back against the wall, went limp. Turning to Thomas, he cried: 'Enough . . . I stop!'

Sir Robert was staring at both falconers – the English and the Russian. But Rivers, who had also got to his feet, was angry.

'Disarm him!' he ordered, gesturing to his servant. The silent man nodded, and fumbling at Kovalenko's belt took the man's poniard from him. Kovalenko offered no resistance, and soon the servant stepped back, with a look at Thomas that meant he should do the same. So Thomas too let go, and moved away. Kovalenko was alone at one side of the room with all eyes upon him.

But it was Yusupov who spoke, in a tone none had heard him use; and every head snapped towards him.

Sitting on the floor, his hair awry, his bruised and reddened face shiny with sweat, the man was a sorry sight. But he had lost none of his skill with words. Looking up, he glared at Sir Robert.

'So the chain is stolen – and yes, I know it! You think Keril Yusupov a fool, for you do not know him! Your attempts to keep an illusion of calm never deceived me, Sir Robert. Neither am I ignorant of the terrible murders done here on your land . . .' He gave a short laugh. 'Your guardianship of the chain has been laughable, sir! To place it in that . . .' He gestured contemptuously towards the heavy chest. 'Without even guards posted, here or outside – how the thief must have scorned you! Why, he even left the lid gaping wide, to mock you!'

There was a sudden silence. Then feeling Thomas's gaze upon him, the secretary turned warily to him.

'How did you know the lid was left open?' Thomas asked.

Yusupov stiffened.

'How could you know that,' Thomas persisted, 'unless it was you who stole it?'

Yusupov drew a hand across his mouth, but still said nothing. Whereupon, at a gesture from Sir Thomas Rivers, his servant stepped forward, gripped the man by the collar and put the point of Kovalenko's poniard to his throat.

But the cry of anguish that followed came not from Yusupov: it came from Kovalenko. And as all eyes turned to him, he shook his head helplessly.

'He not take the chain,' the falconer said, 'for he not know how to break locks! I did it!'

And in the hiatus that followed, the man dropped weakly to one knee, and turned an imploring look towards Sir Robert. 'Now, do as you wish with me, sir,' he muttered. 'For I have no life left. But you will not send me back to prison. I will die first!'

Thirteen

He was a humble countryman who had fallen on hard times. But the hardships he had suffered in his homeland were worse than Thomas imagined. Along with the other men he listened to the falconer's tale, and could not help but feel some sympathy for Pavel Kovalenko. And for the first time he caught a true glimpse of life in distant Muscovy, and of the abject slavery that most of the population endured.

'I told you how little you knew of us,' Kovalenko said, looking at Thomas. 'You are a working man who serves his master – yet he does not hold such power over you as do our *boyars*. As for the Tsar . . .' Kovalenko shook his head. 'Not only can you lose your land and everything you have, at his pleasure – one word from him, you lose your life too!' He turned to Yusupov who stood beside him, the two men like condemned prisoners already. But the secretary made no sound; merely kept his eyes on the floor, as if he had retreated into some private world.

'This man was my saviour,' Kovalenko said softly. 'For it was he who gave me a chance . . . freed me from prison, where I was thrown because I could not pay my taxes. Because I chose to feed my wife and my child first!' The man struggled with his feelings. 'The boy died while I was in prison. As for my farm – that is gone, and my wife too.'

He indicated Yusupov again. 'If he not set me free, but a short while ago, I also would have died! This man it was, knowing of my skill with hawks, who got me into service with His Excellency. True, it was for his own ends – I was not such a fool to think otherwise. I would be his instrument, to call upon when he wished . . .'

Now Kovalenko faced Sir Robert. 'It was here in your house, sir, that I was called upon to pay that debt. To use another skill I have – one I learn in the Tsar's prison.' He pointed towards the chest near the window, that had already been the cause of so much discourse. 'To undo a lock such as that is but a simple matter for me – like opening the casement above.' The falconer sighed. 'I did not mistake in leaving the lid of the chest open – for I was told to do it, so that you would know at once of the theft. What we do not expect . . .' Kovalenko gave a rueful smile. 'We not expect that you hide the theft from our master. That was not in the plan!' The man turned to Yusupov. 'I think you should ask him now, for I not tell more.'

And watched by everyone, Kovalenko turned away and spat heavily into a corner. To Sir Robert, he said: 'Forgive me, sir: in my country, is how we exorcise the devil.'

There was a silence, as every man digested the tale. Finally, with a glance at Rivers, Sir Robert turned his eye upon Yusupov. 'You may take your turn now, master secretary,' he said grimly. 'But after all that's happened – ' the knight's anger rose as he spoke – 'all the wickedness that's been practised under my roof, I should warn you that I'm in no humour for leniency! You will pay for your actions – if not by my hand, then by your master's. And somehow I don't think he will be inclined to leniency, either!'

Then he waited, as did the other men, until Yusupov raised his eyes from the floor.

'We have an old saying in Muscovy,' he said bitterly. '*Scratch a Russian, and you will soon find a Tartar beneath.*' The man glanced at Kovalenko, who would not meet his eye. 'They will always betray you in the end.'

But at that Sir Thomas Rivers bridled. 'You dare talk of betrayal!' he snapped. 'What you have done to your master amounts to—'

'Vengeance,' Yusupov said sharply. 'And you may think what you will, sir: His Excellency's hurts are as nothing to what my family and I have suffered at his hands.'

But Rivers was tired, and his composure was gone. 'I care not a fig for that!' he cried. 'You have caused mayhem and discord here, fellow. And to my mind you are in part responsible for two deaths! The petty squabbles you bring with you are no concern of mine, nor of Sir Robert – nor of our Queen, who sent the priceless gift here in good faith!'

Yusupov stiffened. 'Petty squabbles?' he echoed. 'You think they are only that? And your Queen sent the chain as a bribe for Godunov, that she may be able to better the French in trade with our nation—'

'Be silent!' Rivers was on his feet. 'You will say nothing more – only answer the questions put to you! Or I will have you, and this man too, treated here and now as captured felons. And I think you will find that our own prisons – not to mention our hangmen – are as effective in the final throw as any that exist in your barbarous country!'

Yusupov had gone pale. 'You are not so different to my master, after all,' he said with a bleak look. Turning to Sir Robert, he said: 'You loathe His Excellency like a leper. Yet you feast him and flatter him, even letting him fawn upon your own wife . . . and all the time you cannot wait for him to leave! Yet you pretend you wish him to stay, so that you can search for the chain to save your own reputation . . .' The man's mouth twisted in a cold smile. 'I say this: if you knew more of the man you entertain here in your house, you would hate him as I do!'

Now at last, it was out; and gazing at the secretary, Thomas realized that he had known in his heart that the man's unswerving loyalty to his master had been a sham. Somehow he had refused to face the fact – and now he cursed himself. If he had looked within the ambassador's retinue from the beginning . . . he drew a breath, forcing the bitter notion down, and threw a glance at his master. But now matters were becoming clearer, instead of flying into a rage Sir Robert had become icily calm. Turning to Rivers, he even laid a soothing hand on the Privy Councillor's arm.

'With your leave, Sir Thomas . . . ?'

Stifling an oath Rivers sat down, waving a hand to signify that he was more than willing to let the master of Petbury deal with the business. Whereupon Sir Robert fixed Yusupov with a look that made the man flinch.

'Well now: before we hear your testimony, master secretary – which will be intriguing, I have no doubt – you may clear up one matter that has caused me some concern.' The knight paused. 'Since you have admitted arranging the theft of the Muscovy chain, will you kindly tell us where you hid it?'

Another silence fell. But if Sir Robert had expected a forthright answer, he was disappointed. For with a sudden passion, Yusupov met his eye and said: 'I will die before I tell you!' A scornful look came across his face. 'And it is in the last place you would look!'

Sir Robert bristled, as did Rivers. But for Thomas, the words were a revelation.

For some reason he had been thinking briefly on his discovery of the empty case, at the side of the house. In his ears, he heard again the squeals from the pig-pens. And with a sudden clarity that made him want to laugh, he saw it. To the consternation of his master and the other men, he looked deliberately at Yusupov, and gave a passable imitation of a sow's grunt – whereupon the look on the secretary's face was all he needed. The fellow paled; and it was plain that he understood at last that his plans – whatever their reason for being – were now in ruins.

Everyone was looking at Thomas, as if they believed he had lost his reason. But facing Sir Robert, he said: 'If you will send someone to the pig-pens, sir, bid him find the barrel of caviar and bring it here, I believe you may uncover the chain within it.'

As the discoverer of the hiding place, it was Thomas who was prevailed upon to take the lid off the small barrel and dip his hand into the noisome black jelly. As Petbury folk well knew, the keg was almost full, since even the pigs did not deign to eat its contents. Hence it had stood out in the rain all this time, in a corner of the sties where someone had left it. Its contents gave off an unpleasant smell, but Thomas did not care. He laughed inwardly, thinking how he had passed the chain's hiding place a dozen times. Even when he had found its case a short distance away, he had not thought of the pigsties: in spite of himself he admired Yusupov's cunning in thinking of such a location. But now excitement was upon him, as on all of them. With shirt sleeve rolled up, he shoved his hand down to the bottom of the barrel, and felt his fingers close upon something solid. It was not metallic, however, but covered in what felt like fur. He drew the heavy object out, and wiping the caviar away, placed it on a cloth that had been spread upon Sir Robert's table. And now all became clear: it was a piece of fur that the chain had been wrapped in. Carefully Thomas unfolded it; and a sigh of relief and wonder arose from the other men, as the familiar glint of gold and the dazzling array of sapphires and rubies appeared before them. Here was the Muscovy chain; damp and sticky, but undamaged.

Rivers broke the silence. 'Well, sir . . .' Mastering his feelings, he threw a dry look at Sir Robert. 'I trust that I no longer need to advise you on how to proceed?'

Sir Robert met his gaze. 'I swear to you that the royal gift will not leave my sight again, until I see it safely on its way,' he answered. He turned to Yusupov, who had not moved. Beside him Kovalenko stood, pale and silent.

'Master secretary . . .' Though filled with relief, Sir Robert was not about to let that emotion sway him. 'I had a mind to hear your story, as I did the falconer's. Yet now that your deeds have been laid bare, and the chain recovered, I'm inclined to turn you over to your master and tell him all. Is there any reason you can give me why I should not do so?'

Everyone watched Yusupov. Even Sir Thomas Rivers showed some curiosity now, as to the events that had led to the chain's theft. But the secretary eyed Sir Robert, and shook his head. 'None that would sway such as you,' he replied.

Sir Robert frowned. 'You think me a mere tyrant, like your Muscovy landowners?' he demanded. 'The Dukes of Novgorod, Lords of this and Wardens of that?' He gave a snort of exasperation. 'You have spoiled my sleep for the best part of a week, together with that of my two most loyal servants . . .' this with a glance at Thomas and Martin. 'More, you have led us a sorry dance that sent my falconer chasing shadows across the county . . .' The knight drew a breath. 'And all the while you have watched in secret, knowing that what he searched for was but yards from my own kitchen garden!'

Yusupov spread his hands. 'I could ask your pardon, Sir Robert,' he murmured, 'but such words would mean nothing. You will do with me what you wish. As for the deaths that have occurred . . .' The man looked uncomfortable. 'My soul shrinks within me, to think that I may have occasioned them in any way.'

There was a moment, before Rivers gave vent to his curiosity. 'Why in God's name did you go to such lengths – and take such risks?' he cried. 'Do you wish us to believe that this projection was put into effect merely because of your hatred for a cruel master?'

But before Yusupov could answer, Sir Robert broke in. 'What troubles me more is this: was the plan hatched from the beginning, before you came here – before you arrived in England?'

After a moment, the secretary nodded. 'Before I had even left the Tsar's court.'

There were some intakes of breath, whereupon the man met Sir Robert's eye. 'Perhaps you should know what occasioned it, sir,' he murmured. 'Then you would know more of this man whom you trust to take the royal gift to the *boyar* Boris.'

Sir Robert stared at the secretary, then turned to Rivers. 'Well, sir – I confess that having heard one part of the tale, I am reluctant not to hear all of it,' he said. 'You have ridden all day – will you rest here tonight? That will give us both time to consider what we have heard. What say you?'

Rivers needed little persuasion. He nodded and sat back, as eager as his host was to hear Yusupov's words. So too was Thomas; but as the tale unfolded, he found to his surprise that he viewed even the wily secretary, as he had Kovalenko the falconer, through more sympathetic eyes. And along with the other men he listened intently, finding himself taken to a country where a man's breath could freeze in his throat, and his spittle turn to ice before it hit the ground.

But the story began with a childhood romance.

'The girl's name was Nastasya,' Yusupov said softly. 'I knew her all my life, and she was to be my bride. There was never any question about it, for either of us. She was every-thing . . .' He smiled at the memory. 'I was the envy of every man on the estate! Even my family's hopes, that I enter the priesthood, fell away when they saw how it lay. We would marry, and that was all – that was to be my life.'

His smile faded. 'That was when my father was a wealthy man,' he went on, 'before his estate was confiscated – I should say stolen, for that is the true word. It was stolen by the Tsar Ivan – the one you knew of as the Terrible. The one to whom your Queen sent such generous gifts!'

Sir Robert said nothing. And with growing animation Yusupov began to speak, eager now to spill the story he had kept buried within himself. 'That was fourteen winters ago. Years of poverty followed: years in which I fought to educate myself, determined to prosper – to recover by some means my family's good name. But my father was broken. He never recovered from his losses, and he died a poor man.'

Yusupov looked around, saw every face intent upon his. And there was much bitterness in his tone, as he came to the nub of his story. 'One thing – one ray of gold, sustained me through that time: my Nastasya. She understood, for she was as kind as she was beautiful. She did not desert me, as did my boyhood friends – now the Tsar's lackeys, who outdid each other in treachery to win his praise, and what rewards he chose to sprinkle among them!'

The man clenched his fists. But there was no threat: Yusupov was being listened to, and he burned to tell every-thing. 'Nastasya would have married me still,' he cried, 'had she been allowed to live!' He turned to Kovalenko, who met his gaze with sympathetic eyes. And Thomas saw that these men shared a bond greater than he imag-ined. Perhaps the falconer would not have needed much persuasion, he thought, to make him carry out his part of Yusupov's plan.

'Yes, she died . . .' Yusupov eyed Sir Robert. 'She died when a *troika* fell through the ice.' The man lowered his gaze. 'Our lakes can be treacherous in the spring, when you do not see the thin patches beneath the snow. Even with an experienced man holding the reins, such things happen. So I blame not the Russian winter, nor even the ice, Sir Robert . . .' Yusupov's eyes glinted. 'Nor would I blame the man who drove the *troika* – even though he was fortunate, pulled from the water by wood-cutters, half-frozen but alive. Nastasya was not so fortunate. No!' He shook his head vigorously. 'I would not have condemned him – until I learned who he was, this man who was carrying my Nastasya to his house. For the same man, who was drunk and laughing, not looking where he drove . . . the same man is he who I now learned was to be given my father's estate by the Tsar – the new Tsar, Feodor the fool – as a reward for some petty service!' Yusupov trembled with emotion now. 'As this man was to be given the hand of my Nastasya, too, whether she willed it or no! So, he would have every- thing that was once mine! This man,' he went on, 'who was but a poor *boyar* himself, until he saw ways to gain favour!' The secretary looked directly at Sir Robert, and burst out: 'You know his name: it is Grigori Stanic!'

He had done. With a great sigh, he lowered his eyes to the floor. To Thomas, he looked like a man who no longer cared what befell him. But glancing round, he knew the atmosphere of the small chamber had altered. Sir Robert, Rivers and Martin exchanged looks. Even Rivers' silent manservant was staring at Yusupov, as if uncertain how to judge him.

'I do not understand.' Sir Robert's voice broke the spell. 'I cannot fathom you. If you thirsted for vengeance, why forge such an elaborate scheme? Why not simply have the ambassador killed . . . contrive an accident? From what I can see, in your country such matters are easily arranged!'

A bleak smile spread across Yusupov's smooth features. 'You are right,' he answered. 'That would indeed have been easy. Death has a thousand forms, in the winter forests of Muscovy.' He shook his head. 'But where then would be the retribution, for such wrongs as I suffered? No, Sir Robert: believe me, humiliation and ruin are far greater punishments for a man like Grigori Stanic. To lose the valuable royal gift which had been entrusted to him – even if by your neglect, for that would have been brushed aside by the *boyar* Boris – would be a heavy blow. Godunov is not a man of patience: at the least he would take the loss as a slight – at worst, as theft on the part of his own ambassador! And terrible would be the revenge of the Tsar's kinsman, who is almost Tsar himself, upon Grigori Stanic!'

Yusupov's face glowed now, almost as if his plan had succeeded. 'He would lose everything – as I did, as my father did . . . I even had hopes of regaining our family estate, as reward for my loyal service to Godunov. For when I gave him my account, I would paint my own picture of how the chain came to be lost: and on our return to Muscovy – *vide*! It would turn up, in the private baggage of none other than His Excellency!'

There was a collective sigh; of understanding, even tempered with a trace of humour. And it was Rivers who now favoured the ambassador's secretary with a look akin to admiration. 'Well, Master Yusupov,' he said drily. 'I'm almost sorry that we have spoiled your plans.'

The secretary fell silent. His hopes were lost, and his future now lay in the hands of these men. And there was indeed a moment of indecision on the part of Rivers and Sir Robert. Then it was that Thomas, who had been turning the matter about, voiced the notion that leaped to his mind.

'Sir . . . if I might make a suggestion?'

Sir Robert turned.

'Now that the chain is restored to your keeping,' Thomas said, 'could it not merely be replaced where it was? Indeed, would it not then appear as if it had never been stolen?'

Sir Robert stared, then realization dawned.

'You mean – the ambassador need not know?'

Thomas made no reply. Sir Robert glanced at Martin, who looked stunned. The two Russians remained silent, but

both had tensed visibly. Here was a turnabout that neither
had expected.

There was a snort from Sir Thomas Rivers, which Thomas
assumed was one of contempt. So he was as surprised as
anyone when the Privy Councillor gave a shout of laughter.
'By the Christ, falconer, your wits are wasted on hawks!'
he cried. 'You have thrown us a line, in the midst of this
morass . . .'

He turned to Sir Robert. 'In a stroke, sir, you may put
paid to this muddle,' he said. 'The chain and case can be
cleaned, and the case put back in the chest. And there it
will stay – under guard of course – until His Excellency
goes home!'

The man laughed again, and plucking a kerchief from
his sleeve, wiped his eyes. But on this occasion Sir Robert
was not only abreast of the other man's thinking; he was
ahead of him. He turned to Keril Yusupov.

'Well, master secretary – what say you to that?'

Yusupov shook his head. 'I know not what to say, sir,'
he answered. He turned to Kovalenko, who was speechless.
A moment ago he had seen nothing but a grim execution
ahead of him. Now . . .

'You men should cheer yourselves!' Rivers favoured both
the Russians with a broad smile. 'Can you not see that Sir
Robert offers you a bargain?'

'I do see it,' Yusupov answered in a sullen voice. He
faced Sir Robert, but there was no sign of relief on his face.

'You will say nothing to my master, so that you do not
appear remiss in guarding the chain. Hence he may leave
here as contented as he arrived – and as ignorant.' The man
gave one of his cold smiles. 'My part is also to say nothing,
only—'

'Your part, Master Yusupov, is to comprehend mercy when
it's given!' Sir Robert broke in harshly. 'Then to set aside
your thoughts of vengeance, and do your proper office! And
more . . .' The knight could not resist a dry smile at Rivers.
'More – you will find a means to persuade your master that
it is time for him and his train to leave Petbury. Tomorrow
would seem as good a day to me as any!'

Yusupov said nothing. But Kovalenko was frowning at him – and as if a dam had burst, the man once again gave vent to his feelings in his own language. Those present needed no translation, for they could guess the meaning. With a quick bow, the falconer faced Sir Robert.

'It shall be as you say, sir,' he said in a voice of gratitude. 'By whatever means necessary, we will see His Excellency make decision to go home!' He glanced briefly at Thomas. 'Could it be there is sickness, somewhere on the Downs? That is always good reason to leave a place!'

Thomas looked at Sir Robert. 'There are always rumours of plague, in summer,' he said. 'Some turn out to be merely rumours, while others . . .'

Sir Robert nodded. 'True! And as a good host, it's my duty to tell His Excellency at once, so that he may make preparations for his departure!'

He turned to Martin, who had remained frostily silent throughout the debate. But the old man's disapproval had somehow vanished. 'A most satisfying solution, Sir Robert,' he said stiffly. 'While all of us at Petbury will of course be saddened by the departure of His Excellency, it would seem in his best interests . . .' He glanced at Thomas, who almost laughed.

'Then it's settled!' Sir Robert sat back in his chair. To Rivers, he said: 'The evening's upon us already, Sir Thomas – we seem to have been in this room for days! Will you take a walk in the gardens with me before supper?'

Rivers showed his approval, whereupon the knight turned to Thomas, letting him know he was dismissed at last. Thomas too felt that he had spent if not days, then long hours in the small chamber. As he made his way outside, he threw a glance at the two Russians. Kovalenko met his eye, and there was warmth in his gaze. But the secretary merely stared at the floor again. His sadness he wore like a cloak that he could never remove. Indeed, to Thomas it looked as if he did not wish it.

But for him, the day was not done; nor, despite the reappearance of the Muscovy chain, would he find rest in the night that followed. An hour later he was at the mews, awaiting the return of Lady Margaret, Ned and the ambassador's hawking party with some impatience. But while tending the birds that remained, a groom brought him a hasty and badly spelled message, from someone he had almost forgotten. The news sent him hurrying to the stables for a horse, without asking leave of anyone. And as dusk fell, he was galloping down the Hungerford road towards Great Shefford, all thoughts of Russian ambassadors, quests for vengeance and *troikas* crashing through thin ice pushed aside.

John Hodge had set a watch, and it had borne fruit. Not only had the hooded man been sighted: he had been challenged, as he ran along the river. There he had vanished again, but this time the constable was in no doubt: the man had first appeared in the vicinity of Mary Jeap's house. Hodge would search it again, with others; and if Thomas wished to accompany him . . .

Thomas did wish it. And at that moment, not even the Tsar's army could have stopped him.

Fourteen

He found the small knot of men at the end of the village, near the river. They had lit lanterns against the gathering dark, and the lights swayed when they turned on hearing the thud of hooves. Thomas drew rein, and Hodge quickly came forward.

'Well, master – you've made good time!'

Thomas dismounted and gave his greetings. There were three others: village men he knew by sight, each carrying a billet of oak. They gathered about Hodge as he told Thomas his intentions. 'I doubt he's within,' the constable said, jerking his head towards Mary Jeap's house. 'Indeed, I doubt we'll find anything. But I'm mighty suspicious, for something isn't right . . .' He indicated a stocky little man who was closest to him. 'This is Nat Gower – 'twas he saw the hooded fellow. Tell it again – only make it short.'

Nat Gower nodded eagerly. 'I done my watch as I was bid,' he said to Thomas. 'It was near suppertime, I'd seen naught, so I was off home. Then I saw him, close by the riverbank.' The man pointed into the gloom. 'He moved fast . . . and he had a way of moving, near made my skin crawl. Like . . .'

'Like a dog?' Thomas asked sharply. But the other shook his head.

'Nay – more like a lizard! I shouted, but he darted off. No one else saw him, for the light was going. But 'twas by the hood I knew him: black, like a monk's garb!'

Thomas started. The hooded cloak had puzzled him: a rarity for a woman, let alone a man – or at least, an Englishman. But a monk's cowl . . .

'Which way did he go?' he asked.

Gower shrugged, whereupon Hodge answered. 'We don't know – but he didn't cross the bridge, or he would've been seen.' The constable showed his impatience. 'There's no sense us searching in the dark – but we can shake Mistress Jeap up a little!' He eyed Thomas. 'I wish you and me had been a bit more thorough last time, Master Finbow. I told you she's hidden fugitives before – though for the life of me I don't know where. But this time I'm not leaving until I find out!'

The talking was done. Thomas tethered the horse, and joined the other men as they set off in a determined body along the riverside path. The big house loomed ahead of them, lights burning from several windows. As they drew close the noise of male laughter rose, along with a familiar sound: that of Mary Jeap's lute. Without slowing his pace, John Hodge strode up to the heavy door and banged on it.

As before, it was opened quickly. But at the sight of several armed men, the Cerberus fell back. 'What's this?' he cried. 'And by whose warrant are you come—'

'Here's my warrant!' Hodge retorted, and raised his fist. And though there was anger in the big man's eyes, he backed away along the passage. As the Shefford men crowded into the house, the fellow turned and rapped upon the closed door. At once the strains of the lute ceased, and the door opened to reveal a smiling Mistress Jeap, dressed in her evening finery. But at sight of the intruders, her smile vanished.

'By the Christ, it's high time I swore out a warrant against you, John Hodge! You invade my house, frighten my girls, and—'

'And I'll do it again!' Hodge threw back. 'Only this time I'll tear walls down, if I have to. And if you've harboured a murderer, Mary Jeap – whether we catch him or no – I'll take you to Reading myself, tied to a cart's tail, with a sign round your neck for all of Berkshire to view!'

He had described the common punishment for a pander; but Mistress Jeap was no common bawd. Reddening beneath her periwig, she faced Hodge down. 'Search again, then!' she shouted. 'And when you find naught, and you slink out that door, I'll be watching the whole pack of you, and laughing till I wet myself!'

Hodge did not reply. Angrily he gestured to the others, who began their task with some relish. Their heavy boots thundered on the stairs, causing shouts from above. Soon they had gained the top floor and were forcing their way into dimly lit chambers, disturbing men and women in their passions, or at least in their undress. There were angry words, and Nat Gower even found himself facing a drawn poniard. But at the sight of Thomas's tall frame looming behind him, the antagonist fell back with an oath. Thereafter there was little resistance as the constable's men roamed every floor, coming close to ransacking the house in their enthusiasm.

But for Thomas, it was clear that this enterprise was as fruitless as the last. With Hodge he had been in these rooms only two days before, and once again he found nothing untoward. With the others he knocked on ceilings and panels, opened closets and peered up chimneys. And there was small need for the constable to tear down the walls as he had threatened, for they examined every one. But if there were any hidden space – an old priest's hiding hole, or even a chest with a false base – they did not find it. Considerably deflated, the group assembled at the foot of the stairs, while Mary Jeap's girls assailed them from above with cries of outrage, along with choice slurs on their manhood. Those customers who had not left in a hurry remained out of sight, seemingly confident of the party's taking their leave. And much to the constable's chagrin, a humiliating departure now seemed the only course.

Mistress Jeap stood with arms folded, wearing a triumphant smile. Once again Thomas met her eye, but read nothing. There was a stiffness about her neck, he thought, that might have been due to the starched ruff she wore above her gown of crimson sarsenet. Below its low, square-cut neckline her chest rose and fell rapidly.

'See our guests out, Samuel.' The bawd spoke in a matter-of-fact tone to the doorkeeper. 'And make sure they don't thieve anything as they go!'

Hodge was seething, but he was helpless. With a glare at the woman, he said: 'I may not be back for a while, mistress. But when I do come I'll wipe that smirk from your face, for I'll have a signed warrant, and a parcel of sheriff's men at my back – and they won't want to leave empty-handed. Mayhap they'll burn this nest of whores to the ground!'

Mary Jeap seemed not to hear. She gestured to Samuel, who shoved his way roughly past the group to the front door. But just then, Thomas's glance once again fell on the nearby door to the cellar, which he recalled had been flooded. He turned to the bawd.

'You won't mind if I look down there, would you mistress?' he asked mildly.

Mary Jeap scowled. 'Please yourself, long-shanks. Only I'd take your boots and stocks off first, if I were you.'

With a frown, Hodge bent close to Thomas. 'I've no mind to waste more time,' he said. 'Let's walk the river, see if there's any trace.'

His voice was dull with shame. But Thomas gestured to the door. 'Then let me waste my time, John,' he said. 'There's no disgrace on you, if it's another fool's errand.'

Hodge sighed. 'I'm in disgrace already,' he said. 'Look, then – though what you think to find I can't guess.'

Thomas glanced at Samuel, who hesitated. Then at a sign from his mistress he lifted the latch and pushed the door open. Raising his lantern, Hodge peered down. Again there came a rippled gleam, along with the sound of dripping water. He drew back, and without a word handed the lantern to Thomas.

Holding it before him, Thomas began descending the steps, which creaked alarmingly under his weight. The water appeared, dark and sluggish. The steps vanished beneath it, yet he continued to descend. His boots were soon covered, the noisome floodwater swirling about his knees, but ignoring its coldness he gained the bottom step and felt the floor underfoot. Then, standing waist-deep in the water, he raised the lantern and looked about. To his right was the side nearest the river, which had invaded the cellar with ease. Great runnels of lime and mould streaked the wall above the water-line, where the mortar was badly crumbled. Glancing above, his head barely clearing the ceiling, Thomas saw cracks in the stonework.

The cold water was soaking his breeches. By what instinct he had come down he did not know, yet he stayed. Suppressing a shiver, he held the lantern at arm's length, so that its light was thrown on the far wall, to his left – whereupon he stiffened. Then he shouted, at the top of his voice.

'John Hodge! Come down here – now!'

But from above, out of his view, there was a sudden commotion – a cry, then another, then a scuffle followed by rapid footsteps. And even as Thomas turned and stumbled up the stairs, he guessed what had caused it. He pushed into the hallway – only to see the front door wide open, and two figures disappearing into the gloom. After them, bumping into each other, went Hodge's men, cursing as they ran.

But Hodge appeared at Thomas's elbow – and to his surprise, the constable was smiling. 'You found something, didn't you!' he cried. 'I knew it – even before you shouted I knew, and so did Jeap! She took off like a rabbit, and that great bullfrog with her!' The man's eyes shone in the lantern-light. 'We rattled her, Master Thomas! When I thought we'd lost, you risked another throw – and you were right! We shook the old hen after all, clean out of her wits!'

At last the man paused, and fixed Thomas with an eager look. 'Now – will you show me what it is?'

It was a wall of stone and roughcast, built across the cellar from one side to the other to form a very narrow room behind. Not all of the wall, however, reached to the roof: a section of it stopped short – a section wide enough for a man to pass through, to the space beyond. This opening in fact, Thomas saw, could have been closed off with a board, making the hidden room all but invisible to anyone who chanced to come down here. Though seeing the flood, he thought, few would have wished to investigate the place. And now, as he and John Hodge descended with lanterns, he saw a wooden plank floating by the wall, and gave a sigh of satisfaction: this was how the occupant gained access to his secret chamber. Once inside, he could draw the plank in after him, and close up the gap.

One thing puzzled him: the water level – but that question would be answered soon enough. Eagerly now, the two men waded across the waterlogged cellar. With difficulty, and help from Thomas, Hodge climbed into the opening and shone his lantern inside. Then he called out. 'Come in, and look at this! It's snug as a badger's holt!'

He jumped down inside and disappeared. Thomas clambered into the space after him, struggling to get his long legs through. But when he had eased himself down on the other side of the false wall, he too showed his surprise. For it was indeed as snug as an animal's burrow – and as dry, too.

Because of the narrowness of the chamber, which was in fact more like a passageway, there was just room for a straw pallet at one end. Closer to was an upturned cask with a stub of candle on it. There were a couple of sheepskins for warmth – for despite its dry floor, the room was clammy with damp. Nevertheless, it was the most perfect hiding place Thomas had ever seen. He turned to Hodge, who was gazing about him in amazement.

'Jesu . . . I don't know how long this has been here, or who built it. I'll wager none but Jeap and her people know of it . . . but I see now where she's hid men before – and where this murdering cove's been holed up!'

'Yet he's gone,' Thomas said, his voice flat in the narrow space. Holding the lantern up, he circled the chamber. 'There's no trace of anyone. No clothes – not a crumb of food.' He sighed. 'He's too clever to leave a sign, as he's too clever to come back. He's flown, Master Hodge; and once again, he could be anywhere.'

Hodge nodded. 'Still I'm in your debt, Master Thomas – for no fugitive will be able to hide here again!' He gestured to the opening. 'I've seen enough – will you go first?'

They climbed out through the small entrance, dropped down and waded across the flooded cellar. But glancing back towards the false wall, Thomas halted. 'I see why it's dry behind there,' he said. And he felt a grudging respect for the cunning of the design. Raising the lantern, he pointed. 'Whoever the builder was, he knew what to do. He water-proofed the wall, with tarred leather.'

Hodge followed his outstretched arm; then he frowned. 'One thing troubles me: the way the river seeps through that thick stone so easily . . .' He peered at the far wall, then let out a shout of laughter. 'See now – this cellar didn't let water in of its own accord: it's been flooded on purpose! I'll wager if we searched long enough we'd find a loose block that can be pulled out, then put back to plug the gap!'

Thomas nodded. 'And what if the stone was big enough, or if there were more than one? Might that not be a hidden way out? So that by night, our man—'

'Could come and go as he pleased!' Hodge finished. He shook his head, almost in admiration. 'Well, between us we've teased it out. Now I don't know how it is with you, but I've done enough bathing to last me until Christmas. Shall we go up?'

Despite his great size, Samuel the doorkeeper had escaped.

That much became clear when, a few minutes later, Nat Gower and the other men returned, sweating and out of breath. Yet they were triumphant, for Mary Jeap had been less fortunate. They had caught her on the far side of the bridge, tugging off her shoes. They would have caught Samuel too, had he not downed one man with a single blow, causing the others to halt. They could hardly leave their fellow, they explained, though it soon became clear his bleeding was due to nothing worse than a split nose. As for Samuel: they thought it more important to bring Mistress Jeap back at once. So her servant was allowed to disappear in the dark.

But John Hodge was elated with his success, and magnan-imous in excusing his men. He sent two off to tell the occu-pants the bawdy-house was closed down, and all its customers should make themselves scarce. Meanwhile he, Thomas and Nat marched Mary Jeap into her parlour. The room was bright with candles and comfortably furnished. But the bawd, cold-faced and silent, refused Hodge's request to sit. She stood before the curtained window, and despite the fact that she was barefoot, faced the constable with her defiance intact. Without delay, the man spoke up.

'How long has he been hiding down there?' he asked.

The woman did not answer.

'Let me guess,' the constable went on. 'Four days – five? Was it Saturday he came here, or Sunday?' But for reply, he received only a look of contempt.

'Do you know what that man did?' Thomas asked. When still no answer came, he looked to Hodge. 'Will you tell her how John Doggett's body looked, or shall I?'

Hodge opened his mouth – whereupon the bawd spoke in a shrill voice. 'If I give testimony, 'twill be to a magistrate! You men have no right to question me!'

'The one you harboured had no right to question either,' Thomas countered. 'Yet he did – and those he interrogated died in agony, their bodies awash with blood—'

'It's naught to me!' Mary Jeap cried. 'I've harmed no one . . .' For the first time, the woman showed her anxiety. 'You can arraign me – but for nothing worse than giving a man shelter. I knew not who he was, or what he did—'

'You're lying!' Hodge's anger rose again. 'The whole village knows of the body we pulled from under the bridge – not fifty yards from this house! And a walk in the other direction takes you to a torture hut, where he carved his prisoner up like a slab of mutton! You let this devil go in and out at will, to commit whatever villainy he pleased! What did he pay you, Mary Jeap? I hope it was a goodly sum!'

'He paid me nothing!'

The words flew from her in a shriek; and the moment they were uttered she regretted them. Quickly she regained her control, but her eyes flicked towards Thomas's, and she saw that he had understood.

'No . . . he did not need to, did he?' Thomas gave her a grim look, and turned to Hodge. 'Mayhap you should ask what he threatened to do to her, if she didn't agree to his demands.'

There was a silence. The three men watched Mary Jeap, whose eyes remained upon Thomas. Then at last, she moved. Seizing a cup from a small table she drank from it, before sinking into a chair.

'Well?' Hodge glared at her. 'Will you not speak of that, at least? Then I might view you as human, instead of the she-devil I thought!'

The bawd stared at the cup in her hand. Finally she threw her head back, drained it and set it down. 'He did not need to threaten,' she said, so quietly that the others strained to hear. 'He but told me what he did to a woman in France. Where he placed the knife, and how he worked it. He smiled when he told me.'

She hesitated, then put a hand to her chest. 'He gave me a little sign,' she said, 'of what would follow if I did not do his bidding . . . *uno assaggio*, he called it.'

And as the three men watched, she pulled down the edge of her gown to show a small, livid scar on her breast. Then she looked up and met Hodge's gaze.

'You know not who you deal with,' she said in a cold voice. 'He likes his work. The night he came I welcomed him, for he was not without means. I offered him one of the maids, but he had no taste for that . . .' She looked away. 'I know now what he is: a demon.'

'He's a man!' Thomas said. And the harshness of his tone made the others look round sharply. For he saw the puny, lacerated body of Will Corder; and in his mind rang the shrieks of the boy's mother. 'He's but a man,' he repeated. 'Wicked and of cruel appetite, perhaps – but mortal. He works for money. He came here on a commission, and he cannot afford to fail. Perhaps the consequences for him if he does are grave . . .' He glanced at Hodge, then back at Mary Jeap. 'At least you can tell the constable all you know, so that it helps his search.'

But the woman shook her head. 'Search as you will,' she said dully. 'Corvino will always be gone before you. And he will not give up, until he has what he wants.'

She paused, then: 'I know not what he seeks. But I know he does not bluff. He would do to me all he described – and

he saw that I knew it. He's the only man I've met of whom
I am truly afraid.'

The bawd seemed to be drifting into memory. But when
she looked up at Hodge again, it was with her old brazen-
ness.

'The name he gives is Corvino,' she said. 'He minds not
who knows that, for it's but a colour in his language. *Jet
black* it means, like the monk's robe he wears . . .' She
smiled faintly. 'And as for describing him, what does that
matter? You will never see him again – unless he wishes
you to!'

The night brought a high wind that shook the windows of
John Hodge's cottage. Thomas accepted his invitation to
sleep in the parlour, and was able to snatch a few hours'
rest before the dawn. He was already outside and dousing
himself from a pail when the constable emerged from the
house.

There was little to be said. Thomas would ride back to
Petbury and make report to Sir Robert. Hodge would confine
Mary Jeap as a prisoner until he received instruction from
the sheriff of Berkshire. Mistress Jeap's girls had vanished
in the night, leaving the house empty. Along with the doorkeeper, they were never seen again.

As for continuing the search for the one they now knew
as Corvino . . . Hodge was doubtful. In view of what they
had learned, where should he look?

Thomas had no answer. Taking leave of the constable he
rode back to Petbury, reaching the manor as smoke began to
rise from the chimneys. After returning the horse to the stable
he went first to the cottage, but found it empty: Nell had
stayed in the kitchens again. He changed into a fresh shirt
and breeches, then hurried out to the mews. Ned had not yet
arrived, but he saw that the falcons were on their perches
and had been well tended. Though there was a restlessness
about the great white hawk, that made him uneasy. He came
out again, took a lungful of morning air. The wind had
dropped and the clouds were drifting, promising a fair day.
Exercise was what the bird needed . . . He gazed downhill at

the house, hearing the familiar sounds of the manor coming to life. Sir Robert would still be abed, and he must wait before seeking an audience. His mind drifted back to the previous day, and to the confessions of Yusupov and Kovalenko. He thought of the bargain his master had struck: if all went as Sir Robert hoped, there was every chance the ambassador and his retinue would leave today. Then perhaps things could begin to return to something akin to normal life; that thought, at least, cheered him a little.

He glanced towards the path that skirted the kitchen garden, expecting to see Ned come hurrying along at any moment. If the boy was late, what of it? He had done the work of two men in recent days. To Thomas's mind, he had been remiss in leaving him alone. He would try to make amends . . .

A noise, very faint . . . He turned, thinking it sounded like a groan. It came from behind the mews. He listened, and heard nothing more; but he walked round the side of the wooden hut anyway, hearing the birds stir within. He walked round the back, which was hidden from the house . . . and stopped.

A figure was lying slumped against the wall of the mews. Stifling a cry, Thomas darted forward and dropped to his knees beside the man, who opened his eyes. It was Pavel Kovalenko. And one glance at the clothing, which was torn to shreds – let alone at the caked blood beneath – told Thomas all he needed.

His breath caught in his throat, as he bent over the ravaged body of the falconer. Gently he put his hand under the man's head and cradled it. It was a miracle he was still alive, after losing so much blood.

'My friend . . .' Though his voice was almost inaudible, relief showed in Kovalenko's eyes. He would not die alone, as he must have expected. How long he had lain here in the grass, Thomas could only guess: the best part of the night, by the state of him.

'I came here to say my farewell . . . to Dushenka,' the Russian whispered. 'For we go home tomorrow.' A rasp came from his throat. 'I mean today. Is good, Master Thomas. I not want to die in the dark.'

'There's no need to speak,' Thomas said, struggling with the emotion that welled up. 'I know what happened – I know who did this.'

'You know?' Kovalenko was surprised. 'I not see his face. But Dushenka heard him . . . she rouse on perch, afraid. So I leave her – then when I come out, he take me!' The man gave a cough and tried to move, but he was too weak. Thomas peered into the chalk-white face, and forced a smile.

'We must get you to the house, Master Pavel. My wife makes the best porridge in Berkshire. Salty, hot as coals – and thick enough to stand a spoon in!'

The other man's mouth widened slowly. Then his smile faded, to be replaced by a worried frown. 'I told him, Master Thomas,' he said. 'He knew I would tell what he wanted . . . he's one who understands pain. We have such men in Muscovy, too . . .' He closed his eyes briefly, then opened them. 'I could not bear any more: I told him where the chain is.'

Thomas stiffened. 'Think not upon that,' he said. 'My master and I will deal with this man. He'll not succeed. I swear it to you!'

Another sigh escaped Kovalenko's lips, which had turned an alarming shade of purple. He tried to nod, but his strength was gone. His eyes closed, then opened for the last time.

'My wife too was fine cook,' he whispered.

Then he died.

Thomas laid the falconer's head on the damp grass, and sat back. That was how Ned Hawes found him, a short while later, still staring down at the face of the man who told him he was little more than a slave.

Now at last, he was free.

Fifteen

H is Excellency Grigori Stanic had never shown the true force of his anger in all the days he had spent at Petbury. That much became apparent later in the morning, when the man was roused from his bed to learn that his falconer had been murdered. And the furore that followed in the great hall would remain famous in the manor's folklore for years to come.

Sir Robert too, was beside himself. Having gone to his own bed relieved at the turn of events, he had risen in the expectation that his guests would be packing up to leave. He had even ordered the grooms to ready the Russians' cart. Instead he found Martin the steward waiting with news that made him stagger to a chair.

Sir Thomas Rivers was already up, as was Lady Margaret. So when the ambassador finally appeared in the hall, it looked suspiciously as if his English hosts had closed ranks against him. Whereupon the man gave vent to a deafening tirade, the like of which not even Rivers had heard before. Mercifully, it being in the Russian's language, no one could understand it. And on this occasion Yusupov, who stood in silence behind his master, did not even attempt to interpret but let His Excellency rage at will.

Outdoors there was calm, though fear now gripped the manor as it had not done before – not after the death of John Doggett, nor even that of Will Corder. The body of Pavel Kovalenko, on Yusupov's instruction, was wrapped from head to foot and laid in the chapel. The secretary, who was up early, had been first to hear the news. And though it had shaken him to the core, Thomas was relieved to see the man summon his reserves, and become businesslike.

He would inform his master, he said. And whatever happened, no one should deny the ambassador anything. His every whim must be indulged, or his anger would be terrible, and it could fall on anyone. Eventually, when it had spent itself, Yusupov said, His Excellency would stop, and would then make a big show of grief. It was at this point that his secretary would impress upon him the need for a speedy departure from Petbury. This was an unwholesome place, he would say. There were devils here – and likely sickness, too. His Excellency must collect the Queen's gift and take his leave. The packing would be done quickly . . . as for Kovalenko: it would be impossible to transport his body all the way back to Muscovy. He would have to be buried here, where he had died. It was the least Sir Robert could do. As for hunting down the murderer: let the English take care of that, too.

And so, it fell out. And having begun his day being plunged into gloom, Sir Robert strived to put a brave face on the events. With the departure of the chain, he ventured to suggest, the danger would surely pass with it – away from Petbury. Exhausted by the whole business, he confided as much to Sir Thomas Rivers, after the ambassador had finally come to the end of his rant and stormed off to his chamber.

But Rivers did not like the notion at all. The thought of this murderer being free to learn of the chain leaving Petbury – even perhaps to waylay the ambassador's party on their journey – filled him with alarm. Nor did Sir Robert's offer to provide an armed escort all the way reassure him: they were dealing with no common thief, he retorted. Whatever the reasons for this man's obsessive quest, he suggested, there was some driving force behind it, and it troubled him greatly.

He and Sir Robert left the house to walk in the gardens, both men pleading headaches after the fury they had endured in the great hall. Lady Margaret walked with them while Martin trudged behind, leaning on his staff of office. There Thomas was at last summoned to attend them, around midday, and to tell his tale in full: from receiving Hodge's message the evening before, to the events at Mary Jeap's house, and finally his discovery of the dying Kovalenko. When he had done, it was difficult to judge who was more shocked: the master and mistress of Petbury, or the Privy Councillor.

'It's a shambles, sir!' Rivers said, not for the first time that day. 'I've no choice but to make full report to the Lord Lieutenant – and to the Queen's Council. There's some purpose behind this . . . someone perhaps who has a strong interest in the chain never reaching Muscovy. Whoever he is, we have woefully underestimated him. And what is more, your reliance on plodding villagers as instruments of justice has made you a laughing stock!'

Sir Robert was too chastened to reply. He threw a forlorn look at his wife, who was walking between the two of them.

'Indeed, Sir Thomas . . .' Lady Margaret was at her most sympathetic. 'It is all most distressing. You must do as you think fit . . . we have but tried to do our duty, in entertaining the ambassador at Petbury. It was not my husband's wish that the chain come here – indeed, perhaps it would have been better kept in the Tower under guard, and presented to His Excellency as he left England.'

Rivers frowned. 'The whole object, my lady, was not to attract too much attention to the bauble,' he replied testily. 'In that regard we have failed dismally. All of us!' he added, seeing Sir Robert's wounded look.

Lady Margaret did not answer. Instead she exchanged a private glance with Thomas. If anyone had the resources to find a way out of this difficulty, she seemed to be saying, it was he. And indeed, having turned the matter about all morning, a notion had occurred to Thomas – though one he hesitated to suggest. But drawing a breath, he made bold to outline the plan as cogently as he could.

Corvino – who now seemed to know his way about the manor well enough – had left Kovalenko for dead. He did not expect his victim to live until morning – hence, he did not know that others were aware that he now knew the whereabouts of the Muscovy chain. Given the man's dogged persistence, it seemed likely to Thomas that he would make a final attempt to steal it before the Russians left – which meant tonight. It was no secret that Mikhailov and Piotr were already packing the ambassador's belongings, but the day was too far advanced now to begin the journey to London. The word from Yusupov was that the party would leave early next morning – by which time Corvino, if he had the chain, would expect to be far away. A locked window, Thomas thought, should present no obstacle to such a man. A locked chest . . . he shrugged: they would have to count on his self-confidence. But in any case, by the time he had reached that, the trap would have been sprung.

The trap? They heard Thomas out in silence, if not with unease. Whereupon Sir Robert was quick to make objection.

'The risk is too great,' he said. 'At the first sign of armed men about the place, this rogue will know what we're about. It's clear he's as cunning as the devil! And if we have too few posted – well, from what I can discern, he seems able to overpower a small army by himself!' He frowned. 'Besides, there's been enough blood spilled on Petbury soil. I won't have it in the house – especially in my private sanctuary.'

But Sir Thomas Rivers gave one of his disdainful snorts. 'Is that your chief concern, sir?' he asked. 'Do you not see an opportunity here to redeem yourself? Surely you agree that if a chance exists to apprehend this devil before he wreaks further havoc, we should take it! Moreover . . . not only has your falconer reasoned well: I have an inkling he also has an interest in being a party to the man's capture.' He turned to Thomas, and there was respect in his gaze. 'Do I hit the mark, Master Finbow?'

'You do, sir,' Thomas replied.

'And would you be one of those who lies in wait?'

Thomas nodded. 'Two or three well-armed men could hide in the chamber. I could speak with Gale the constable – we should have men outside too, well concealed but ready to come at a signal.' He faced Sir Robert. 'There is indeed a risk, sir; but the prize is great. And I would ask your blessing in doing my utmost to seize it—'

'Or die in the attempt?' Sir Robert blurted. Unhappily he turned to Lady Margaret, who gave him a sardonic look.

'What other course do you propose, sir?' she asked. 'There have been deaths already . . . the Lord Lieutenant himself will soon know how many. Your duty is to dispense justice here. The goodwill of His Excellency the ambassador is not our only concern – nor even is it the safe despatch of the Muscovy chain. What of the fears of our own people, indeed of all the Downland folk, if this murderer is not caught?'

After a moment Sir Robert sighed. 'Well, then . . .' He looked at Thomas. 'There's none at Petbury more skilled at trapping wild creatures than you. Though this is no dumb beast . . .' The knight looked away. 'And even you may find yourself put beyond your limits this time. I pray to God you will succeed!'

There was a flaw in the plan: Tertius Gale.

That was clear to Thomas even before he went to Chaddleworth and acquainted the constable with the whole tale. And when he realized how little he had been told of recent events, the man took immediate offence.

'So: your case of jewels that went missing, was a royal gift – of which a man of my humble office was to be kept in ignorance!' He wore one of his severe looks. 'Though Hodge down at Shefford seems to know all about it . . . and now you tell me there's been another death in my parish. On top of all this, you ask my help! When it looks like the search I've made – to which good men have given time of their own free will – has been naught but wasted effort!'

The man's long neck craned alarmingly. 'Well, Master Finbow – since you're jack-a-dandy who knows so much, suppose I tell you to deal with the matter yourself?'

Thomas sighed. 'I thought it was Will Greve you searched for,' he said. 'Have you had no sight of him?'

Gale bristled. 'I suppose you know well enough that I haven't!'

'I didn't know,' Thomas replied. 'But as for calling on

you for help, it's Sir Robert who does so. I ask pardon for
not telling you all. I was bound to secrecy.'

He looked Gale in the eye, and there was an edge to his
voice. 'Do you know what a bitter taste I've borne since
Will Corder died?' he demanded. 'You knew the boy, as I
did – is not the chance to avenge him enough?'

Gale said nothing.

'All I ask is that you assemble a few good men,' Thomas
persisted. 'To come to Petbury and keep watch. I'll wait in
the chamber where the chain is kept. Then tonight if—'

'If this murderer comes, you will snatch him and reap
the reward!' the constable sneered. 'No doubt your master
will show his gratitude as always . . .' He gave a grim smile.
' 'Tis no secret how Lady Margaret regards her loyal falconer
– and now I hear your daughter entertains the Muscovy
men in the park. Mayhap she's had more sight of Will Greve
than I've had!'

Thomas stood up. 'I was unsure whether to come to you,
master,' he said quietly. 'I should have heeded my own
doubts. We'll mount our own watch, of Petbury folk.
Gardeners, grooms and servingmen they may be – and likely
frightened out of their wits. But after what happened to
young Will, they'll risk their lives readily enough. And I
doubt the notion of reward will occur to any of them.'

At that Gale also stood up, the two of them face to face
in his tiny parlour. 'Don't you preach at me, Finbow!' he
cried. 'I'll do my office! I came to your aid before – who
was it went to the Dagger seeking the men who beat you?
Your master knows as well as any that Tertius Gale is a
man of honour!'

Thomas made no reply. Outside the bell of St Andrew's
suddenly clanged. There was a moment, before the constable
seemed to collect himself.

'I've known the Corders all my life, like you,' he said.
'And I wager there will be no shortage of Chaddleworth
men to avenge the boy . . . But you may do me a service
in return.'

Thomas eyed him. 'What's that?'

'You can show you respect me – by letting me wait with

you in the chamber where this chain lies. Then if our efforts bear fruit, you let me make the arrest. That will be my reward!'

It was not as Thomas wished, but this was no summer stroll he had embarked on. And any man who knew what Corvino had done and was yet willing to face him did indeed deserve respect. He gave a nod.

'So be it,' he said. 'Only if I were you, I'd arm myself with more than an oak billet this time.'

Gale did not answer.

It was a long night. Quiet had settled over Petbury, broken only by the calls of night birds and the snicker of horses in the paddock. The men Tertius Gale had brought, some half a dozen in number, had been positioned since dusk at strategic points about the manor, with instructions to remain out of sight. Others – gardeners and grooms, as Thomas had said – were also hiding, armed with whatever weapons Sir Robert would provide. Meanwhile, in the great hall, he and Sir Thomas Rivers, neither of whom could have slept even if he wished, sat up by candlelight with a jug of strong water to sustain them.

In Sir Robert's private chamber, Thomas and Gale waited in silence. Indeed, they had not exchanged a word since the constable's arrival. He had accepted Thomas's suggestion, and lay in a dark corner where he could not be seen by anyone climbing through the window. Thomas had chosen a point against the side wall near to Sir Robert's table, from where he had a clear view not only of the window but of the iron-bound chest. The chest, like the window, was locked; but the Muscovy chain was not inside it. Rivers had been adamant on that score, and would take no chances. The case was there, but anyone who succeeded in taking it, whatever the odds against such an event, would find it contained nothing but a few horseshoes to give it weight.

Thomas had ceased to notice the stiffness in his limbs. He sat on the rush-strewn floor, and had forbidden himself to change position. His poniard was unsheathed, and lay beside him. He could not see Gale, nor to his relief had the

man made a sound. From time to time Thomas squinted at
the window, a latticed casement through which a faint
glimmer of moonlight had showed earlier. But that seemed
a long time ago now. Clouds had drifted in, bringing the
threat of more rain. His hope was that if Corvino made an
appearance, the weather might prove a hindrance to him
and a help to his capturers. But somehow he doubted it.

Corvino . . . he had had more than enough time, these
past hours, to think about the man he faced. His mind had
drifted back to the first sighting of the hooded figure, by a
hysterical Lady Jane Rooke. Who could have imagined what
was to follow: the torture and cruel deaths of Doggett and
Will Corder – and the discovery that all along their murderer
had been hidden in the cellar of Mary Jeap's bawdy-house.
Then, the murder of Kovalenko, which had changed everything. To Thomas's mind it now seemed a miracle that
Corvino had only now discovered where the chain was.
Sitting cramped against the wall, he turned the matter over
once again, shaking his head slowly. Until the previous
afternoon the chain had not been here either, but hidden in
a keg of stinking caviar. By some quirk of fate, when
Corvino had finally managed to seize someone who could
tell him where it was, he was almost too late. And had
Kovalenko not gone outside to say farewell to the great
white falcon . . .

He drew a deep breath, forcing himself to concentrate
on what mattered. Regrets were useless, while the capture
of Corvino was everything. Though Thomas knew only too
well that he had staked all on this one hope: that a man
like Corvino would not – perhaps could not – leave the
Downlands empty-handed.

But now the night was almost spent. Stiff and tired,
Thomas forced aside the disappointment that threatened to
overwhelm him. He did not know the time, but guessed it
was barely an hour before dawn. From across the room, he
heard Gale stir at last. The constable must be as uncomfortable as he was; his only hope was that the man would
not give in to despair, and abandon the watch. But how
long should they wait? Corvino only ever worked by night;

Thomas was certain of that. The fellow must have a cat's eyes, he thought grimly, to see so well in the dark. Not for the first time he fell to wondering what he looked like under that hood. And Mary Jeap's words came back to mock him: *You will never see him – unless he wishes you to!*

He bit his lip, so hard that the pain made him wince. For he knew that he had almost fallen asleep, and berated himself. He blinked, wondering at last if he should call out to Gale. Perhaps he could risk movement, and rub some life into his limbs. Then he frowned: what if the constable had fallen asleep?

A click.

Thomas caught his breath, alert in an instant. Focusing on the window, he waited . . . then felt his neck hairs spring up. For with a suddenness that surprised him a figure appeared, crouching by the casement, fingers working deftly. There was a scrape of metal, another click, then the faint squeal of hinges. At once the window swung wide, and a man was climbing through the opening.

Thomas was motionless. Across the room, he knew by instinct that Gale too was alert. But mercifully the incomer had no knowledge of their presence, for he did not wait to check if he was safe. In the near-darkness he simply moved around the great chest and stooped to examine the lid. Then he fumbled in his robe – for a robe it was, after all – and brought out something that jangled. Bending to his task the man fitted keys to the lock, selecting and rejecting them in turn. Finally there was a squeal and a clatter as the heavy mechanism yielded. It was then the work of a moment for the thief to throw back the lid.

His pulse racing, Thomas's immediate thought was that the man had no light – how would he see the case? The plan was that he be allowed to take it before he was apprehended. Tense in every muscle, Thomas prepared to spring. He could only hope the numbness in his limbs would not impede him. Surely he should wait no longer? But the next moment the decision was taken out of his hands – for from the other side of the room came a voice that made his heart sink.

'Hold! You are arrested by an officer of this parish! Stand still, or be taken by force!'

What followed was like a puppet play Thomas had once seen – but faster, and in almost total dark. He scrambled to his feet, feeling the blood rush to his legs, pausing only to snatch up his poniard. Across the room he sensed that Gale too had risen – but his eyes were on the figure before him. And in a moment he saw what would happen – even as he knew that he was powerless to stop it.

Corvino did not spring. He seemed to glide over the few feet of floor that separated him from the constable. There followed a dreadful scream: and it was made by Tertius Gale. Thomas thought he heard the knife sink into flesh, a second before the cry. But it mattered not; the constable was a vague shape, slumping to the floor. While his assailant . . .

He turned with the agility of a cat, dropping to a crouch, his face a blur. Thomas crouched too, the handle of his poniard cold in his palm. He was aware of Gale groaning in the corner, but his every sense was tuned to his opponent. Oddly, his comforting thought was that the man had not succeeded in stealing the case.

'You won't get clear. There are men outside.'

Thomas's own voice came hoarsely from his throat, after so many hours of silence. But he wanted to speak – to engage with this man, to make some beginning. He wanted it, very badly now; and yes – Sir Robert's hasty words flew into his thoughts: even if he died in the attempt . . .

Corvino made no answer. Instead he lunged, so suddenly that Thomas was wrong-footed. He barely saw the knife – a faint, fleeting gleam – as it cleaved the air. But he felt it – as he felt relief: for it had missed his body, and merely pierced his arm.

The pain made him hiss. Again he faced an assailant in the dark, as he had faced two, on the road near the Dagger Inn. How long ago that now seemed . . . he made a thrust with his poniard, but found only empty space. For the other man was faster, and far more accurate. Without any waste of effort, he sliced through Thomas's upper arm, severing the artery.

The pain doubled, but Thomas no longer cared. And though blood pumped warm and wet through his jerkin, he paid it no heed. He spoke again.

'You can kill me, but it won't help. You were expected.'

Still there was no reply. Perhaps he understood little English, Thomas thought, fighting the growing numbness in his left arm. At least in the other he still had the poniard. He made a sweep with it, having a notion that he could force his opponent back, away from the window. Surely Gale's cry would have alerted someone?

It didn't work. Indeed whatever he tried, he knew this man would anticipate him. Buying time was not the answer. As Thomas lunged, the other simply twisted away. *Like a lizard*, Nat Gower had said . . . His arm was becoming heavy now. Desperately he struck out again. But all he got for his effort was a blinding pain across his hand that made him stagger – and drop his poniard.

There was a moment that seemed long to Thomas, though it was merely seconds. Feeling the blood well from the deep cut, he kicked out. To his surprise his foot found a target. And for the first time the other man made a sound, though it was only a grunt. But it made no difference . . . Thomas was out of his depth this time, and he knew it. Was it pride had made him think he and a clumsy village constable could overcome such a one as this? He was alarmed, for he had almost lost his balance. His hope was that the other would want to make his escape while he still could. And that looked like a strong possibility . . .

A noise, but not from outside the window. It came from beyond the door – and there followed a voice. Someone was in the passage! Now, Thomas cried out.

'He's in here! To arms!'

The last words he directed towards the open casement. And at last there came a distant shout. At the same time the door of the chamber was flung open . . .

But Corvino was not to be taken; indeed, he appeared quite unhurried. Ignoring Thomas, who was struggling against faintness, the man stooped and rummaged in the oak chest. The next moment he had drawn out the case.

And even as Sir Robert burst into the room with sword drawn, the man leaped to the casement and squirmed through it. Then he was gone, with barely a sound. From outside, the shouts were closer; but to Thomas, they sounded utterly futile.

'In God's name . . . bring lights!' Sir Robert blundered across the chamber, his sword clattering. From the passage came raised voices, that of Rivers among them. But they were too late. Thomas could have laughed; in all his life, he had never felt such a sense of utter failure. Better indeed if he had died – so long as Corvino died too . . .

But he was not done. Some strength, he knew not whence, seeped through his hurt body. He stooped and fumbled on the floor for his poniard, before finding it beside his foot. Then ignoring his master's shout, he stumbled to the window and put his bloodied hand on the sill. The other arm was all but useless, but he ignored that. In a moment he was through the opening, scraping head and knees but oblivious to further pain. He landed in the soft earth of the flower bed – and to his relief, his legs did not buckle. Then he was running through the dark, across the gardens towards the paddock. And at that moment he could have shouted with joy – for he heard the horses wheel in alarm, and knew that by pure chance he had chosen the right direction.

Somewhere, Corvino ran ahead.

Sixteen

Which way would he go?

The question burned through Thomas's mind as he ran across the gardens into darkness. The Hungerford road was at his back. Ahead was the deer park, giving way to open fields and Downland. To the left the park sloped away towards the farmland that lined the river. To his right was the paddock – and Thomas veered towards it. If he were Corvino, he reasoned, his best chance would be to steal a horse.

There was no moonlight, but his keen eyes adjusted quickly. His left arm troubled him. He knew that he should stop and bind it, to staunch the blood, but he would lose too much time. He ran on, towards the faint outline of the paddock fence. There came a shout, from somewhere by the stables, which was answered by another from behind him. The hue and cry was raised, but Thomas merely gritted his teeth: the watchers knew not where to run, or indeed what they faced.

The horses were more than nervous: they were afraid. He sensed it as he reached the fence and clambered over, landing heavily on the other side. Swiftly he scanned the enclosure, but there was no sign of his quarry. Then, what had he expected? *Search as you will; Corvino will always be gone before you . . .* Mary Jeap's words mocked him as he moved towards the bunched animals, speaking softly. Then he almost laughed at his foolishness. There had been no sound of hooves. And surely even Corvino, no matter how well mounted, could not leap a high fence in the dark?

He stopped, catching his breath, listening intently. Men were calling, from several directions. But their efforts were

useless; he knew it now. Corvino was unlike anyone they
had faced, or ever would. He was a force from elsewhere
– from some other domain, where different standards
prevailed. He accepted pursuit as merely one more obstacle
to overcome. Perhaps he had never experienced failure;
hence, he did not even consider it. Standing weakly by the
fence, dripping blood, Thomas was only too aware of his
own mortality. Finally, knowing it would buy him only a
little more time, he tore at his shirt sleeve, wrenching it
from the shoulder. Transferring the poniard to his left hand,
with his right he fashioned a crude bandage about his blood-
soaked arm, pulling it taut with his teeth. As he fumbled
to tie it he heard more voices, and running feet. How much
more noise could the pursuers make? Yet he had not the
heart to blame them, even though this was fast becoming
a comedy. The more they shouted, the better clues they
gave Corvino as to which way to run.

He drew a deep breath, forced himself to reason. Corvino
was on foot, and sooner or later he would have to strike the
road east towards Reading, or south towards Hungerford. The
way north, to Wantage, Thomas rejected. This man came from
across the Channel – he had spoken in the Italian tongue. He
must reach London, then, or the coast . . . but surely he would
not try to cross the swollen Lambourn in the dark? Hence he
must double back, towards the Petbury gates . . .

Suddenly one of the horses whinnied. The man was close
by – he had to be. Crouching, holding the bottom rail of
the fence, Thomas peered into the gloom. He could see the
small trees that dotted the deer park, but beyond that nothing.
Behind him, lights had sprung up in the great house.

At last – a shape looming out of the dark, ahead and to
his left. His heart thumped, for there was no mistaking the
gait. A lope, someone had said . . . and in a moment, Thomas
had shinned over the rail, to land on his back in the grass.
Then he was on his feet again, and running. But his quarry
heard him, turned and shot away. And with sinking heart
Thomas knew that, weakened as he was, he could not outrun
this man. Bitterness welled up, like bile in his throat: Corvino
would escape . . .

Whereupon something happened that made him lurch to a halt.

Out of the darkness, from the direction of the house, a great bulk of a man appeared, moving surprisingly fast – and converging on the path of the running figure. It was the last person Thomas expected to see. He would have shouted had the other been able to understand him. But the next moment, he saw that it didn't matter.

'*Pogano!*' Mikhailov shouted . . . and Corvino slowed. Swiftly he changed direction – but so did the other. At the same moment there was a clatter; and from thirty yards away Thomas saw the reason. The *sotnik* captain had drawn his fearsome-looking sabre.

Unbelievably, there was hope. If between them they could cut off the man's escape, long enough for those from the house and stables to move up . . . but Thomas realized Mikhailov had not seen him, so he shouted.

'Don't let him past! Look to your left!'

Startled, Mikhailov looked round – and Thomas cursed his mistake. The big man may have been agile, but his thinking was less swift; and he hesitated long enough for Corvino to seize the advantage. But to Thomas's alarm the man did not run away: instead he darted forward, putting his left hand to his belt. In his right hand, Thomas now saw, he carried the black case.

He cried out – but his warning was wasted. Too late Mikhailov turned, to face the lithe figure that bore down upon him. He shouted angrily and swung his blade, but Corvino simply dived under it. Then Thomas too shouted, finding his legs at last, and began to run forward; but he was too late.

Corvino's upward thrust caught the big man full in the abdomen, stopping him in the act of raising his sword again. He dropped his arm, and went rigid. And even in the gloom, Thomas saw the puzzled look that came over Mikhailov's features. He peered at his assailant, and said something in Russian. It was a dumb-show, with only one end – but Corvino did not wait for that. Even as Thomas lessened the distance between them, he saw the robed figure lean back and pull the knife from Mikhailov's body. Then as the Russian howled in pain, the other raised his foot and pushed, sending him falling backwards on to his rump. There sat the *sotnik* in the grass, helpless and bewildered, looking down at the ugly wound. Without another glance, Corvino turned and sprinted off.

But Thomas chased after him. With a renewed strength that he barely understood, he sped past the seated Mikhailov. Help would come – he would not concern himself with the bodyguard now. He had one thought left, that drove away all others: to catch Corvino. And he allowed himself a moment of encouragement: for the man was not running east towards the road after all. In one respect at least, Mikhailov had succeeded: he had made the fugitive change direction. Now he ran south, where the park sloped away to grazing land. Beyond was the river.

But first there were trees, which offered cover . . . Thomas's lungs heaved, his body racked with pain and fatigue. Yet never did he take his eyes from the dim shape before him, even as it gained distance and began to fade in the dark. He knew this country – every tree and hollow of it. Boxwell Farm was below them – upriver lay South Wilby; but that direction would not be Corvino's. He still had to work his way east, to strike the road . . .

He was nearing the southern edge of the park. The foliage thickened ahead, even as the ground dipped under Thomas's feet. He slowed . . . the man could be waiting behind a tree. He was trotting now, relieved that he had managed to hold on to his poniard. Though the thought of another knife-fight with Corvino was not one he liked to dwell on . . .

He scanned the trees on either side. There were cries as night birds flapped from the branches above. He could not see them, but he heard woodcock . . . and in the distance, the bark of a dog fox. Otherwise, nothing: no running feet, no one crashing through bushes. Despair rose inside him, and he slowed almost to a halt; he had lost his quarry. Or had he . . . ?

There came a very faint sound, one that only Thomas

would have heard – and in that moment he knew he was beaten. For it came not from ahead of him, but behind.

He snapped round – and sure enough, here was the robed figure that had almost become familiar to him. But once again, Corvino did not hurry. Panting, dropping to a crouch, Thomas watched the man emerge from the gloom, left hand extended. He could not see the knife, not yet . . . and he cursed himself now for his carelessness. For Corvino had indeed concealed himself behind a tree, then simply moved around it as Thomas ran past, to come up from the rear. How many times, he wondered, had he played that trick as a boy, in Poughley woods? How could he be so careless!

Grim-faced, he held his poniard before him, trying to guess which way the other would move. Either way, he doubted if he could be fast enough. There was but one small consolation, that fed his innate curiosity: he would see the face of the man, after all.

Corvino walked towards Thomas with small, neat steps; the steps of a dancer perhaps, or of a fencer. He stopped; the hood was thrown back – and Thomas stifled a gasp: for the face that appeared was frightful. At first he thought of a skull; then saw that he was mistaken. There was a pair of sharp eyes under thick brows – but beneath them only a ridge of flesh, filled by two gaping black cavities. At some time in his past, this man's nose had been sliced off.

He struck: a crosswise blow. Thomas tried to leap back, but the other's reach was long, and too quick. The point of the blade raked Thomas's chest, an inch below his heart. He staggered, but felt relief: the cut was not deep . . . it was not a death blow.

He lunged in reply, but it was hopeless. He was back in Sir Robert's chamber, with Tertius Gale groaning in the corner, and wondering where the blade would strike next. Again his poniard met nothing but air. Whereupon the other used Thomas's brief loss of balance to deal his next blow – which he did with ease, and what seemed to Thomas like delight. Dimly he saw the mouth, twisted in a hideous grin.

This time the pain was acute, but it was not where he expected it. The slash was delivered with a backward stroke, across his chest and right shoulder. The knife was double-edged, and sharp as ice. Thomas gasped, feeling the muscle cleave; his arm went limp, and his poniard dropped soundlessly into the grass. A moment later he sagged, then sat down. And there he stayed, both arms all but useless: a carcase for the other to carve as he would. As no doubt he had carved John Doggett . . . the picture of the body rose before Thomas with stark clarity. So, he thought – it comes to me now. And for some reason, he wanted to laugh.

Less than an hour ago, he seemed to have had so much to do: for the falcons, for his master, for Nell and for Eleanor; but now, it looked as if he was not going to do them. In fact he was not going to do anything very much, now; except die.

He looked up, into the ghastly face of his assailant. 'So, what will you do?' he asked weakly. 'Make me a eunuch, like the other? Though you prefer your victims bound, do you not? Bound or too weak, like the boy . . .'

Corvino watched him. Then at last, he spoke.

'You want it?'

With a mocking grin he held up the black case – and at once Thomas understood. To this man's mind there could be no other reason why someone would pursue him so doggedly. He assumed Thomas wanted the chain as badly as he did!

And then Thomas remembered what was in the case.

'That?' He managed a surprised expression. 'Why would I want a box of horseshoes?'

Then he flinched – for without warning Corvino dropped to his knees beside Thomas. Feebly, Thomas glanced round for his poniard. He felt something sharp under his thigh, and realized that he was sitting on it.

'Horseshoes . . . ?' Almost casually Corvino reached forward and swiped his blade across Thomas's chest, below the other cut. Thomas blinked, more at the speed of the movement than with pain. He glanced down, saw the dark stain that was already soaking his shirt. Wincing with the effort, he raised his bandaged arm . . . but there was no feeling in it. With a groan, he let it fall.

Corvino ignored him. He had put the case down and was fumbling with the catch. Finding it locked, he looked quickly at Thomas. 'Key?'

Thomas said nothing. Whereupon, seemingly for no particular reason, Corvino slashed him across the left shoulder, then twice across the stomach again. Then bending intently over the case, he put the point of his knife to the lock and forced it. It gave easily – indeed, too easily. And the moment the man saw what was within, he stiffened from head to foot.

To Thomas, he now appeared like some crazed monk from long ago. He had heard of penitents who once travelled about Europe, lashing themselves with whips woven with thorns. This man however, preferred to inflict pain on others. Thomas was in a great deal of pain now, and weakening by the minute, his life-blood oozing into the grass. He could still shout – but shouting, he realized, would avail him nothing. He was out of earshot of Petbury; he doubted if anyone knew where he was. And now, in spite of himself, he dreaded what would happen.

Corvino picked up a horseshoe and examined it closely. Then from eye-height, he opened his fingers and let it fall back into the case with a crash.

'You knew?' Abruptly Corvino pushed his dreadful face towards Thomas's. 'You knew what was here, yet you came after me? Why?'

His English was good, Thomas thought; the accent soft. He met the man's eye, tried to remain calm. Under his thigh he still felt the hard outline of his poniard, but he knew that he would not have time to reach it. He could have laughed long and loud at his predicament.

'Why? To avenge the boy you killed.'

Corvino seemed to consider that. But when he spoke, Thomas realized that his thoughts ran on a different tack.

'But you know where the chain is,' he said. 'The chain with the white hart made of jewels.'

'White hart?' Thomas echoed. 'You mean the white bear, made of sapphires?'

Corvino stared. Then, again without warning, the blade

darted past Thomas's face. He winced, as his ear was slashed. Warm blood ran down his neck. He thought he could feel the lobe, dangling by a shred of skin.

'Bear . . . ?' Now a glint of understanding showed in Corvino's eyes. Black as charcoal, Thomas noticed, with an odd light behind them. *Jet-black it means, like the colour of the robe he wears . . .* Mary Jeap was talking in his head again. He realized he was growing faint.

'So the English jeweller re-made it . . .' The other's thin lips parted in a smile. 'What skinflints the Queen's nobles are! They do not commission, but buy ready-made, and have the pendant altered!' He gave a shriek of laughter, and shook his head.

'What tales that chain could tell you, *signor*. The pendant was once a wedding gift to the most beautiful woman in France . . . who bore a son, who is less beautiful!' His smile faded. 'She treated him so badly . . . he grew up a cruel and bitter man. Yet to regain his mother's jewel, fashioned as his family crest, he would give everything – and pay anything!' He paused, gave another little shake of his head. 'So many hands it has passed through . . . though the owners of some of those hands have paid dearly. But you . . . you do not know what it is.'

Idly Corvino flicked the point of his poniard towards Thomas's eye, laughing when he flinched.

'Well – then my work is not done,' he went on. 'For you will now tell me *where* it is!' And merely for emphasis, he made a cut on Thomas's cheek.

Thomas caught his breath, as more blood ran. He must try to summon what strength he had left – he must not believe it was too late. Was he really dying? The futility of it, along with the ease with which he had let himself fall into this man's clutches, now made him sick with anger. Suddenly, surprised to find that he could, he lifted his right hand and tried to grab Corvino's poniard. But all he got was a slash across the palm, and a harsh laugh from his captor.

'Now . . .' Corvino grew businesslike. 'You know what happened to others, so I need not tell you. Nor need you take so long as the first – you know the pain will be too great. So favour yourself, *signor* tall fellow, and tell me where the chain is now. Quickly is best!'

'The chain . . . ?' Thomas tried to focus, but the other's face was indistinct. Dimly he became aware that dawn was breaking . . . a greyness, from somewhere to his left. A feeling almost of elation came over him: he would see a new day, after all . . .

There was movement. Corvino was waving the knife in front of Thomas's face. Behind it his disfigured features twisted in a snarl. 'Come, you are not a fool!' he cried. 'Tell me and you die quick. Try to thwart me, and you die slowly. You know it's the truth – so speak!'

After a moment, Thomas did speak. 'How long is it you've been hereabouts?' he asked, so quietly that Corvino frowned and cocked his head. 'Not so long . . . so you don't know us Downland folk. We're a cussed lot when we choose to be.' He managed a faint smile. 'You see, I've a mind to make things difficult.'

But Corvino merely turned aside and spat. 'Difficult?' he snapped. He drew back and sat on his haunches, looking down at his victim. 'There is no difficulty for me, *signor* – none at all!'

Thomas steeled himself; he would try to roll aside, seize his poniard, do whatever it took. It was that, or die slowly and uselessly . . . he stiffened, watching Corvino's left hand, trying once again to judge which way he would strike. He saw the man move – it was time—

A faint noise came out of the dark . . . a *ssssswww!* of rushing air, followed by a loud thud. To Thomas's alarm Corvino fell forward, half across him, pinning him flat. He heard choking noises, though they were muffled . . . he gasped and reached out, but he was too fatigued to heave the heavy body off his. Feebly, with his one hand that still worked, he grabbed at the hood. But all he succeeded in doing was to raise Corvino's head a few inches. To his amazement the man was wide-eyed and gasping, fighting for his life. His hands worked uselessly, clawing at the grass.

Then at last he saw the arrow, protruding from Corvino's back. It was fletched with the feathers of a wild hawk.

Weakly Thomas sank back, letting his head rest on the soft grass; it was so comfortable. His eyes wandered, from the writhing form that pressed him to the ground, to the trees beyond . . . from which a shambling, stubby figure now emerged, his face framed by long greasy hair. A bow was in his hands, a second arrow already fitted; but it was not needed. Taking in the situation at a glance, Will Greve slackened the string and laid the weapon down. He stepped forward, took Corvino by the shoulders and yanked his body off Thomas's. Then he stooped and rolled the man over on to his back. With a crack, the arrow's shaft snapped beneath him.

The poacher straightened up, and looked down at the one he had shot. 'That was for young Corder,' he said.

Thomas tried to raise himself, but fell back. With a grunt Greve came forward, put his hands under Thomas's armpits and sat him up. 'Here's a turnabout,' he muttered, and jerked his thumb towards Corvino. 'I seen him – that night your daughter was walking with her swain . . . foreigner, an't he? That one was lucky he didn't get shot in the arse!'

He grimaced. 'I'd taken the boy with me. Said he could show me where Sir Robert's deer lay. But I lost him . . . by the time I heard voices . . .' The poacher sniffed, then turned suddenly and delivered a savage kick at Corvino, who twitched. He gave a hoarse cry, then went limp.

'Is he dead?' Thomas tried to turn, to get on to his knees. But pain came from so many directions he gave up again.

'Nay, but he soon will be.' Greve frowned. 'Why – did you want to say summat to him?'

Thomas breathed steadily. The tension was draining from him now. He had been spared . . . the notion astonished him. Would he live, after all? To the consternation of the poacher, he laughed.

'What's tickled you, Finbow?' Greve demanded.

Thomas shook his head slowly. 'Of all the men I'd expect to save my life . . .' He laughed again.

There was a grunt of pain: Corvino was trying to move.

Thomas turned to look, but Greve muttered a curse, swung round and stalked over to the man. He bent down, wrapped his brawny arms about the murderer's body and dragged him towards a nearby tree. Then he propped him unceremoniously against the trunk and stepped back.

They faced each other, from what seemed like a great distance: Thomas, and the man who had come closer than anyone to killing him. But if Thomas wanted answers, he was too late. He knew it, even before he saw the bloody point of Greve's arrow protruding from the man's ribcage. It had passed right through his body.

'I wanted to see England . . .'

Corvino had spoken, making Greve jump. 'I'll finish him!' he snapped, as if the man were a rabbit he had wounded. 'He would 'a done for you – like he did for the boy!'

'No . . .' Thomas tried to raise his hand. 'Let me hear . . .'

In the faint light he struggled to focus on the man's dreadful, skull-like face. After a moment, Corvino spoke again.

'I wanted . . . to see this land, that's ruled by a maid . . . though I did not expect it would be my grave!'

He gave a choking laugh that brought blood welling from his mouth. 'I have one regret . . .' His voice was hoarse, and failing. 'I will never see the look on the face of the Seigneur de Maisse, when he knows he has lost . . .'

The assassin's head drooped. He looked down at the arrow-point and sighed. Then his eyes closed. Slowly his body slid down the tree trunk, to land softly in the grass.

Greve dropped to one knee beside him, felt the artery in the neck, then stood up. 'Gone,' he said, and sniffed. He peered at Thomas, squinting in the dim light.

'What now? See, I'd a mind to make myself scarce . . .' He shrugged. 'There's another of my arrows back there in the park, sticking out of a nice buck. You passed within a few yards of it.'

Thomas managed a smile. 'Then your eyes aren't failing, after all.'

Greve hesitated. And as he surveyed Thomas's many

wounds, a frown creased his brow. 'You need a surgeon bad, Finbow,' he muttered. 'Else you'll be joining that whoreson bastard . . .' He indicated Corvino's still form. 'Who in God's name was he?'

'No one knows,' Thomas answered. 'But in the end he wasn't much of a thief. All he got was a few horseshoes.'

He met the poacher's eye. 'If you're going back to the park, I'd be obliged if you'd tell someone you found me. Then you can make yourself scarce. I doubt they'll see the dead deer, in this light.'

Greve considered. 'Then we'd be all square, you and me?'

'Square? I'll be in your debt for the rest of my days,' Thomas answered.

The poacher snorted. 'I never knew how you fadged in the Low Countries, Finbow,' he muttered. 'You've not the killing urge – a soldier needs that. A poacher, too.'

Then he turned, picked up his bow and trotted off through the trees.

Thomas watched him go. Slowly he turned his head, towards the growing light from the east. The clouds were thinning; it had not rained after all. In fact the sun would rise soon, above the trees. He would watch it come.

He no longer felt any pain. Instead a deep calm pervaded his body. He knew he could not stand, but thought he could crawl, perhaps out of the trees; then he decided against it. He could sleep here; it was so peaceful . . .

Then the dawn birds began, above his head and all about him. One, another . . . and soon a myriad chorus of songs, that seemed to be just for him.

Epilogue

The barber-surgeon arrived from Wantage in mid-morning, bad-tempered after a frightening ride on a fast horse. The horse had been brought for him by a groom from Petbury, who had ridden so hard his own mount was flecked with foam. When the two men clattered into the stable yard, they found Martin the steward waiting anxiously. Even as the surgeon dismounted, the old man was speaking. There were two men needing his skills, he said – most urgently. One was the constable from Chaddleworth. He should be seen first, Martin said, for he had grave fears about the man's chances. He continued talking as he led the way; but the barber-surgeon had ceased to listen.

The men were lying on pallets in the great hall, amid a deal of toing and froing by members of the household. Among them the newcomer recognized Lady Margaret Vicary. Carrying his case of instruments, he walked forward stiffly and made his bow: a crabbed, white-bearded man in the customary black gown and skull-cap. He was past his sixty years, and had been a member of the Barber-Surgeons' Company for half of them. And one look at Lady Margaret's face told him his journey had been in vain.

'The constable died a few moments ago. We staunched the blood, but it wasn't enough . . .' Lady Margaret's face was drawn tight, as she nodded to the still form against the wall. Bright sunlight streamed through the windows.

The barber-surgeon walked over to the pallet. A maid stood by, and at his sign folded back the linen sheet. There was a moment, as the surgeon peered down at the rigid form. Then he turned to face the mistress of Petbury.

'You are right, my lady – there's naught I can do for this

man,' he said shortly. It was not the wasted journey that irked him, so much as the waste of a life. He looked round the huge room. 'I'm told there is another . . . ?'

Lady Margaret pointed with her chin. For the first time the surgeon was aware of two men in heavy coats, standing beside the other pallet watching him. As he walked towards them, one, a slim man with a scholarly air, spoke in an accent he did not recognize.

'Our friend is very sick. The wound needs stitching, and then—'

'Are you a surgeon, sir?' the barber-surgeon snapped.

The other shook his head. 'I am Yusupov, secretary to His Excellency the Russian Ambassador. This man is his bodyguard—'

'Then move aside!'

Yusupov blinked, and did so. Beside him stood a younger man who looked bewildered by their exchange.

At last the barber-surgeon had something to do. Accepting a stool, he sat down beside the prone figure. The man was huge, and barely conscious. He was bare to the waist and had been bandaged, but the blood had soaked through. His breathing was slow; nor did the barber-surgeon like the man's pallor. Briskly he set to work – but first he looked round at the two Russians.

'What happened to him?'

'He was stabbed,' Yusupov replied.

'I see that! What with?'

The secretary shook his head.

The barber-surgeon sighed. 'I'll do what is in my power,' he said. 'But he's lost a deal of blood. He must not move, but rest here and take the physic I will give you—'

'No.' Yusupov was suddenly firm. 'We must leave this afternoon. His Excellency has ordered it – he will not stay a day longer at Petbury.'

'Impossible!' the barber-surgeon retorted. 'This man is not well enough to travel . . .' He frowned. 'Leave?' he echoed. 'Leave for where?'

'Muscovy,' the secretary replied. 'We go home.'

For a moment the other was lost for words; then finally

he stood up. 'Does your master know the condition of his bodyguard?' he asked. When no reply came, he went on: 'He would die before you even reached your ship – likely before you got twenty miles. The roads are slow and choked with mud. No matter how carefully you bore him the wound would open—'

'That, sir, is not your affair.'

Yusupov turned to the younger man and spoke a few words in his language. Piotr nodded and walked away. Then the secretary faced the barber-surgeon again.

'Let me explain,' he said. 'If the bodyguard dies, he dies a contented man; for he was brave, and did his office. He tried to avenge his friend who was killed – he even risked his master's wrath, by going outside against orders. And yet he has protected our master throughout his stay here, as he swore to do. So believe me, sir . . .' Yusupov met the man's stare with a steady gaze. 'Sotnik Mikhailov would not wish it any other way. Nor would he want to delay us.'

The barber-surgeon had been about to make some retort, but he saw it was useless. So he gave a sigh, and turned back to his patient.

'Then I will do what I can – and you'd best pray to God!'

Piotr was in the sunlit garden, standing beside his master, Grigori Stanic. The young man having made his report, the ambassador dismissed him curtly. Then with a stiff nod in the direction of Sir Robert, who stood with Sir Thomas Rivers, His Excellency swung round and stalked off back to the house. He and his train would leave as planned. The events of earlier this morning had made the man more determined than ever to keep to his decision of the evening before. The entire household now knew of the departure; but only Grigori Stanic was ignorant of how relieved they were, to the last man and woman, to see him go.

Sir Robert and Rivers watched the man walk away. Both were exhausted, having had no sleep. Dawn had brought only mayhem and tragedy. When Martin the steward appeared, walking heavily across the lawn towards them, he looked like a defeated old man. He drew near, and without preamble told Sir Robert of the death of the constable, Tertius Gale.

Sir Robert passed a hand over his brow. 'And the body-guard?'

'He lives. And though the barber-surgeon spoke against his being moved, the Russians insist he goes with them.' Contempt showed in Martin's gaze. 'The ambassador leaves one man behind dead,' he added. 'I venture he feels it would reflect badly on him, if he were to lose two.'

Rivers snorted. 'On his own head be it!'

He looked to Sir Robert. 'Be assured of this, sir: I now consider the chain safely delivered into my keeping. Henceforth my servant and I will be beside the ambassador, every step of the way back to Richmond Palace. From there an armed guard will escort him and his men to their ship.' He paused. 'And I will make a point of informing the Queen's Council that you have performed your duties fully and admirably!'

But Sir Robert barely nodded; he no longer seemed to care what the other man said. 'The search parties have scoured the manor, in every direction,' he said to Martin. 'Hence we must widen the circle – beyond the Ridgeway to the north, and Greenhill Down on the west. On the south, we must look to the river. If necessary, I'll wade it myself!'

Martin nodded. 'Everyone is eager to do their part, sir,' he said. 'More men are coming from Chaddleworth . . .' He frowned. 'The constable's death will be a bitter blow to them.'

'And it happened in my house.' Sir Robert lowered his eyes. 'I will bear that stain on my conscience for the rest of my days. To think of the bloodbath, in my private sanc-tuary . . .' Angrily, he looked up. 'The room will be cleared of everything, save that wretched chest! Then I want it sealed – for ever! Do you understand?'

Martin signalled his assent.

Rivers glanced at his host, but said nothing. Finally Sir Robert mastered himself, and spoke to Martin again.

'What of the poacher?'

'His body is taken to the chapel,' the steward answered.

'The man who killed him is most distressed. In the semi-darkness, he thought it was the fugitive. He challenged Greve – but when he failed to answer, the fellow fired off his caliver. He's a Chaddleworth man, like the poacher. He but came to offer his help . . .'

Sir Robert sighed. 'Tell him he's not to blame. Will Greve's been a trial to us for years – it was his fate to die on my land!'

At last, he turned to Rivers. And seeing the look in his eye, even the Privy Councillor flinched.

'So many deaths – all of them hard, all of them futile!' Sir Robert cried. 'And all due, some might say, to the presence of the chain – that I never wanted here in the first place!' He stared fiercely at Rivers. 'How many more must perish before that bauble leaves our shores? And all so that it can be handed to another preening tyrant, who may or may not decide to grant our merchants a few rights in return . . .' The knight broke off, and took a long breath. 'Tell me, Sir Thomas – from your heart: do you truly think it was worth all this?'

Rivers hesitated. His instinct had been to utter some retort; now he found he had no stomach for it.

'I know not, Sir Robert,' he answered tiredly. 'I but serve my Queen and do her bidding, as must we all. Beyond that . . .'

He shrugged; then a worried frown creased his brow. 'Will you send word to me?' he asked. 'When there are any tidings, I mean?'

The other two looked at him stonily.

'The falconer,' Rivers added, somewhat testily. 'Do you not think I care what has befallen him?'

After a moment, Martin gave a brief nod. But Sir Robert merely turned away from the man, and walked off towards the house.

Nell and Eleanor stood beside the falcons' mews, gazing anxiously to the west. Neither had moved from the spot for the past hour; nor had they exchanged a word in that time. An unspoken bond placed them together, side by side but not quite touching. The grooms, gardeners and other men who were still roaming the manor had left the two women alone. But now at last Eleanor raised her hand to shade her eyes from the sunlight, and pointed.

Nell peered into the distance, and stiffened. Out of the haze Ned Hawes came running, cleaving the long grass with his stride. Then abruptly, both women sighed. The boy was alone.

He drew close, panting hoarsely, and halted. Sweat dripped from his face. They waited, still as statues, while he found his breath.

'Nothing,' he said finally. 'I crossed the Ridgeway, ran into a couple of Chaddleworth boys. They'd come all the way from the village, but there's been no sign. You ask me, we must look in another direction.'

He made a vague gesture southwards. Eleanor's face was blank. But after a moment Nell spoke gently to the boy.

'Rest a while,' she said. 'There's no sense driving yourself to a standstill. Others are searching . . .'

She broke off, working her fingers. Eleanor looked, and realized she had never once seen Nell fret – not since before she and Thomas had married; those days when she used to blush and fumble with her ladles whenever the tall falconer stopped by the kitchen with birds for Sir Robert's table.

'I'll go,' Eleanor said. 'I'm no use here.' She glanced at Ned, saw the drawn look on the boy's face. It had not left him since the moment he arrived, soon after sunrise. It seemed he had not stopped running since.

Nell looked at her. There was a moment then that even Ned understood. And at once he turned away, embarrassed by the emotion of the two women. They had embraced, he knew, though he did not look. Not until he heard Eleanor hurry off down the slope towards the paddock, her shoes swishing through the grass. He looked round to see her break into a run, holding up her skirts. She looked then like the simple Downland girl he had fallen in love with all those years ago, before she became a woman-in-waiting. Eleanor had no idea how relieved Ned had been to hear that she and the young Russian man were no longer seen together. Piotr would go back to his country, while Eleanor would stay with her mistress, where she belonged. What else should a falconer's daughter do?

He forced himself to meet Nell's gaze. They had never been close; like many of the younger folk at Petbury, he feared her famous temper. But now the man they each loved in their own way was missing; a circumstance neither had known, or anticipated. It made things different.

Nell broke the silence. 'There's hope,' she said. 'You know there is.'

The boy nodded.

'I'd best go back,' Nell said. She looked away, towards the kitchen garden, and the archway through which she walked on those mornings when she had been able to sleep at the cottage. There was a numbness in her that she had spoken of to no one, not even Eleanor. It felt like a cold poultice wrapped about her heart.

Ned frowned suddenly. 'Something shook me this morning, when I got here,' he said. 'I took the great white hawk out – and she was fair raging at me! Before I knew it she'd tore the jesses out of my hand and lifted herself. I fear she's gone!'

Nell gave a start. 'Which way did she fly?'

'South,' Ned said, and pointed. 'Across the paddock and the deer park. I lost her then, where the trees start . . .' He blinked, then came to a decision.

'I'm going to follow Eleanor,' he said. And without further word he ran off, picking up speed as he descended the hill.

Nell watched him until he was but a distant speck, trotting across the park. Then the sun slipped out from behind a cloud, and dazzled her. When she peered into the distance again the boy had disappeared.

She stood for a moment, hearing the falcons stir on their perches behind her. Then she began to walk down the slope.